"You felt that?"

She sandwiched his hand between both of hers. "At first, I thought there was something odd about handshakes, but I felt nothing when the others held my hand. It is most . . . curious, don't you think?"

"Marielle." He winced when she brought his hand to her chest. He could feel the soft fullness of her breasts. His sight darkened, turning red.

She tilted her head, regarding him curiously. "I've been trying to understand this. I thought it might be lust, but I've always considered sin to be ugly and ultimately destructive. This doesn't feel like that. What would you call it?"

He swallowed hard. "Desire. Longing."

Her eyes widened with wonder. "Yes. That's it, exactly."

He grabbed the back of her neck to pull her forward, then halted with his mouth less than an inch from hers. Bloody hell, he had sworn he wouldn't do this.

She released his hand and wrapped her arms around his neck. "Yes," she repeated, and all restraint was lost . . .

By Kerrelyn Sparks

KERRELYN SPARKS

Vampire Mine

WITHDRAWN

AVON

An Imprint of HarperCollinsPublishers

AVON BOOKS
An Imprint of HarperCollins*Publishers*
10 East 53rd Street
New York, New York 10022–5299

Copyright © 2011 by Kerrelyn Sparks
ISBN 978-0-06-195804-5
www.avonromance.com

First Avon Books mass market printing: April 2011

Avon Trademark Reg. U.S. Pat. Off. and in Other Countries, Marca Registrada, Hecho en U.S.A.
HarperCollins® is a registered trademark of HarperCollins Publishers.

Printed in the U.S.A.

10 9 8 7 6 5 4 3 2 1

In loving memory of
Caden Joshua Grajkowski
Heaven welcomed a perfect little angel
August 28, 2009

Acknowledgments

I risk sounding redundant in the acknowledgments of each book, for I keep thanking the same group, but I truly find it touching that these dear people continue to support me and watch my back. I am so grateful to them all! First of all, many thanks to my dear friend and agent, Michelle Grajkowski, who has been with me for ten books now and believed in me long before Roman lost a fang. My thanks also to Erika Tsang, who loved the fact that Roman lost a fang and has been my fabulous editor ever since. Thank you, all the folks at Avon/Harper-Collins, from editorial, marketing, and sales, to publicity and the art department, where Tom creates the most beautiful covers in the business. My thanks to my critique partners—M.J., Sandy, and Vicky—who keep me sane (reasonably sane). To my husband and children—you are always there for me. And many, many thanks to all you readers! Thank you for the enthusiasm and support that has made the Love at Stake series continue for ten books. With readers like you, the Undead can live forever!

Vampire Mine

Chapter One

*A*fter four hundred and ninety-nine years of existence, Connor Buchanan arrived at an inescapable conclusion regarding himself. He was a coldhearted old bastard.

He slowed to a walk after checking the extensive grounds at Romatech. He'd enjoyed zipping through the trees at vampire speed with the cool breeze whipping at his face and filling his nostrils with the heady scent of newly budded leaves and flowers. But then he'd realized why he welcomed the coming of spring. Not for the warmer temperatures. Not for the promise of rebirth and renewal, since he would remain the same as he'd been for centuries. No, to be brutally honest with himself, it was the shorter nights he was looking forward to. That meant longer days and more death-sleep. More time spent in utter oblivion. No thoughts. No memories. No remorse.

The main building at Romatech Industries came into view, and he slowed his pace even more, struck by a sudden reluctance to reenter the facility. More and more these days, he preferred to be alone.

Why bother with companions? Was there any conversation he hadn't already experienced a dozen or more times? And if he even hinted at the black despair that threatened to engulf him, he would only receive knowing looks from other Vamps as they doled out the usual diagnosis. He was nearing his five hundredth birthday, and apparently, hitting that mid-millennium marker could plunge the most stalwart of Vamps into a mid-life crisis.

Bull crap. Roman and Angus were both older than him, and they were content with their lives. *They're happily married*. He shoved that thought aside. He wouldn't fall prey to that form of insanity, no matter how old he got.

No, he was fine with being a coldhearted old bastard. He was good at it. He'd been perfecting the condition for years. He strode through a flower bed, trampling the new blossoms underfoot.

At the side entrance, he slid his ID card through the security console and pressed his palm against the scanner. When his ultrasensitive hearing detected the faint click of the lock releasing, he pushed open the side door and trudged down the hall to the MacKay security office.

His footsteps echoed in the empty hallway. No one came to Romatech on Saturday night except those who attended Mass on the far side of the facility.

He let himself into the security office and scanned

the wall of surveillance monitors. Parking lot clear. Corridors empty. Cafeteria empty. Heart empty. He pushed aside that errant thought and focused on the screen showing the chapel.

Out of habit, he searched the small congregation to make sure Roman and his family were all right. Connor had been officially watching over Roman for more than sixty years now as a MacKay S&I employee, first as head of security at Romatech, and in recent years as personal bodyguard. Since Roman Draganesti was the inventor of synthetic blood and the owner of Romatech where it was produced, he presented a tempting target for the Malcontents who considered synthetic blood an insult and threat to their murderous way of life.

But the hatred went deeper than that. Casimir had been the one to transform Roman back in 1491. The Malcontent leader had thought it would be an amusing slap at the face of God to turn a humble monk into a bloodthirsty, homicidal vampire. But Roman had refused to turn evil. He'd made his own group of good Vamps, so they could fight the Malcontents and protect humanity.

Connor was dying on a battlefield when Roman changed him. He owed his existence to Roman. And his sanity. Keeping Roman and his family safe gave him a noble purpose, noble enough to almost make him forget what a coldhearted old bastard he truly was.

He watched on the monitor as Father Andrew gave his final blessing, and the congregation moved from the chapel into the hallway. Connor's heart squeezed at the sight of Roman's children, Constantine and Sofia. They were as close as he'd ever get to having children. Tino had celebrated his fifth birthday last month in March, and Sofia would be turning three in May. He touched the screen that showed them prancing about the hallway. Having to sit still during Mass must have left them with pent-up energy that was now bursting free. He smiled as they skipped into the nearby fellowship hall, no doubt eager for punch and cookies. Their mortal mother, Shanna, gave Roman a quick hug, then chased after the children.

Connor's smile faded as he watched his Vamp friends emerging from the chapel, nearly all of them with a wife at his side. Most of the men had succumbed to the silken trap of love. Poor romantic fools. How could they remain single for centuries, then out of the blue, one after another, plummet off the cliff like a dazed herd of sheep? Not only had they made themselves personally vulnerable to the heartache and despair that came with love, but they endangered the entire vampire world as more and more mortal women learned of their existence.

The men seemed happy enough for now. Ignorance was bliss, Connor supposed. They didn't see the risk. They didn't feel the cold shadow of doom hovering just outside their gilded cage. They had no idea how love could drive a man to commit desperate, unthinkable acts, destroying his own soul along the way.

He turned his head and focused instead on the monitor that was playing the Digital Vampire Network. A black animated bat flapped its wings while underneath a message announced: *DVN. On 24/7 because it's always nighttime somewhere.*

The *Nightly News* came on, so Connor turned off the mute button.

"One last item." Stone Cauffyn picked up a piece of paper that had been pushed across his desk. "A Vamp in Los Angeles believes he saw Casimir several nights ago." The newscaster scanned the paper, his face blank as usual. "I'm afraid we cannot confirm the report at this time."

Connor snorted. Last week, a Vamp claimed he'd seen Casimir paddling an outrigger canoe in Bora Bora, and the week before, someone swore he'd spotted Casimir milking a reindeer in northern Finland. The leader of the Malcontents had become the bogeyman of the vampire world, spied behind every tree and whispered about in dark rooms.

"And that concludes our broadcast for the night," Stone continued with his bland voice. "For all the latest news on the vampire world, keep your televisions tuned to DVN, the world's leading vampire network."

Not a stellar achievement considering it was the world's only vampire network. Connor muted the volume as the ending credits began to roll.

He glanced back at the monitor showing the hallway in front of the chapel. Most of the congregation was moving into the fellowship hall. Father Andrew appeared to be in deep conversation with Roman, who was solemnly nodding his head. They shook hands, then Roman proceeded into the fellowship hall while the priest walked toward the foyer, his leather briefcase in hand. He was leaving earlier than usual.

Connor switched his attention back to DVN. A commercial had started for Vampos, the after-dinner mint guaranteed to get rid of blood breath. A handsome male Vamp, dressed in an expensive tuxedo, slipped one of the mints into his mouth, then kissed his date, who, oddly enough, was dressed in a skimpy bikini in the dark in the middle of Central Park. On horseback. A likely scenario, Connor thought with a wry twist of his lips, although his gaze did linger over the woman's curvaceous body.

Bugger. How long had it been? Thirty years? Fifty? Too damned long if he couldn't even remember. No wonder he was a coldhearted old bastard.

Gregori, who always kept a roll of Vampos in his coat pocket, was constantly nagging Connor to go with him to the vampire nightclubs. Apparently, his plaid kilt and Scottish accent would make him an automatic "babe magnet." There was a multitude of "hot chicks," as Gregori called them, who wanted to relieve the boredom of immortality with a night of screaming wild sex. Gregori claimed it was their manly duty to keep all those Vamp women happy.

So far, Connor had declined. Attempting to cure his loneliness with a long line of faceless, nameless, desperate, Undead women didn't seem appealing. Or very honorable. *Hypocrite,* a small voice in the back of his mind needled him. *Who are ye fooling, pretending to be a man of honor? Ye know what ye did.*

He struck the voice down and glanced back at the surveillance monitors. Father Andrew had reached the foyer, and he set his briefcase on the table where Phineas had checked it earlier in the evening. As a safety precaution, all items brought into Romatech had to be searched.

The priest had left his overcoat on the table earlier, but instead of putting it on and heading out the front door, he strode across the foyer into the hallway on the left. Connor frowned, wondering what the old priest was up to. The hallway was empty except for . . .

"Bugger," Connor whispered as the priest marched straight toward the MacKay security office.

He couldn't pretend he wasn't here. With a groan, he pushed back a long strand of hair that had escaped the leather tie at the nape of his neck while he'd been running about the grounds.

He opened the door and stepped into the hallway. "Can I help you, Father?"

The priest smiled. "Connor, good to see you again." He shook hands, then peeked inside the office. "Fascinating. I've never seen this room before. May I?"

Connor motioned for him to enter, then followed him inside.

Father Andrew pivoted, scanning the office. His eyebrows rose at the sight of all the weapons in the caged-off area in the back. He turned toward the wall of surveillance monitors. "I wanted to let you know how much we appreciate you keeping us safe during Mass."

Connor inclined his head. It wasn't an idle compliment. The Malcontents had tried bombing the chapel before. With Roman in attendance, along with Angus MacKay and other high-profile members of the bottle-drinking Vamp world, they were practically begging for an attack.

The priest gestured to the screen showing the chapel. "So you were still able to watch the service?"

"Aye." Connor didn't admit that he'd kept the volume turned off. "I wasna here all the time. I did four perimeter checks."

"You're very vigilant," Father Andrew said with the hint of a smile. The silver fringe of hair surrounding his bald crown indicated an advanced age, yet his clear blue eyes and smooth skin lent him an oddly youthful and innocent appearance. "Roman and his family are fortunate to have you."

Connor shifted his weight. "Roman is verra important."

The priest's smile widened. "You are all important in the eyes of the Lord. I was wondering why you volunteer to guard us every week. Surely you could take turns with the other men? I haven't seen you at Mass for months now."

Connor winced inwardly. He should have known this was coming.

"I'm concerned about you," the priest continued. "Perhaps it's my imagination, but I feel like you've grown more isolated and . . . unhappy in the last few years. Roman agrees—"

"Ye talked to Roman about me?" Connor snapped.

The priest's eyes widened, but he remained quiet

until Connor felt a twinge of guilt for raising his voice.

"Roman tells me you're approaching your five hundredth birthday," Father Andrew said in a soothing tone. "I've heard that can cause feelings of depression or—"

"Bull crap."

"—or anger," the priest finished his sentence with a pointed look. "In your case, I fear you're shutting yourself off from your friends, which will result in you feeling even more alone. What do you think, Connor? Do you feel isolated?"

Not isolated enough since he was forced to endure this conversation. He shoved the annoying strand of hair behind his ear. "'Tis no' the same anymore. All the men are getting married."

"I heard that you disapprove of their relationships."

Connor shot him an irritated look. "'Tis no' that I want them to be lonely and miserable. They just doona see the risk they're taking. There's nothing more important to vampires than keeping our existence a secret. That has been our top priority for centuries, and they're foolishly flaunting it."

"They're in love."

Connor snorted.

"You don't believe in love?"

Connor grimaced as if he'd been poked with a spear. Oh, he believed in love all right. Love was a bitch.

Father Andrew watched him closely. "There's no

need to feel alone, Connor. You could come to Mass with your friends and take Holy Communion."

The wily priest was going for the jugular. Connor was purposely avoiding Communion. He'd been raised to believe he would have to go to confession first.

Father Andrew slipped on his reading glasses and removed a Day-Timer from his coat pocket. "I'd like to set up an appointment with you."

"I'm busy."

The priest ignored that remark as he thumbed through the pages. "Roman would give you the time off."

"No thanks."

"How about next Thursday evening at nine? I could meet you here."

"Nay."

With his hand resting on an open page of his Day-Timer, Father Andrew peered over the rims of his reading glasses. "I've been a priest for over fifty years. I can tell when a man is in need of confession."

Connor stepped back, his jaw clenched. "I confess nothing."

Father Andrew removed his glasses and fixed his blue eyes on Connor with a hard stare. "You won't scare me away. I will fight for you."

A chill crept over Connor's skin. The fight had been lost centuries ago.

The priest closed his Day-Timer with a snap and stuffed it into his coat pocket. "I assume you fought in the Great Vampire War of 1710? And until Roman invented synthetic blood in 1987, you survived by feeding off humans?"

Connor folded his arms across his chest. So in lieu of a confession, the priest was attempting an interrogation.

"I've learned a great deal about your world in the last five years." Father Andrew slid his glasses back into his chest pocket. "I seriously doubt there is anything you could tell me that I haven't heard before."

He was wrong about that. Connor motioned toward the door to indicate that the meeting was over.

A hint of amusement glinted in the priest's eyes. "You're a man of few words. I like that." He took one last look around the room, and his gaze fell on the screen showing DVN. "That woman looks familiar. Wasn't she the one who tried to wreak havoc on Jack's engagement party?"

Connor glanced at the monitor, which displayed a close-up of a woman whose bright red lips were twisted into a smug smile. "That's Corky Courrant. She hosts the show *Live with the Undead*."

"So this is the vampire channel?" The priest stepped closer. "I've never seen it before."

Connor sighed. The old man seemed fascinated with anything from the vampire world. Along the bottom of the screen, a message announced that Corky was about to interview her mystery guest. Corky quivered with excitement as the camera moved back and the shot widened.

Connor's jaw dropped. "Bloody hell!" He leaped toward the screen and punched the buttons to record and turn up the volume.

"—reached the pinnacle of my journalistic career," Corky said, motioning to her guest. "It is an honor to have you on my show, Casimir."

Father Andrew gasped. "That's Casimir?"

Connor zipped over to the desk and hit the alarm button that emitted a sound too high-pitched for human ears. The Vamps and shifters in the fellowship hall would hear it and rush to the office within seconds.

Connor glanced down at the dagger in his knee sock while he reached overhead to make sure his claymore was in place. "Tell them I went to DVN," he told the priest, then teleported away.

There was a big sign posted just inside the Brooklyn headquarters of the Digital Vampire Network. *Auditions tonight for* All My Vampires! *Male romantic lead role.*

Connor frowned as he pushed his way into the crowded waiting room. Apparently, over a hundred young Vamps wanted to star in DVN's most popular soap opera. They'd come dressed for the part, most of them in black tuxedos. Others had opted for costumes: a gladiator, a matador, a Dracula with a long silk cape. Connor wrinkled his nose at the staggering scent of cologne and hair gel.

"Hey!" A young Vamp in a black trench coat and dark sunglasses nudged him. "You have to get in line first to fill out the forms." He pointed a black-painted fingernail at the queue that snaked around the room.

Connor reached overhead and pulled out his claymore. With a chorus of gasps and squeals, the lads parted like the Red Sea.

"Aw, shoot, he brought his own props," muttered a young Vamp in a cowboy costume. "And that kilt looks awesome. I wish I'd thought of that."

"Damn." A Mr. Darcy impersonator tugged at his lacy cravat. "I knew I should have gone with the butch look."

Connor strode toward the receptionist desk.

The girl's mouth dropped open at the sight of his drawn sword. "I—I—"

She appeared incapable of communicating in a coherent manner, so he skirted the desk and headed for the double doors behind her.

"Wait!" the receptionist cried. "You can't go—"

Her words were cut off when the doors swung shut. He hurried down the hallway, hoping to find the recording studio before Casimir could escape. If he could kill the bloody bastard tonight, the Malcontents would scatter in disarray. Countless human lives could be saved.

He spotted the red flashing light outside a studio and resisted the urge to rush in with a war cry. Instead, he quietly opened the door and slipped inside. It was dark by the entrance, but across the room, two dim lights illuminated the stage. Connor weaved silently around the cameras, which appeared to be turned on, although they were unmanned.

"You know I love you," a male voice whispered

behind a monitor. "You make me look so good."

Connor groaned inwardly. The voice didn't belong to Casimir, but to Stone Cauffyn. Apparently, now that the *Nightly News* was over, the newscaster was dallying with a lover, perhaps a makeup artist who made him look good.

Connor rounded the monitor and discovered Stone in a passionate embrace with . . . his hairbrush.

"Aagh!" Stone jumped and his brush clattered onto the floor. "I say, you scared the dickens out of me."

Connor didn't know which was more bizarre: a man who used the word *dickens* or a man in love with his own hairbrush. "Where's Corky Courrant?"

"Look what you made me do." Stone grabbed his brush off the floor and inspected it for damage. "Dash it all, I could have scratched it."

"Where the hell is Corky Courrant?"

"No need to use such coarse language. And I strongly suggest you put away that medieval monstrosity of a weapon." Stone turned toward the monitor where he could see his own image and ran the brush through his thick hair. "I say, I do sorely miss the good old days. Regency England, don't you know? When genteel people behaved with proper etiquette and—"

"Ye bloody whoreson, tell me where Corky is!"

Stone huffed. "Miss Courrant is not here. Thank God. She wanted to sully this stage with an unsavory character."

The studio lights turned on.

"What's going on here?" A bald-headed man stood

by the studio door, his hand on the light switch. He eyed Connor suspiciously. "I've called security."

"I *am* security," Connor replied. "Where's Corky Courrant?"

The bald-headed man sighed. "This is about that stupid interview with Casimir, isn't it? I told her it would cause trouble."

"Unsavory character." Stone Cauffyn shuddered.

Connor gave the men an incredulous look. "He's a wee bit more than unsavory. He's a bloody terrorist."

"You think I don't know that?" the bald-headed man asked. "His pal Janow held people hostage in this studio. Thankfully some MacKay S and I guys showed up— Hey, is that where you work?"

"Aye." Connor strode toward him. "Where is Corky?"

"She threw a hissy fit when I said she couldn't interview Casimir here. I told her to take a few weeks off to cool down. Next thing I know, she's sending me a DVD of her interview—"

"From where?" Connor interrupted.

Before the bald-headed man could answer, he was shoved farther into the room by Angus MacKay and three other Vamps who had attended Mass at Romatech. All four of them had their swords drawn.

"Where is Casimir?" Angus demanded.

"I don't know." The bald-headed man nodded toward Phineas, Ian, and Jack. "I remember you guys from the Janow incident. You're from MacKay Security and Investigation."

"I'm Angus MacKay. And ye are?"

"Sylvester Bacchus, station manager."

"Tell me." Angus stepped closer. "Are ye aiding and abetting a known terrorist?"

"No!" Sylvester ran a hand over his bald head, which was gleaming under the bright lights. "I told Corky I didn't want any part of it. I sent her on vacation, but then she sent me the DVD—"

"From where?" Connor asked again.

Sylvester shrugged. "She didn't say. The package was postmarked California, a few days ago. Hollywood, I believe."

"I say, what a fortuitous coincidence." Stone patted his hair as he regarded himself in the monitor. "There was a report that someone spotted that unsavory character in Los Angeles."

"Several nights ago," Connor muttered. "That's when the interview must have been recorded. Casimir could be anywhere by now."

"The devil take it." Angus sheathed his sword.

"Merda," Jack grumbled. "I was hoping to kill him tonight."

"Yeah," Phineas agreed. "And the really shitty part is that bastard's back in America."

Stone shuddered. "Such coarse language. Thank God this isn't being broadcast to my listeners."

"Sod off," Connor told him.

"Humph." Stone lifted his chin and marched toward the door. "You're just jealous because your hair is unruly and barbaric."

"You mean your hair is real?" Phineas asked as Stone passed by. "I thought it was a rug."

Stone gasped and ran from the studio, clutching his hairbrush to his chest. Phineas grinned and did a high five with Ian.

"Sylvester, do ye still have the envelope Corky sent?" Connor asked. "We need that, and the DVD she made."

"Sure." The station manager rushed out.

Angus retrieved his cell phone from his sporran. "I'll call J.L. Once we get a location in California, he can check it out."

Connor nodded as he sheathed his sword. J. L. Wang was a fairly new Vamp, but as a former FBI special agent, he knew how to get the job done. "We should check every place in America that Casimir has teleported to in the past." Those locations would be embedded in his psychic memory, so he was more likely to use them than risk an unknown destination.

"Aye," Angus agreed. "Jack, go with Lara to the compound in Maine. If Casimir's there, call for backup."

"Will do." Jack teleported away.

"Ian, go to New Orleans to warn the coven there," Angus continued. "Then go to Jean-Luc's place in Texas to let him know. Is the school well guarded?"

"Aye, Phil is there with his werewolf lads." Ian teleported away.

"Phineas, I want you and Robby to check out St. Louis, Leavenworth, and those farms in Nebraska," Angus ordered. "As soon as I get Corky's DVD, I'll be returning to Romatech, so call me there to report."

"Got it." Phineas teleported away.

"That leaves the campground near Mount Rushmore," Connor said quietly. The accursed place where Casimir and his minions had slaughtered innocent people twice before. The same place where Robby MacKay had been held captive and tortured. If Connor had to lay a bet, he would wager this was Casimir's favorite location in America.

Angus sighed. "I dinna want to send Robby back there."

"I understand." Connor knew what it was like to be burdened with bad memories. "I'll leave right away."

Angus reached out to stop him. "Ye shouldna go alone. Drop by Romatech and take one of the shifters with you. Carlos or Howard."

"I'll be fine."

"That wasna a suggestion, Connor. It was an or—"

He teleported away before Angus could finish.

Chapter Two

A strong wind whistled through the forest, rustling the trees and welcoming Connor with an unmistakable odor—the scent of death. Connor swore silently as he weaved among the trees. How many mortals would have to die at this campground before the place was permanently closed? Sean Whelan of the CIA had covered up the last massacre by telling the media that a flu virus was to blame. No doubt the owners had cleaned the place up and invited more happy campers. More victims for Casimir and his minions to terrorize and kill.

Connor stood in the shadow of a large tree while he scanned the surroundings. Casimir could be long gone, or he might be hiding in the nearby caves.

A storm was brewing, building pressure and moisture in the air. Thick gray clouds swept across the three-quarter-full moon and blotted out the stars. A banging noise echoed through the campground, an unlatched door or shutter abused by the wind.

A sudden gust flipped his kilt up in the back, and he winced at the chilly air on his bare arse. He twisted at the waist to push his kilt down, and the wind ripped another lock of hair free from the leather tie at the nape of his neck. He hooked it behind his ear and continued his silent surveillance. Far off in the distance, he could spot the carved presidential heads of Mount Rushmore, the granite gleaming white among the dark hills. No doubt Casimir enjoyed the irony of mentally enslaving and murdering Americans so close to a monument of their strength and freedom.

In the clearing, the wooden cabins were dark. Connor couldn't hear any sound coming from them, no moans from dying mortals, no heartbeats. He would check them later, but for now, he assumed they were empty.

The banging noise and odor seemed to emanate from the main lodge, a rustic building made of stone and varnished logs. He sprinted toward the lodge, positioned himself next to a window, then peered inside. A large leather couch, several wooden rocking chairs, a table with a half-played game of checkers. Glowing coals in the hearth of a large stone fireplace. A homey, friendly-looking place if you didn't count the lifeless bodies on the braided rug.

Anger and disgust roiled in his gut. There was nothing he could do. Casimir and his minions were probably gone. The bloody bastards had already done their worst.

Still, he didn't want to be caught unprepared, so he drew his sword before teleporting inside. He checked the entire building. Empty. He latched the banging door, then returned to pay his respect to the bodies left in a neat row on the braided rug. Seven bodies. Throats slit to conceal bite marks, but not a drop of blood to stain the rug. They'd all been drained dry. Rigor mortis had not set in, so they'd died this evening, probably soon after sunset.

His anger grew, threatening to erupt. His grip tightened knuckle-white on the hilt of his sword. The Malcontents would have used vampire mind control on the campers to force them to submit. Two families, he assumed, since there were two sets of parents. Two lovely mothers. Three beautiful, innocent, young children. The controlled fathers would have watched helplessly while the Malcontents murdered their wives and children.

Rage flooded him, making his heart race. Emotion this intense made the blue of his irises glow, tinting his vision with an ice-cold blue. His fists clenched with the need to kill. *Please, let them still be in the caves.*

He teleported outside, his claymore raised and ready for battle. He would kill them. Every last one of them.

He stormed down the dirt path that led to the nearby caves. The wind blew stronger, tossing the trees and littering the path with small branches and pinecones. Loose locks of hair whipped across his face. He shoved the strands back and glanced up at the moon. It was an eerie blue, almost completely enshrouded with thick clouds. Good. The darkness would conceal his attack. They'd never know he was coming until his sharp blade plunged through their black hearts.

Kill them. Kill them all.

He halted with a sudden slap of clarity. Déjà vu. The same cold rage. The same black night. The same icy-blue vision. The same storm-tossed trees and scent of pine. *Kill them all.*

His extra-sensitive, glowing eyes stung with the biting wind. What a fool he was. Did he have no more control over his rage than he'd had centuries ago? What if Casimir had fifty minions with him? A hundred? Was he so damned bloodthirsty that he would walk into a trap?

He slipped into the woods, leaned back against a tree trunk, closed his eyes, and took deep breaths. *Control yerself.* His heartbeat slowed. The rage dimmed.

He opened his eyes, and his sight was back to normal. He retrieved his cell phone from his sporran. No signal. *Bugger.* He didn't want to leave the area unguarded while he teleported to Romatech. He headed back toward the lodge. Still no signal. He couldn't risk sending Angus a telepathic message since any Malcontents nearby would be able to hear it.

His gaze fell on the gleaming granite heads in the distance. Mount Rushmore. He could probably get a signal there. And he'd have a bird's-eye view of the entire area. If anyone ventured from the caves, he'd spot them.

The world went black for a second, then he was there, his feet making contact with solid rock. Before he could gain his bearings, a hard wind slammed into his back and shoved him forward. *Damn.* He'd landed too close to the edge of Washington's forehead. He skidded to a stop as a few loose rocks skittered over the precipice.

With his feet more firmly planted, he gazed down the mountain. Pinging noises echoed in the wind as the rocks bounced their way to the bottom. He'd come close to plummeting, but it probably wouldn't have killed him. He would have simply teleported to a safe place before hitting the ground.

On the hill in front of him, rows of aluminum benches climbed the slope like a giant staircase, forming an outdoor theater. The hill was topped with a visitor center and parking lots. All empty. A good thing since he didn't want an audience to witness him teleporting about. Or see his cold arse every time the wind tossed his kilt up.

With an annoyed growl, he shoved his kilt down again, then focused on the nearby hills. His superior vision zeroed in on the campground. No movement there. He spotted the rocky outcropping nearby that housed the caves. Quiet for now.

He punched in Angus's number, and the call went through.

"The devil take it," Angus growled. "I told you no' to go alone. Do ye have a bloody death wish?"

"I have a report if ye care to hear it."

"I care about following orders," Angus shouted.

"Maybe ye doona value yer own sorry hide, but—"

"Seven dead in the main lodge," Connor interrupted. That should put a stop to the annoying lecture. He was awarded by a moment of silence.

"Seven?" Angus asked quietly.

"Aye. Casimir's usual MO. The victims were drained dry, throats cut." His jaw clenched. "Three children."

Angus cursed in Gaelic. "That bloody bastard. Any sign of him? Nay, forget that! Doona do a damned thing until we get there."

A strong gust of wind pummeled Connor, and he raised his voice. "The murders occurred earlier this evening. Casimir could be long gone."

"Or he could be holed up in those bloody caves," Angus said. "I'll gather some men. Stay out of sight until we get there. Do ye hear me? Doona investigate on yer own. That's an order."

Connor's gaze flickered south, distracted by a bolt of lightning. "Bugger." There he was, standing on top of a mountain with a sword in his hand during a lightning storm.

"What?" Angus demanded. "Did ye see something?"

A vision of himself fried to a crisp. Connor tossed his sword into the forest behind the carved heads. The sky flickered again, and he whirled around to catch the end of another lightning flash. Strange. The lightning had hit in the same place twice.

"Connor!" Angus yelled. "What's going on?"

"Something . . . wrong." He narrowed his eyes. "A few miles south of the campground."

Another flash lit up the dark sky.

His breath caught. It wasn't coming from the sky. "I'll call ye back."

"Connor, doona—"

He hung up and dropped the phone into his sporran. He debated fetching his sword, but decided to leave it behind. Instead, he retrieved a wooden stake from his sporran. No sense in drawing the lightning to him. Although he wasn't quite sure it was lightning.

A drop of rain plopped onto the top of his head, and he glanced up. Another raindrop splattered on his nose, then rolled a chilly path across his cheek. He wiped his face, then focused on the area where he'd seen the flash of light. Everything went black.

He materialized in the dark shadow of trees, his feet landing on the soft cushion of pine needles. The light patter of raindrops sounded overhead, not yet heavy enough to filter through the thick canopy of treetops. He moved silently through the forest, tracing the scent of burnt wood and smoke.

When he heard a man's voice, he edged close enough to hear the words but remained hidden behind a large tree trunk.

"You left them still alive!" the man yelled. "I had to go back to finish your job."

Connor stiffened. Either these were Malcontents, or he'd stumbled across some mortals on a murdering rampage.

"We received our orders," the man continued. "The humans were all supposed to die."

Malcontents. A mortal never referred to his own

kind as *humans*. Connor tamped down on the rage that seethed within. He needed to stay calm and controlled. His grip tightened on the wooden stake. He had four more in his sporran and the dagger in his knee sock. But before he attacked he needed to know how many bastards he was up against.

A female whispered a response, too faint for him to hear. Even so, the timbre of her voice lifted the hairs on the back on his neck. It brushed his skin like a caress. *Bugger*. This was no way to react to a bloody Malcontent.

Her voice grew stronger as she made her final declaration. "I can no longer do this."

Was she rebelling? Connor's heart lurched. If he could capture her alive, she could tell them all sorts of information.

"You must follow orders," the man snapped.

"There was no reason for them all to die," she argued. "I only wished to spare the children."

"You have failed to follow orders, Marielle," he growled. "You must pay the consequences."

"No." Her whisper trembled. "Zack, *please*."

The fear in her lovely voice made Connor's gut clench, and he was seized with an overwhelming need to protect her. Bah, protect a Malcontent? She deserved to die.

"This is your third act of disobedience," the man announced in a booming voice. "The decision has been made. You will be banished."

"*No!*"

The anguish in her voice was more than Connor could bear. *Bloody hell*. He would save her.

He slid the dagger from his knee sock. As far as he could tell, there were only the two Malcontents: the male called Zack and the female, Marielle. He'd take the male by surprise, turn him to dust, then grab the female and teleport her to Romatech where he could thoroughly question her.

A dagger in one hand, a stake in the other, he zoomed toward their voices.

An intense flash of light stunned him, and he halted, his eyes squeezed shut against the pain. Bugger, how could he save her when he couldn't see?

Her scream tore through him.

"Nay," he growled. He fought through the pain and forced his eyes open. His vision sparkled with stars so badly, he stumbled over a fallen branch and bumped against a tree trunk. Still, he could discern a glowing fire ahead, and he headed toward it. The scent of burnt flesh wafted toward him, and a sick feeling coiled in his gut. Had the bastard set her on fire?

She screamed again. To hell with this. He ran toward her, shoving branches out of the way.

A ball of fire exploded with another searing, blinding light. He turned his head, eyes squeezed shut.

Boom. A blast of air whooshed against him, tossing him through the air and slamming him against a tree. His head hit hard, and he collapsed onto the ground.

He lay there dazed, pain thrumming in his head. What the hell was that? Some kind of bomb? Even with his eyes shut, stars twinkled with painful brilliance against his closed eyelids. He rubbed his eyes, willing the stars and pain to go away. Somewhere in his confused mind, he realized his weapons were gone. And the rain had stopped.. How much time had passed while he lay there helpless?

He pried his eyes open. The glimmering lights faded away, and he was once again surrounded by a dark forest. The scent of charred wood and scorched earth tainted his nostrils. In the distance, he spotted the red glow of dying embers.

Could she still be alive?

A memory flitted across his mind. His beloved's dead body. And their wee babe. He'd cradled them in his arms and cried. The last tears he'd ever shed.

He shoved that mental picture away and looked instead for his weapons. His dagger glinted a dull gray in the moonlight. He grasped it and rose wearily to his feet.

Please let her be alive.

He stumbled toward the glowing ember. It was a branch, hit by a fire that was dying instead of spreading. Strange. There was a line of trees, alive and green on one side, and charred black on the other. The half-burnt trees formed a circle around a large clearing that was void of vegetation. A foot of smoke hovered just above the ground. The air stank with charred earth and flesh. The two Malcontents appeared to be gone.

He walked into the clearing, the smoke thick around his ankles. Burned grass crunched beneath his shoes.

A roll of thunder rumbled overhead, and a strong

wind blew into the clearing. The smoke began to move, agitated by the wind, whirling around the circumference of the circle like a hurricane, dark clouds spinning around a black center. The smoke rose higher, past his knees, up to his waist.

He covered his mouth and nose till the smoke rose above his head and dissipated into the night sky. And then he saw it—the black, scorched pit in the middle of the clearing.

He ventured toward it, afraid of what he might see. Sure enough, there was a soot-covered body in the bottom of the pit. He was too late. Again.

A gentle rain began, as if to make up for the tears he no longer cried. The raindrops sank into the black earth and formed little rivulets that serpentined into the pit.

Memories of his beloved wife returned to torture him. *This is no' her*. He knew that, and yet he still felt a terrible sense of loss. Over a Malcontent.

He blinked. Maybe not. Like any vampire, a Malcontent would turn to dust with death. This woman must be human. Or she was a vampire who was still alive.

He skidded down into the pit for a closer look. She was curled into a ball like a newborn babe. Rainwater sluiced off her body, washing away the soot and revealing white, supple flesh.

"My lady?" he called to her. "Lass?"

She moaned.

She was alive. The rain continued to wash away soot and dirt. She seemed remarkably unharmed, even beautiful. His gaze drifted over her bare white arms, folded over her chest. Her legs were bent, drawn close to her core, but they appeared long and smooth, the skin beautifully luminescent.

And yet, he could still smell burnt flesh and spilled blood. The blood's aroma was strong, heady, so much richer than the synthetic blood he was used to drinking. Against his will, his body reacted. His gums tingled as his fangs sought release.

He clenched his jaw. The poor woman had just been attacked, and he was tempted to bite her? What a coldhearted bastard he was. He ventured closer, circling around to examine her from the back.

He gasped. *Holy Christ Almighty.* Burn marks crossed her lower back, red and ugly welts. Higher up, across her shoulder blades, blood oozed from gaping wounds. She must have run, and the bastard had attacked her from behind.

"My lady." He leaned over her. "I'll take you to a healer." Roman could help her.

No response. He couldn't see her face. Her long hair was a tangled mass, covering her face and shoulders. The ends were singed and dark with blood, but he detected a glint of gold in the curls that tumbled over her face.

"Lass?" he whispered, and brushed the hair back from her face. The locks felt silken against his hand. As fine as the hair on a newborn babe.

His chest tightened at the sight of her face. In five hundred years, he'd never seen such loveliness. Such fragile elegance. There was a pearlescent luster to her skin as if she was glowing with beauty from the inside out.

Raindrops fell on her face, and she flinched.

"Doona fret," he said softly. "I'll take you somewhere safe."

She moaned and shook her head.

He unpinned the length of tartan that he wore over a shoulder, then draped it over her hips.

Her eyes flickered open, then widened with horror. "No!"

He straightened. "Lass, I willna harm you."

She shook with a sudden tremor. "Don't touch me!" She kicked her legs, attempting to scramble away from him. When she rolled onto her back, she cried out in pain.

She collapsed, her eyes falling shut. "Don't touch me," she whispered, then lost consciousness.

Chapter Three

_C_onnor approached the side entrance of Roma-tech with the woman wrapped in his tartan and cra-dled against his chest. Teleporting straight into the facility would have caused an alarm to go off and incited panic, so he'd arrived in the side parking lot. Whoever was in the security office should have no-ticed him on the monitors, so hopefully they would let him in. With his arms full, he couldn't reach his ID card.

He paused outside the glass door and spotted An-gus's wife, Emma MacKay, zooming down the hall-way at vampire speed.

She opened the door, and her gaze shifted to the woman in his arms. "You found a survivor."

"Aye." Connor stepped into the hall. "I'm taking her to the clinic. Can ye alert Roman?"

"Of course." Emma touched the unconscious

woman's shoulder. "Poor thing. She smells of blood and burnt flesh. They must have tortured her like Robby. Did you find her in the caves?"

"Nay. She was attacked a few miles south of there."

Emma gave him a confused look. "Did you see Angus? He teleported to the campground about five minutes ago."

"Must have missed him." Connor hurried down the hallway. "Tell Roman I'll be in the clinic."

Behind him, Emma let out an exasperated sigh. "You didn't follow Angus's orders, did you?"

He kept walking. No time to explain his decisions when the woman was bleeding in his arms. Not that he usually bothered to explain himself.

"Is Angus right, then?" Emma called after him. "Do you have a death wish?"

"Nay." He reached the foyer and turned left. Why would he want to die when he'd go straight to hell?

He strode through some double doors and into a hallway lined with glass on one side. Through the glass, he could see the garden and basketball court, illuminated by bright outdoor lights. The children, Constantine and Sofia, were bouncing basketballs while their mother, Shanna, sat on a nearby bench, chatting with her sister.

Down the hallway, Roman emerged from his office. His eyes widened at the sight of the injured woman. "She barely has a heartbeat. What happened?"

"She was attacked. Nasty wounds on her back."

Roman glanced out the window at his wife and

children. "We'll get Laszlo to help." He banged on the office door next to his and called out to the short chemist.

"Yes, sir?" Laszlo peered out, then gasped. "Oh dear." He rushed along beside them as they headed through a waiting room into the dark clinic.

The strong smell of antiseptic cleansers assaulted Connor's nostrils. He laid the woman gently on her side on a sheet-covered gurney, then made sure his tartan covered up the essential areas while leaving the wounds on her back exposed.

"So what's the story?" Roman asked as he hit the light switch.

Connor winced at the sight of the woman's injuries so clearly illuminated. "I discovered her being attacked a few miles south of the campground at Mount Rushmore."

"You witnessed the attack?" Roman asked as he and Laszlo washed their hands in a large stainless steel sink.

"I heard it. There was an angry man named Zack, a Malcontent, I believe, and he was yelling at her for no' killing all the humans. She was—"

"Is she a Malcontent, too?" Roman interrupted, drying his hands.

"Perhaps. She was clearly rebelling, and then the man attacked her."

"Does she have fangs?" Laszlo asked as he snapped on some synthetic gloves.

Connor felt a momentary cringe of embarrassment. Such a simple thing, but he'd forgotten to check her teeth. Although he'd certainly looked over the rest of her. Thoroughly. But only to determine her injuries. A man would have to be dead not to notice a beautifully shaped female with a lovely face and dewy soft, lustrous skin. And he wasn't dead. At least, some of the time.

He leaned over her and whispered, "Doona fash. I willna harm you." He pressed a fingertip against the woman's upper lip and gently prodded it up. Dainty white teeth. No fangs.

She must be human.

But what about Zack? He'd referred to people as "humans," and he'd said something about the master ordering their deaths. He definitely sounded like a Malcontent. Had he attempted to use vampire mind control on this woman to force her to kill? But what vampire could cause the flashes of light and the blast of air that had thrown Connor forty feet through the air? What had burned the trees and scorched the earth? How had Marielle survived such an attack?

He straightened slowly. Roman was watching him curiously while Laszlo readied a tray of surgical instruments.

"Well?" Roman tugged on his gloves. "Is she a vampire?"

"Nay." Connor took a deep breath. "I doona know what to make of her."

"How dramatic." Laszlo gave him an amused look as he set a stack of towels on a table close to the gurney. "She's definitely female. She doesn't have the scent of a shifter, so I think we can safely assume she's human."

"Ye doona think her blood smells a wee bit odd?" Connor asked. " 'Tis verra rich."

Laszlo tilted his head, sniffing. "True. I can't quite detect her blood type, and I usually can."

"Enough talk." Roman marched up to the gurney. "Let's take a look at her before she bleeds to death." He whisked the bloody tartan away and tossed it on the floor.

"Nay!" Connor quickly pushed her onto her stomach and shot Roman an annoyed look. "I've already checked her for injuries." With vampire speed, he nabbed a towel off the nearby table, flipped it open, and covered the woman's rump. " 'Tis only her back that needs tending."

She moaned a few mumbled words.

" 'Twill be all right, lass," he answered as he carefully tucked the towel around her hips. Did the sound of her voice affect the other men like it did him? Perhaps not, since Laszlo possessed the same politely helpful expression he usually had.

"Did she just say, 'Don't touch me'?" Laszlo asked.

"Aye. She said that when I first found her. She may be afraid her nudity will incite men to abuse her." Connor noticed that her hair had fallen over her face when he'd shoved her onto her stomach. He brushed her hair back to make sure she could breathe. "Doona fash, lass, we willna harm you."

"Don't . . ." Her eyelids flickered, then closed.

"Och, she's out again." Connor straightened and discovered Roman regarding him again with a curious look. His cheeks grew warm. So he was displaying some normal human kindness. Was that so strange? He lifted his chin. "So do ye plan on helping this woman or letting her bleed to death?"

Roman's eyes glinted with amusement. "Let's get her cleaned up, Laszlo."

The short chemist passed Roman a bottle of antiseptic cleanser and some gauze pads. When Roman doused her burns with antiseptic, the woman moaned.

"Ye're hurting her," Connor protested.

"We have to protect her from infection." Laszlo smoothed some ointment over the burns. "This will help with the pain and promote healing."

"She may end up with some scars," Roman commented as he began to clean the wounds across her shoulder blades.

She flinched, then moaned again.

Connor grimaced as he saw the two cuts now clearly defined on her back. Each one looked about six inches long. Fortunately, they had stopped bleeding.

Roman finished cleaning her wounds, then tossed the bloody strips of gauze into a metal pan. His eyes narrowed as he examined the cuts. "This is . . . odd. At first, I assumed the slashes were caused by a sharp instrument like a knife or sword, but if you look closer, you'll see the skin is burned."

"Perhaps she was cut by a laser?" Laszlo leaned over for a closer look. "It *is* odd." He glanced up at Connor. "Are you sure this was an attack of violence?"

"Of course it was violent. She was bloody well wounded."

Laszlo frowned as he fiddled with a button on his lab coat. "The two wounds are perfectly symmetrical. I would wager the lengths are exactly the same down to the millimeter. This sort of precision would not occur in a normal fight."

"Laszlo makes a good point." Roman selected two forceps off the surgical tray and gently examined one of the wounds.

"What are ye doing?" Connor asked. "Ye should be closing the wounds, no' opening them."

Roman drew in a sharp breath. "Laszlo, look at this."

Laszlo nudged Connor aside so he could get closer. "What is that? Some sort of bone or cartilage?"

"Yes," Roman whispered. "And it's been severed."

Laszlo straightened with a jerk and grabbed a button on his lab coat. "I've never seen anything like that on a human." He turned to Connor, his eyes wide. "What have you brought here?"

Connor swallowed hard. She wasn't human? He touched a lock of her hair. She felt so human.

"Is there anything else you know about her?" Roman asked. "Did you hear anything—"

"They were arguing." Connor closed his eyes briefly, struggling to remember everything that had happened before he'd been blasted into a tree and had the sense knocked out of his head. "The man, Zack, was yelling at her. She had disobeyed three times. She was being banished." He opened his eyes and gazed down on her beautiful face. "He called her Marielle."

Roman's eyes widened, then his gaze dropped to her wounds. "God's blood," he whispered. "Surely it can't be."

"What?" Connor asked.

Roman stepped back, his face pale. "Gabriel, Michael, Rafael."

Laszlo shook his head, nervously twirling the button on his lab coat. "No. Just because her name happens to rhyme, that doesn't mean—"

The clinic doors swung open, and Shanna ran to the sink to wash her hands. "Why didn't you call me? I just heard about the injured woman. Emma thought the Malcontents might have tortured her."

Connor shot a worried look at Roman. The medieval monk appeared awestruck. Laszlo was clutching a button so hard his knuckles were white. If they were thinking what Connor suspected they were thinking, they had to be wrong.

Shanna dried her hands and grabbed a pair of synthetic gloves. "Why so quiet?" She gasped. "She hasn't died, has she?"

"Nay," Connor said. "She's unconscious."

Shanna snapped on the gloves as she approached. She grimaced at the sight of the wounds. "How terrible. Did you give her a local anesthetic?"

Roman shook his head. "No."

"I think you should before you stitch up the wounds," Shanna said.

"I'm not sure what to do," Roman murmured. "I think we'd better call Father Andrew."

"Why?" Shanna's eyes widened. "You mean for Last Rites? Surely we can save her." She placed her hand on Marielle's head in a protective gesture. Her eyes rolled up, and she crumpled.

"Shanna!" Roman grabbed her as she fell.

"Oh my!" Laszlo rushed toward them.

"Shanna?" Roman patted her face. Her limp body sagged in his arms, and he settled her on the floor. "Shanna?"

Connor watched, his innards growing cold with horror. He didn't want to believe his eyes. Or his ears, for no matter how hard he strained, he could barely hear a heartbeat. Laszlo had to be thinking the same thing, because he fell to his knees and grabbed Shanna's wrist to feel for a pulse.

"Shanna!" Roman screamed and shook her.

"Sir," Laszlo told him quietly. "She's fading fast."

"No! She's going to be fine. She— Oh, God." He seized his wife's face. "Shanna, wake up!"

"Roman!" Laszlo shouted, his eyes glittering with emotion. "She's dying."

Roman glared at him. "No. She just fainted, that's all. She—"

"She's going to die," Laszlo yelled. "You have to change her now!"

"It's too soon! The children are too young. Sofia's only two!"

"You have no choice," Laszlo gritted out.

Roman shuddered, then gazed down at his wife. "Oh God! I can't lose her." He looked wildly about the room, and his gleaming eyes landed on Connor. "What have you done?"

Connor stepped back from the accusing eyes. "I dinna mean . . . please, change her before it is too late."

"You're supposed to protect my family," Roman hissed. "You brought an angel of death here!"

Connor's blood ran cold. Holy Christ Almighty, had he truly brought death to the family he had sworn to protect?

Roman pointed at the woman on the gurney. "Get her out of here before she kills my children, too!" With a hoarse cry, Roman tilted back his head and shot his fangs out. He sank them into Shanna's neck.

Connor didn't know which was worse: the sound of Roman frantically sucking all the blood from his wife, or the wrenching sound of his sobs while he did it.

My fault. Connor doubled over, nausea churning his gut. *My fault.* Shanna had trusted him to protect her, and he'd brought death to her. Just as he had his own wife and newborn child.

He fell to his knees. Failure again.

"Connor," Laszlo whispered.

He glanced up to see Laszlo standing by the gurney.

"You need to take her away."

He glanced at her, then at Shanna, dying in her husband's arms on the floor, then back at Marielle. Could Roman be right? Was she truly an angel of death?

Connor rose to his feet and lurched toward her,

grabbing the edge of the gurney in his fists. "Why dinna ye kill *me*?" he growled. God knew he deserved it.

"Perhaps she couldn't," Laszlo said quietly. "We're already . . . dead."

Connor snorted. One little request, and God couldn't grant it for him. "Ye'd think He'd want me in hell."

Laszlo frowned at him. "Take her away from here. Quickly."

He tugged the sheet loose from the gurney and wrapped it around Marielle. How could she look so sweet and innocent when she was so deadly? He gathered her in his arms.

She moaned as his arm came in contact with her wounded back. "Don't touch me," she whispered.

"Aye. I should have listened to you, lass." With one last glance at Shanna, he teleported away, taking the angel of death with him.

Chapter Four

*P*ain. It flooded her senses, drowned her body, and made it nigh impossible to think of anything other than the torture she endured. With every breath she drew, the pain swelled and sucked her deeper into a black hole.

Marielle had never realized before how sensitive the human body was. No wonder some people begged her to take their souls early. She'd always felt guilty when ordered to grant such a request, fearing the act made her a murderer, but now, for the first time, she realized Zack had been right all along. The Deliverers weren't angels of death, but of mercy.

Was that why Zackriel had punished her? Was she being forced to endure pain in human form so she would appreciate God's mercy and stop questioning orders?

With her eyes still shut, she began to pray. *Heavenly Father, please forgive me. I was wrong to ever doubt Your infinite wisdom. I have learned my lesson. Please return me to Your favor so I may continue to serve You.*

No answer.

Her eyes flew open. Why couldn't she hear an answer? The Heavenly Father always answered His angels. And she was still an angel. Wasn't she?

Panic seized her. She struggled to sit up, even though it caused her more pain. A white sheet was wound tightly around her like a shroud, frightening her even more. *I'm not dead yet!* She tugged the sheet down to her waist and fought against the pain, just enough to clear a bit of her mind.

Glory to God in the Highest, she called out mentally.

Silence.

Her breath caught. Where was the Heavenly Host? They should have responded with the usual refrain—*And on earth, peace, goodwill toward men.*

Hundreds of thousands of angels—Guardians, Messengers, God Warriors, Healers, and Deliverers—all part of the Heavenly Host and always there, connected in spirit. They'd been with her since the dawn of her existence. At any given moment, there was a chorus of angels who were singing, and others joined in between assignments. It was a constant, never-ending liturgy of praise that filled them with joy and peace.

She frantically opened her mind. They had to be there. If she could just get past the pain, she would hear their beautiful voices. *Glory to God in the Highest!*

Silence.

A sob of disbelief escaped her mouth.

Banished. No singing. No words of comfort. No communication at all with her fellow angels. No response from the Heavenly Father. She was absolutely alone. Abandoned and racked with pain.

She had to get back. Somehow.

She willed her wings to spring forth, but two lightning bolts of pain stabbed her in the back. She cried out, but the torture robbed her voice and only a gasping croak escaped. She twisted to look over her shoulder. Dear God, no! She hadn't dreamed it. Zack had taken her wings. No wonder she was in so much pain.

No wings. She covered her mouth to stifle a sob. How would she ever get back to heaven? She was earthbound.

With a sharp twinge of fear, she realized she had no idea where she was. She'd been so distracted by pain and so focused on the spiritual realm, she'd not given her surroundings any thought.

The forest was gone. She was in a dark shelter of some kind. Sitting on a cushioned chair. No, larger than a chair. It was what humans referred to as a couch. How had she arrived here?

She recalled a shadowy dream that had entwined itself like a velvet ribbon around the onslaught of pain. There'd been a voice, a deep male voice with a lilting accent she'd found soothing. Strong arms that had held her tenderly. She'd thought it naught but wishful imaginings. No human could touch her without dying.

But someone, or something, had brought her to

this dark place. Most likely not one of the Heavenly Host, not when she'd been banished from them. *They're not the only angels.* Her skin prickled with a terrible thought. What if she was considered a fallen angel now? What if one of Lucifer's servants had collected her?

Terror struck her so hard, she forgot the pain. She looked frantically about the dark room. Looming shadows of unknown objects surrounded her. A sudden creaking noise made her jump and strain her ears. There was someone nearby. Just outside the room. Footfalls moving back and forth, occasionally striking a board that creaked. Heavy footfalls, most likely a male.

Who was he? Was he guarding her so she couldn't escape? She dragged the sheet up to her chin as if she could hide from whoever was outside.

Her gaze wandered about the room. She gasped when she spotted a pair of glassy eyes staring down at her. Unblinking. Inhuman. Her gaze inched higher, and her heart lurched. The horns of the Beast!

She screamed.

The door flung open, and a man burst into the room, flipped on the lights, and slammed the door shut. She froze in shock at the fierce look on his face and the gleaming dagger in his hand. Was she to be murdered for the pleasure of the Beast?

She turned back to the glassy inhuman eyes, and a grateful squeak escaped her mouth. It was naught but the head of a deer mounted on the wall. There were several hunter trophies: a moose head over the fireplace and a tusked boar on another wall, close to a rocking chair and bookcase. She sent up a quick prayer on their behalf and winced when it was met with silence.

Still, she could feel some relief that the poor beasts were no threat to her. Unlike the man with the dagger. With the sheet still clutched tightly under her chin, she glanced in his direction.

He scanned the room quickly, then focused on her. "Are ye all right?"

She nodded although she felt far from all right. She was hurting, frightened, confused, and strangely unnerved by this man's presence. He was regarding her with an odd look. Cautious and alert. Curious, perhaps, though the intensity of his gaze hinted at something stronger, something she couldn't place.

He had the look of a warrior, but not a God Warrior. There was nothing angelic about him. Whether from heaven or hell, both angels and demons tended to assume a flawless human form with spotless, rich apparel.

This man had to be human. A Scotsman, perhaps, since he was wearing a plaid kilt. His shirt was torn and stained, his kilt old and faded. Dirt and mud coated his knee socks and shoes. He was large with a raw and rugged edginess to him as if he'd just done battle. *Earthy.* His long hair was a tangled mess, blown by the wind, a beautiful fiery red. His eyes, they still watched her, the grayish-blue irises reminding her of the sky just before a storm unleashed its raging winds. Earth, fire, and wind—three elements fused together in one gloriously fierce creation.

Her gaze shifted to his dagger. Did he mean to harm her or protect her?

"Och." He reversed the dagger with a fluid movement. "I dinna mean to frighten you. I thought ye were in danger."

His voice. It was his voice she'd heard while slipping in and out of consciousness. The lilting accent reminded her of the music she was accustomed to hearing in her mind.

She watched closely as he leaned over to slide the dagger into a sheath beneath a knee sock. Apparently, he'd rushed into the room, ready to do battle in her defense. God might not have answered her prayer, but He'd provided her with a protector. *Thank you, Lord.*

With a sigh of grateful relief, she lowered her hands and the sheet to her lap. "May I ask your name?"

He glanced up at her, then straightened with a jerk. "Holy Christ Almighty."

She frowned. "No, I don't believe you are."

"I dinna mean—" He shifted his gaze to a spot behind her and whispered, "Oh, Christ."

"Is He here?" A surge of hope swelled inside her. She twisted to look, but pain ripped across her back. She cried out, doubling over to grip her knees.

"Och, lass." He moved toward her. "'Tis sorry I am for yer suffering. Is there anything I can do?"

She moaned, willing the pain to subside. The cushion she sat upon jiggled, and it took a moment for her to realize he'd taken a seat next to her on the brown leather couch.

"No." She straightened, wincing at the pain. "You must keep your distance from me. I . . . I could be dangerous." Her wings were gone, her psychic connection to the Heavenly Host was gone, but she couldn't be sure that all her angelic powers were gone. If this man touched her, he might die.

His gaze dropped to her bare chest, then jerked away. "We have to do something about yer brea— I mean, yer wounds. On yer back. Ye probably need stitches."

Sew up her wing joints? "No!" She pressed a hand to her chest. Beneath her palm, her heart beat wildly.

He glanced at her hand, then looked away. "We canna leave the wounds open. I—" He grimaced, squeezing his eyes shut. "Lass, I canna talk to you like this."

He looked like he was in pain. She wished she could comfort him, but she didn't dare touch him. "Is something ailing you?"

He opened his eyes, shooting her a fierce look. "Ye doona know?"

The rough edge to his voice made her skin prickle. His eyes darkened with a reddish tint. Her heart stuttered. She'd never seen human eyes do that. Demon eyes could, but she could have sworn this man was human.

"For God's sake, lass, cover yerself."

She was so stunned by the changing color of his eyes that she didn't realize that he'd grabbed the edge of the sheet till she saw him lifting it up to her chest.

She gasped. "Don't touch me!" She squirmed back on the couch, kicking at him from under the safe barrier of the sheet. Her frantic actions ripped the sheet from his grip and caused them both to lose their balance.

She fell back, gasping when her back hit the cushioned arm of the couch just as he fell on top of her, his outstretched hands landing firmly on her breasts. She froze, terrified that she might have killed him.

With their faces only inches apart, their eyes met. The red sparks in his irises faded until only the smoky blue color remained. Seconds stretched into an eternity as she caught her first glimpse into his soul. A human soul. On the surface: honor, courage, strength. Beneath: loneliness, regret. And there was more. He was hiding something dark, something that caused him great pain.

He blinked, and she realized he'd been staring into her eyes with the same intensity. He exhaled, his breath soft against her cheek. He was still alive.

"You're touching me," she whispered.

He reeled back, lunging to the other end of the couch. "Forgive me. I—"

"And yet, you still live."

"Aye, I should be struck down." He closed his eyes and rubbed his brow. "God help me, I just groped an angel."

"You know who I am?"

"Aye." He collapsed against the back sofa cushion. "I dinna mean to . . . assault you."

"You did nothing wrong." She sat up, wincing at the pain. "You simply fell and caught yourself."

He snorted. "Aye, and I have verra good aim."

She glanced down at her breasts. With the warmth of his hands gone, the nipples had reacted by turning tight and pebbly. "How . . . interesting."

With a moan, he dragged his hands down his face. "Just kill me now."

"I mean you no harm."

"Then cover yerself before my eyes explode."

She recalled how Adam and Eve had covered themselves in shame. "I'm so sorry." She dragged the sheet up to her chin. "I didn't realize I was . . . offending you."

He made an odd noise, somewhere between a snort and a groan.

"I'm not accustomed to looking like this. We do occasionally take human form when we need to interact with mortals, but it's merely an illusion. This body is different, though. It feels . . . real."

"That it does," he muttered.

"The pain is certainly real." She sighed. "I fear I was given this body so I could fully experience pain."

He turned his head toward her. "Ye've never had a body before?"

"No." She peeked underneath the sheet at the breasts he'd found so offensive. They looked fairly normal to her.

Her eyes widened at the thatch of hair at the apex of her thighs. "Good heavens!" She clutched the sheet against her chest. She'd never looked like that before.

He sat up. "What's wrong?"

"I—I appear to be more human than I thought."

His gaze drifted down to her lap, then slowly back up.

She realized, then, that he knew exactly what she was referring to. Her cheeks flooded with heat, a sudden and odd sensation, and she pressed a hand against her face. "I believe I'm running a fever."

His eyes twinkled with amusement. "'Tis called a blush, lass."

"Oh." A dozen different emotions swirled inside her. Embarrassment, confusion, curiosity, pain, remorse, a terrifying fear that she'd never make it back to heaven, another fear that she was venturing into a dangerous unknown world of human sensation and emotion, and in the midst of it all, she felt a overwhelming urge to touch this man. It had been so long since she could touch a human without causing death.

"You—you never told me your name," she whispered.

The amusement faded in his eyes. "I'm Connor. Connor Buchanan."

"You found me in the woods. You saved me."

He shrugged. "Anyone would have—" He froze when she touched his cheek.

"I remember hearing your voice. It was soft and lilting and gave me comfort." She brushed her fingers along his jaw, marveling over the prickle of his whiskers against her fingertips. Angels never needed to shave. When they assumed human form, their skin was always smooth and perfect.

"Connor Buchanan," she whispered, and noted his throat moving as he swallowed. "It's so amazing that I can touch you. I've always found humans fascinating. So wild and imperfect." She smoothed a finger over a small scar close to his chin where no whiskers grew. "And yet, so beautiful."

His jaw shifted beneath her hand, and she drew back, feeling her cheeks grow warm once again. "Of course, I find all the Lord's creations to be beautiful."

"Really?" His mouth curled up. "Even a cockroach?"

Her cheeks blazed hotter. "Well, I must admit you look considerably better than a cockroach."

"Such flattery. Be still my heart."

She smiled. He was teasing her, much like her friend Buniel enjoyed doing. Her smile withered as she wondered if she'd ever see her best friend again. Or any of the Heavenly Host. Her predicament crashed down on her with a sudden onslaught of grief for the world she'd lost. Her shoulders slumped. "I don't belong here."

"Marielle—" Connor nodded when she looked at him. "I heard that man Zack call you by name. And I heard yer screams when he attacked you."

"His name is Zackriel. He's my—*was* my supervisor."

"Ye're better off without him. He sorely abused you."

She bowed her head. "I was being punished."

"Why? Did ye do something wrong?"

She glanced at him, worried that he might be judging her, but all she saw in his eyes was a tender concern. "Angels strive to be perfect in every way. I . . . have failed."

"Ye look perfect to me."

Her heart swelled at his compliment, although she knew she had fallen short. "I'm not very good at following orders, not when they don't make sense to me."

He nodded slowly. "I understand."

She had a feeling he really did understand. She was sorely tempted to touch him once again, but winced when she felt something wet trickle down her back.

His nostrils flared. "Ye're bleeding again. I know a doctor in Houston who can sew up yer wounds."

Sew her wing joints shut? Her eyes stung with tears. How could she do that? How could she give up what she was?

But was she still an angel? She was disconnected from the Heavenly Host. She was no longer a Deliverer, for her touch had not killed Connor. Her body was now human, frail and sensitive, susceptible to injury and disease. She could actually die.

A tear rolled down her cheek. She'd lost more than heaven and her friends. She'd lost her immortality.

"Och, lass." He touched her cheek, brushing away the tear with his thumb.

Her skin tingled, and she marveled at the frisson of emotion that skittered through her. Such a strong reaction to such a light touch. It must be caused by the novelty of her new body. Or perhaps she was suffering from loneliness, cut off from the Heavenly Host. But when she looked into Connor's eyes, she knew it was more. She was drawn to this man. She wanted him to touch her. And she wanted to see more of his soul.

She covered his hand with hers, holding it against her face. Perhaps all hope was not lost, for she still retained a little angelic power. Whenever she touched the dead or dying, their souls opened up to her like a book, and she could witness their entire life in an instant. With Connor, the skill was greatly diminished. He didn't die, but as long as she touched him, she could still catch a glimpse into his soul.

And there it was, hidden far beneath his outer shield of honor and forbearance. A deep dark pit of despair and remorse. It was a painful place, too painful to visit with the suffering she was already experiencing.

She released him. "I'm sorry I'm not a Healer."

"Aye," he said gruffly. "'Twould be good if ye could heal yerself."

"I was referring to you." She touched his chest. "You're carrying a dark pain inside you."

"Nay." He jumped to his feet and moved away from her, his face pale and rigid. "'Tis yer wounds we must be looking after. I'll—" He stopped when a ringing sound emanated from the leather bag he wore in front of his kilt.

"I need to take this." He pulled a communication device from the bag and lifted it to his face. "Angus, how is Shanna?"

He listened awhile, then an expression of relief swept over his face. He walked toward the back of the room. "I'm at the hunting cabin."

He glanced back at Marielle. "I'll be just outside the door. Doona go anywhere. I'll be right back." He opened a back door and stepped outside.

She glimpsed a starry sky before he shut the door. Her gaze wandered to the front door that Connor had used earlier. If she went outside, she could call for help from the Healers. Her best friend, Buniel, was a Healer, and he was probably aware that she was missing from the Heavenly Host. He had to be worried about her.

But Connor had told her to stay put. Another order that didn't make sense. If Buniel could help her, it was worth a try.

She stood slowly, her body stiff and aching from her wounds. She wrapped the sheet around her, wincing as it touched her back. She slipped out the front door and gasped when she was enveloped with chilly night air. She'd never felt the temperature before. She wrapped her arms around herself and shuddered. To her surprise, her breath frosted in the air.

She crossed the wooden porch and descended the steps to the clearing in front of the cabin. The brown grass felt icy cold beneath her bare feet. No wonder humans were so fond of clothes and shoes.

She pivoted, taking in her surroundings. In the light of the moon and glittering stars, she could see the snowy silhouette of gentle mountains. Patches of white snow gleamed in the shade of the nearby forest. Newly budded leaves filled the air with the scent of spring. How amazing was the Lord's handiwork. *Glory to God in the Highest!*

No answer.

She willed herself to be strong. Just because she could no longer hear the angels, it didn't mean they couldn't hear her. She dropped the sheet in a pool around her feet, then with a shiver, she stretched her arms up to the heavens.

Chapter Five

*C*onnor shut the back door so he could talk on his cell phone without Marielle overhearing. She didn't seem to have any memory of the disaster at Romatech, and he was in no hurry to remind her. She was suffering enough already.

He scowled at the night sky, bright with stars and the three-quarter-full moon. It was chilly here in the Adirondacks, but much calmer than it had been in South Dakota. Even so, an angry storm was brewing inside him.

He wanted to curse the heavens and one angel in particular—Zackriel. The bastard had cruelly abused Marielle, and for the life of him, Connor couldn't imagine what she could have done to warrant the torture she was enduring. She had questioned Zack's orders in order to protest the killing of children. What was wrong with that?

She was gentle and kindhearted, everything he would expect an angel to be. She'd been more concerned about causing him harm than easing her own suffering. She'd even wished she could heal him instead of herself.

In spite of her good intentions, that moment had scared the hell out of him. Had she managed somehow to see into the black pit of his soul? It had to be some sort of angelic talent, but it made her dangerous. It made him want to flee. Even so, he knew he had to stay. The lass needed protection. She was so damned innocent, she didn't even know it was wrong to expose her breasts.

And what breasts. Full and soft. The luminous white skin made a startling contrast to the rich red color of her nipples. Nipples that had been pressed into the palms of his hands. Even now, his hands itched to touch her again. That soft, sweet skin.

Bugger. He slapped himself mentally. She was an angel, an innocent, sweet angel, and he was lusting after her. Again. Even for a sorry bastard, he was stooping to a new low.

She was just so damned beautiful. Any man would be reduced to a blithering idiot in her presence. And it wasn't just her beautiful body. Or face. Or voice. There was something about her eyes. He'd gazed into them and a strange sense of peace had enveloped him . . . until he realized he was groping her lovely breasts.

"Connor?" Angus's voice sounded impatient. "Are ye still there?"

"Aye." He rested an elbow on the wooden railing that surrounded the back porch.

"Ye dinna answer my question," Angus growled.

What question? Connor winced. His mind had wandered again to Marielle's breasts. "Could ye repeat it?"

Angus grunted with frustration. "I asked about the woman ye found. Is she really an angel?"

"Aye, she is." Admitting it out loud seemed bizarre, so he changed the subject. "Did ye investigate the caves at the campground?"

"Aye, but they were empty. Casimir and his minions must have moved on after killing those puir families."

Connor groaned inwardly. It always seemed to go that way. They could track Casimir by the dead bodies he left behind, but that left him always one step ahead. And it left them unable to protect his next group of victims. "Was there any sign of him at the other places?"

"Nay. We have no idea where he is."

Connor took a deep breath. "How is Roman?"

"He's pissed. What do ye expect?"

"I thought ye said Shanna was going to be all right."

"We think she will be. She did finally accept some of Roman's blood. But it took about fifteen minutes, and in that time, Roman was going out of his mind. He thought he'd lost her." Angus sighed. "Laszlo thinks it took a long time because Shanna's subconscious dinna realize what was happening."

"Aye," Connor agreed. "It all happened verra suddenly."

"She drank a small amount of Roman's blood, then fell back into the vampire coma," Angus continued. "We willna know for sure if she's transformed until tomorrow night."

Connor swallowed hard. Like all Vamps, Roman would wake just after sunset, and hopefully, his wife would wake with him. "How are the children?"

"Their aunt, Caitlyn, has taken them home. She and Carlos will stay with them. They . . . doona know what has happened."

A surge of guilt swept over Connor. If Shanna died, it would be his fault. The bairns would be motherless. The family he had sworn to protect would be destroyed.

"I've asked Robby and Olivia to act as bodyguards for Roman and his family," Angus said quietly.

Connor stiffened as if he'd been struck in the chest. He was being replaced.

"This is for the best," Angus continued with a rush. "Olivia is a psychologist, so she'll be able to help the children adjust."

Connor gritted his teeth. "I've kept Roman safe for over sixty years."

There was a pause before Angus responded. "Roman requested someone new."

Connor flinched. "Nay."

"Ye doona ken how upset Roman is. He was ripping the clinic apart with his bare hands. I've never seen him like this before. Emma had to teleport Father Andrew here to calm him down."

With a sigh, Connor leaned forward on the railing. He knew the danger of uncontrolled rage. "I never meant to harm his wife."

"I understand, but if I canna trust ye to follow orders . . ." Angus's voice trailed off.

Connor had a sinking feeling he was about to be

fired. It was unthinkable. Not that he needed the money. He'd stashed away plenty over the centuries. It was the fact that he was being seen as a failure, a traitor. "Angus, there was no way I could have predicted what happened to Shanna. Who the hell would have believed that I'd find an actual angel—"

"I know. That was explained to me in great length. I was verra close to firing you, but ye have a strong advocate here who convinced me ye were no' to blame. Father Andrew thinks verra highly of you."

Connor jerked upright with surprise. The priest had saved his job?

"In fact, Father Andrew believes this has all happened for some sort of divine purpose." Angus snorted. "He hasna convinced Roman of that yet. Nor me. I'm still pissed that ye canna follow simple orders. If ye had, Shanna might still be alive."

Connor didn't think so. Even if he'd gone back to the campground to meet Angus, he would have still seen the fireballs in the distance and gone to investigate. Could Father Andrew be right? Was he supposed to find Marielle tonight? Only a Vamp could have picked her up and helped her. Any mortal would have collapsed after touching her, just like Shanna had.

He sighed. Father Andrew had to be wrong. God would never cast his barbaric, undead hide in a noble role. The priest was trying to interpret signs that didn't exist. Or trying to see goodness in a Vamp where it had long withered away.

A breeze rustled the trees in the distance, then

swept toward Connor. The minute the air hit his face, he felt more awake, more alert. His senses sharpened, anticipating . . . something. He scanned his surroundings and listened carefully. Nothing.

"Father Andrew is eager to meet the angel," Angus said. "Roman doesn't want her here at Romatech, so I thought I'd have someone teleport the Father to the cabin."

"No' now. She's wounded and bleeding. I need to take her to Dr. Lee in Houston." Connor referred to the Vamp doctor who had delivered both of Shanna's children and regularly patched up Vamps and shifters. "And I need some clothes for her."

"I'll ask Emma to take care of that. Let me know when ye're back."

A stronger breeze whipped Connor's hair across his face, and he pushed the strands back. An awareness sizzled through him that something was off. His senses strained, expecting something. Soon.

And then he heard it. Marielle's voice. Clear and beautiful. Singing a melody so sweet it made his heart ache.

"Christ," he whispered.

"What?" Angus demanded. "Are ye all right?"

"I'll call you back." He disconnected and dropped the phone into his sporran.

Her voice continued, ringing clear in the night air. She must be outside. So much for following his orders.

He descended the porch steps, and a strong wind shoved him toward the side of the cabin. Now he realized what was off. The wind should be chilly, but it wasn't. He rounded the cabin, and the wind still blew at him. Strange. It seemed to be circling the cabin. Another warm gust pushed him toward the clearing in the front.

He halted with a jerk when she came into view. She was naked, standing with her back to him. Her skin glowed in the moonlight, and her curly blond hair tumbled to the small of her back. Her hips flared into an arse that could inspire poetry. Unfortunately, he'd never been a poet, so it simply inspired another round of lust.

Snap out of it, he mentally snarled at himself. She was an angel. And she was up to something strange. Her arms were extended overhead, reaching for the stars. She tilted her head back as she sang to the heavens, and her hands moved gracefully with the music, the lovely expressive hands of a dancer.

He'd heard once that the body was a temple, but he'd never believed it till now. She was so beautiful. And her voice—only an angel could sound so good and pure.

The wind picked up, whirling around the cabin and playing havoc with his kilt. As he watched the trees sway and bow, he realized Marielle was in the center of the circle.

A breeze lifted her golden hair, and the long tresses seemed to float about her shoulders. Some of the locks were dark and matted at the ends with her blood. He winced at the sight of her wounded back. Dark trickles of blood meandered down the white glowing skin.

She had to be in pain, and yet her song sounded

so joyful. It made him ashamed for all the years he'd spent grumbling and rueful. But how was he to feel when he'd lost the only woman he ever loved, and that love had driven him to destroy his own soul?

He jerked when something warm touched his cheek, something feather soft. He looked about, but saw nothing. Wait, over there, a glimpse of movement, something sheer and white in the wind. It rushed past him, then faded to nothing.

A tinkling sound like wind chimes floated through the air, in and out of his hearing, and he strained to listen. Yes, there it was. He couldn't tell if it was bells or harps or perhaps both, but he'd never heard anything so enchanting. So peaceful, as if his wandering soul had finally returned home.

Then the voices began. Male and female. Perfect in pitch and harmony, singing the same melody as Marielle. And beneath it all, he could hear and sense a low, steady vibration that stirred the air. Constant like a heartbeat. The beating of angel wings.

He closed his eyes, feeling like a lowly sinner who had accidentally stumbled upon something sacred, something no human was ever meant to see. But he couldn't close his ears. The voices continued, so achingly sweet, he never wanted it to end.

More wisps of movement brushed across his face, and each time it happened, a small burst of joy would warm his heart. He opened his eyes and stepped toward Marielle. His body tingled as the warm wind enveloped him. His heart matched the rhythm of the wings beating the air. Such joy and peace—it was addictive. Bright green grass sprouted in the circle of wind, and he felt an overwhelming urge to lift his arms to the heavens like Marielle.

Before he could move, a flare of light stunned him. He blinked, trying to stay focused on her. She'd stopped singing and stood frozen, surrounded by a bright light. It flashed with an intensity that forced him to shut his eyes.

"Thank you," Marielle whispered. "The Lord is good."

He opened his eyes as the light dissipated. Her back was completely healed. No marks or bloodstains, just her white glowing skin. Even her hair was clean and shiny gold.

The wind grew stronger again, and he could feel the whirling cyclone moving upward. The voices faded away.

"No!" Marielle cried. "Don't leave me!"

Her hands appeared to grasp something that Connor couldn't see, then to his amazement, her body rose off the ground. She wasn't levitating, he realized. Rather, she was being lifted by whatever she was holding.

"Please." Her voice trembled with emotion. "Take me with you."

Was she returning to heaven? Was she forgiven? Connor's heart raced as he watched her body rise higher and higher. Four feet off the ground. Six feet. Was there hope for those who had fallen short?

Was there hope for him?

"No!" Marielle screamed as her hold was broken. She fell to the ground, and with a final whoosh, the wind was gone.

All was quiet except for the sound of her weeping. The air grew chilly again.

Connor felt his whole body sag. He should have known there was no hope. No forgiveness for the likes of him.

But Marielle—dammit, she was different. Her heart was pure. She still believed God was good. It made his heart ache to listen to her tears.

He walked to where she was huddled on the ground, leaning forward on her elbows, her shoulders shaking. "Are ye all right?" He winced at the stupid question.

"They left me behind," she cried. "I'm all alone."

"Nay, lass." He fell to his knees, then picked the sheet off the grass and draped it over her back. "Ye're no' alone."

She turned her head to peek at him. Her cheek glistened with tears. "Did you hear them? Did you hear the music?"

"Aye."

She sat up, and the sheet slipped off her back. "Then you know how beautiful it is."

"Aye." He hastily wrapped the sheet around her.

She continued, oblivious to his roving eyes. "And now you understand why I need to go back. It's where I belong."

He tied the ends of the sheet over her right shoulder. "I couldna really see them, but I heard them. And felt them in the wind."

She nodded. "The Heavenly Host. I've always been with them, since the moment of my creation. Their music is always in my head. We're all connected, always sharing our thoughts and praise."

"Always?" He grimaced. "Ye doona tire of the constant noise?"

"Noise?" She gave him an indignant look. "You're calling our music noise?"

"It was beautiful," he conceded, then drew a deep breath. "'Twas the loveliest sound I've ever heard. I've never felt so full of joy and peace."

She smiled. "Then you do understand."

He shook his head. "'Twas no' real."

"Of course it was real. You felt it."

"It was . . . alluring, but it canna be. I live in this world where we canna escape death and suffering. Besides, I wouldna want the constant voices in my mind. Nor would I want anyone else to hear my thoughts. I need my privacy."

She looked at him, stunned. "You prefer to be all alone? You'd rather suffer than be at peace?"

"I prefer to be myself."

She touched his chest. "Even with the pain you carry?"

He scooted back, out of her reach. "At least it is my own."

Frowning, she rose to her feet. "I never realized before how frightening and lonely it is to be human. How do you bear it?"

He shrugged and stood. "Some rely on faith."

"What do you rely on, Connor Buchanan?"

He winced. "I'm no' a good person to ask. I just keep going . . . out of stubbornness."

Her mouth tilted with a smile. "Then I shall be stubborn, too." She shivered, then shifted her gaze to the stars. "I will find my way back. And I will count my blessings, for the Lord is good."

Connor stifled his snort, but she still glanced at him as if she could sense his doubt.

"The Lord *is* good," she insisted, "for I have been sent a fierce protector."

He almost looked over his shoulder to see who she was referring to. It was laughable to consider him a "fierce protector." He'd failed his wife and bairn. He'd failed Shanna.

"And the Lord let Bunny heal me," she continued with a smile.

He blinked. "Ye were healed by a rabbit?"

She laughed, the sound like the tinkling of wind chimes. "Bunny is a nickname for Buniel. We've been best friends for ages. He's an excellent healer."

"He?" Her best friend was male? And a perfect angel, too. *Bugger.*

Her smile faded. "Bunny wanted to take me with him, but . . . he couldn't."

Connor's jaw shifted. "I wouldna have let you go."

Her eyes widened with surprise. She stared at him, speechless, while he fought to keep his desire from showing. Time stretched out, and the air felt thick between them. He balled his fists to keep from touching her, from drawing her into his arms.

Her gaze drifted down his body, then back up. His heartbeat quickened. He looked at her mouth, wondering if she could possibly react like a real woman. Could she be aware he was studying the pink plumpness of her mouth?

She licked her lips.

Yes. He smiled slowly.

Her cheeks blushed a pretty pink, and she turned away. "A mouse just died," she said in a breathless voice.

"Excuse me?"

"A mouse has died. Carried off by an owl."

He strained his eyes, but couldn't see an owl in the night sky. "Where?"

"About thirty miles away." She gazed at the forest with a pensive look. "Not all my powers are gone. I can still sense death."

"Ye know when something's dying? How far can ye sense it?"

She shrugged. "Anywhere in the world. It's how the Deliverers know where to go when people are dying."

She can sense death. Connor paced toward the cabin, then back. This was a valuable skill. If she could sense people dying while Casimir and his minions were attacking them, then she might be able to help the Vamps find him.

He glanced up at the stars. Had God sent him a secret weapon that would help them defeat Casimir once and for all? Then Father Andrew might be right. He was meant to find Marielle.

He looked at her.

She was gazing at the distant mountains. "I have always thought the Earth was full of beautiful places. Now I can experience them as a human. It should be very interesting, don't you think?" She turned to him with a hopeful expression. "'Weeping may last through the night, but joy comes with the morning.' "

He winced. Morning always brought him death. He was going to have to explain what he was. He could only hope she wouldn't be disappointed. Or disgusted.

She shivered and hugged herself. "I never realized how much humans feel the cold."

"Ye should come inside." He motioned toward the cabin, then froze when he heard a noise in the forest.

She heard it, too, whirling around to face the line of trees. Leaves shuddered as something pushed through the bushes.

Connor whisked the dagger from the sheath beneath his knee sock. A black snout poked out from the bushes. A wolf? No, it was wolflike, but bigger. The black, furry beast emerged from the forest.

Marielle stiffened with a gasp.

Connor widened his stance, his dagger ready.

She touched his arm. "You cannot fight it. It's here for me."

The beast moved to the side, keeping its dark eyes focused on her. Then the eyes turned red and began to glow.

Connor inhaled sharply. "What is it?"

Her voice was whisper soft. "A demon."

Chapter Six

*M*arielle squared her shoulders and glared at the black beast, feigning a courage she wished she had. She'd dealt with fallen angels before, but always with the vast power of the Heavenly Host to back her up. Now she was alone.

Not entirely alone. Connor stepped in front of her, but his protective move only increased her fear. Didn't he realize he was no match for a demon?

"Go inside," she whispered.

He shook his head slightly, never taking his eyes off the beast. "Nay."

He hardly knew her, yet he was willing to risk his life for her? Emotions swirled inside her, strong human emotions she wasn't accustomed to feeling. She didn't know whether to hug Connor or yell at him. One thing was certain, she didn't have time to deal with the confusion now. She had to make sure he survived.

She eased away from him as she glared at the demon. "Begone!"

The wolflike creature tilted its head to watch as Connor moved close to her once again. She groaned inwardly. Was he determined to get himself killed? She should have yelled at him.

The beast drew her attention with a low growl. Its red gleaming eyes focused on her. Its lips pulled back to reveal a row of long, pointed, yellow teeth.

"I have come to escort you to your new home," it rasped in a masculine voice. "I suggest you come along quietly."

She lifted her chin. "Never."

"I could rip you apart," it hissed.

"Try it, and I'll send ye back to hell in pieces!" Connor shouted, lifting his dagger.

The beast snorted. "A savior? I love killing those." It narrowed its bloodred eyes on Marielle. "Are you willing to let the fool die for you? In that case, hell would be the right place for you. Of course, you could act like a little angel and rescue him from the jaws of death. Come with me, and I'll leave him alone."

Connor grabbed her arm. "She's no' going with you," he said hastily as if he were worried she would sacrifice herself to keep him safe.

The swirl of emotions inside her came to rest, and she knew then that she'd much rather hug Connor than yell at him. He had a good and noble heart.

She laid her hand on top of his. "I won't let it hurt you."

The beast made a huffing noise. "So you refuse to

be frightened or coerced into submission. No big deal. I have other strategies." It snarled, baring its long, yellow teeth. "One way or another, I will succeed."

Its body glimmered, then reshaped, taking the form of a human male. A very handsome male with flowing red hair, bright blue eyes, a bare muscular chest, and a plaid kilt. A perfect body with flawless skin.

She felt Connor stiffen beside her. No doubt he was shocked to see an enhanced version of himself.

The demon flashed a brilliant white smile at her. "Now do you like me?"

The demon must think she was attracted to the Scotsman if he was attempting this ploy. With a small jolt, she realized he was right. Still, the trick wouldn't work. Connor was real, and his rough, imperfect exterior only made him more beautiful in her eyes. "Begone."

"Before I can even introduce myself?" The demon assumed a wounded expression. "Come, Marielle, didn't they teach you better manners than that up in heaven?"

She swallowed hard. He already knew her name.

"Oh yes." He nodded his head, knowingly. "We've been watching you for some time. Poor little angel who keeps getting into trouble. We knew it was only a matter of time before those sanctimonious snots decided you weren't good enough for them."

Her skin crawled with goose bumps. Connor's grip on her arm tightened.

"My name is Darafer, by the way. My friends call me Dare."

"Go back to hell," she said.

"Of course. And I would be honored to take you with me." His mouth curled with the hint of a smile. "If you dare."

"I will never go with you."

"You will," he snapped, his smile vanishing. "You'd be a fool to want back into heaven. Look what those prigs did to you. They tortured you. Cut off your wings. Left you in the dirt to die."

She winced inwardly. In her mind, she knew better than to heed the words of a demon, but there was enough truth in what he said to make her heart squeeze in her chest. *Banished.* Connor seemed aware of her pain, for he drew closer.

Darafer's upper lip curled in disgust. "Even your best friend rejected you."

And that slashed at her more painfully than having her wings ripped off. "He had to follow orders."

"Did he? Why didn't he disobey?" Darafer's blue eyes glittered. "You have the courage to disobey. You're more like us than you realize."

That shocked her out of her pain. "I will never be like you! You spread evil across the world."

He waved a dismissive hand. "Yeah, yeah, it's a dirty job but somebody has to do it."

Anger flashed inside her. "You make light of it when millions of people suffer because of your evil?"

His eyes turned solid black. Beside her, Connor tensed.

"I wasn't joking," Darafer snarled. "Somebody

does have to do it. Your precious Father in Heaven couldn't play the good guy if we weren't doing our part. He needs us as much as He needs you. Where would Jesus be without Judas? By joining us, you can play a valuable role in the grand scheme."

She shuddered. "You're twisting the truth to suit your own purposes."

"You think so?" Darafer snorted. "Maybe now that you're disconnected from the all-holy collective, you'll start thinking for yourself." He stepped closer. "Who created us, Marielle? All of us fallen angels—who made us the way we are?"

She stiffened. "The Lord is good. It was *your* decision to rebel against Him."

Darafer smirked. "And wasn't it your decision to rebel, too, little angel?"

Her skin chilled. Connor gave her arm a tug as if he wanted to move her back. She held her ground, even though inside, she cringed with fear. Was there any going back now? What if she'd already doomed herself?

Darafer's eyes turned back to blue, and he gave her a knowing look. "Yeah. Free will. It has a way of coming back to bite you in the butt."

Her heart raced. "Just because I disobeyed a few times doesn't make me like you. I was trying to protect the innocent. You derive a sick pleasure out of tormenting them."

He shrugged. "All in the grand scheme, angel. Sometimes a little torment drives the sheep right back into the Father's arms. You could say we're doing Him a favor." Dare's mouth curled. "Of course, sometimes it leads them straight to hell. Speaking of which—" He extended a hand toward her. "Are you ready?"

With a shudder, she stepped back.

Darafer chuckled. "It's a bit warmer there. You'll like it."

She shook her head. "I will never go with you."

Connor remained close by her side. "Ye have yer answer, now go."

Darafer gave the Scotsman a bland look, then turned back to Marielle. "Have you ever heard of a banished angel being reinstated?"

No, she hadn't. Panic swelled inside her, and she fought against the surge of fear and despair. She couldn't give up hope.

"The longer you stay on Earth, the more human you will become," Darafer continued. "Do you really want to lose all your power? How about your immortality? Do you want to grow old and turn to dust?"

She forced the words past the lump in her throat. "Better to lose my immortality than my honor."

Connor inhaled sharply, drawing her attention. He was staring at her, his eyes gleaming with strong emotion. He inclined his head. "Well said, lass."

Her heart expanded in her chest. He understood. He approved of her even when heaven had rejected her. A spring of gratitude and affection bubbled up inside her, and the panic faded away. "Thank you."

Darafer snorted. "Pardon me while I puke."

She glared at him. "I'm not going with you. Begone."

"You're so naïve," Darafer hissed. "You have no idea what kind of parasite is clinging to you, do you?"

Connor stiffened. "She told you to go. Now leave!"

"Looks like I hit a nerve." Darafer smirked as he looked Connor over. "I suppose Marielle could do worse for a bodyguard. Hell knows you've shown a distinct talent for violence."

Connor lifted his dagger. "Doona tempt me."

"Oh, I do. That's my job, Connor Buchanan." Darafer chuckled when the Scotsman flinched. "Yes, I know who you are. You've been on our list for a long time."

Marielle touched Connor's arm and winced at how tense he was. "Pay him no heed. He's a deceiver."

Darafer snorted. "Who's deceiving whom? Maybe for your sake, angel, I should take out the trash. Wouldn't want the parasite to soil your dewy innocence." He smiled slowly as he looked her over. "I'm planning on doing that myself."

"Ye willna touch her!" Connor yelled.

Darafer shot him an angry look. "Do you really think you can stop me? Try it. Then I won't have to go back empty-handed tonight. Looks bad on my résumé, you know."

Marielle's heart lurched when the demon's eyes turned red. He was planning to attack.

Connor realized it, too, for he jumped away from her and assumed a defensive stance.

Her heart pounded. Connor couldn't possibly

defeat a demon. And still, in the face of death, he tried to protect her. He kept moving to the side to draw the demon away from her. His dagger gleamed in the moonlight as he raised his arm.

Darafer stepped back and his body shimmered, shifting back into the beastly black wolf. He crouched, preparing to pounce. A low growl rumbled in his throat.

Oh God, no. She couldn't let Connor die. She shot up a desperate plea for help, but heaven was silent. It was up to her. Curling her hands into fists, she hoped she still retained enough power to keep Connor from being ripped to shreds.

The beast leaped.

"No!" She threw her arms out, her hands splayed. A massive burst of air exploded around her, shooting out in all directions. It blew the beast back, tossing him forty feet into the forest. He crashed into some bushes.

Unfortunately, the blast also knocked Connor back forty feet and he landed on his back, thumping his head hard on the ground.

With a growl, the beast jumped to its feet.

Marielle raised her hands, hoping she could muster enough power for another attack. Fear crept along her skin, making her shiver. Darafer had the same abilities she had, but even more since he could change his form at will. He could also call for assistance from Lucifer's other servants.

She, on the other hand, was trapped in a human body and cut off from the Heavenly Host.

He morphed into a male human form. Long dark hair, emerald-green eyes, luminous pale skin. This was most probably his preferred look, and she hated to admit he was striking. Dramatic and elegant, too, in his black leather pants and long black coat.

"You don't want to get into a battle with me, angel," he said quietly. "You know you'll lose."

She swallowed hard.

"Luckily for you, I'm not allowed to force you to accompany me," he continued. "Free will, you know. Sometimes the black beast strategy works, and the poor sap says he's willing out of fear. You didn't fall for it, though, so I'll have to wait until you *want* to come with me."

"That will never happen."

He smiled slowly. "I was hoping you would be a challenge. Makes the final surrender so much more sweet." He lifted a hand, palm up, and a red glowing light appeared, then condensed into a solid red object. He tossed it toward her.

The object rolled toward her feet. A shiny red apple.

"Let me know when you're ready to take a bite." With a whoosh, black wings sprang from his back, and he was gone.

Marielle drew in a deep breath. Thank God. She was safe for now. And Connor? She ran toward him.

He was still flat on his back. The poor man must have hit the ground hard.

With a gasp, she stumbled to a stop. *Good heavens.* The blast of air had blown his kilt up to his chest.

"Oh," she breathed. She'd never seen an angel

look like that. Come to think of it, she'd never seen a
human look like that. As a Deliverer, she'd seen her
share of naked human bodies, but they tended to be
old, or ill, or injured. And they were usually gray,
shriveled, and dead.

She stepped closer. Definitely not gray. Rather
pink and healthy. And most definitely not shriveled. Even his hair was interesting. Red and curly, it
looked very soft and . . . touchable.

She tilted her head, marveling at the size and
structure. It was all so . . . out in the open. Blatant.
Masculine.

The invasive purpose of the design was so obvi-
ous, she reacted instinctively and pressed her thighs
together. That was . . . curious. Oddly pleasurable.
A shiver ran down her arms, but she didn't think it
was caused by the cold. She felt strangely . . . warm.

Connor groaned, and she jerked to her senses.
Good heavens, he'd been lying there, possibly hurt,
and she hadn't even checked him for injuries.

His eyes opened, and he blinked at her.

She crouched beside him. "Are you all right?"

"Is the demon gone?" He struggled to sit up.

"Yes, we're safe now."

"Och, good." He fell back and with a moan,
rubbed his head.

"Are you injured?"

"Head hurts," he mumbled. "Keep getting
knocked—" His eyes widened. "That was you who
blasted me into a damned tree earlier? When Zack
was attacking you?"

"I tried to defend myself. You were caught in the wind?"

"Aye." He propped himself up on an elbow. "How long was I out?"

"A . . . few minutes."

He glanced at himself, then jolted into a sitting position and jerked his kilt down to his knees. "Damn." He shot a fierce look at her.

She jumped to her feet. "I—I beg your pardon." Her cheeks grew warm. "Pray, do not be troubled. It is truly a . . . small matter."

"Small?"

"Yes. Of little consequence."

"Little?" He arched a brow. "Do ye need another look?"

"For goodness' sake, I was not referring to your size. The Lord knows you're definitely—" Her cheeks blazed hotter, and it didn't help that he appeared to be enjoying her discomfort. She turned away stiffly. "In truth, I hardly noticed."

The minute the words escaped, she froze in shock. What was she doing? Never before in her entire existence had she uttered a falsehood.

Her gaze fell on the apple Darafer had tossed onto the grass. A reminder that the longer she stayed on Earth, the more human she would become. The more susceptible she would be to sin. As in hiding the truth. Telling lies.

Or feeling lust.

Good Lord! She'd never get back to heaven if she fell into sin.

"Marielle?" Connor asked softly, and his voice sent a shiver down her spine.

She dashed to the cabin and let herself inside. She paced around the large room, weaving a trail around the couch and through what appeared to be a kitchen and dining area. Around and around she went, and her heart kept pounding, thundering in her ears. This wasn't helping. She felt caged in. She'd always had wings before. She'd always had the ability to fly anywhere she wanted.

She had to get back to where she belonged. There had to be a way.

She stopped and brought her clenched hands up to her face. *Don't panic. Think.* Unfortunately, her thoughts seemed to bounce around, echoing in the empty cavern of her mind where she was used to hearing thousands of voices. Voices that sang praises and offered a constant stream of encouragement and comfort. They were all gone. She was so alone.

Don't panic. Darafer was counting on her panic and fear so he could lure her in. No doubt, he figured she would miss the company of angels so badly, she'd be willing to join the fallen ones just to regain some sense of belonging. But the lure was false. There would be no comfort in hell.

There had to be a purpose to what she was enduring. The Heavenly Father was always big on learning through experience. He was forgiving, too. She just needed to find the right path, the right penance that would convince Him she'd learned her lesson.

Maybe there was something she was supposed to do here on Earth. Some noble mission. And once she'd proven herself worthy, she'd be allowed back into heaven.

She resumed her pacing. That had to be it. She was simply being tested. The Father would never completely abandon her. She was not a fallen angel. No matter what Darafer said.

Like all of Lucifer's servants, Dare was a deceiver. He would try anything, say anything to confound her. And without her connection to the Heavenly Host, she had succumbed too easily to fear. She couldn't let that happen again. She would have to be strong. Fearless. Gird herself with righteous armor.

She jumped when the door clicked shut. Oh great, that was real fearless of her. She gave Connor a wary look.

He stood by the door, watching her with an intensity that sent a shiver down her back. His hand gripped his dagger once again. He must have found the weapon somewhere on the grass. He leaned over to slip it into the sheath beneath his knee sock.

The cabin felt much smaller with him there.

She took a deep breath to calm her racing heart. "I'm sorry you had to experience a demon. He'll come again, so it's not safe for you to be with me. I appreciate your noble intentions, but it would be in your best interest to leave."

"Ye think I turn tail and run that easily?" His blue eyes glittered. "Ye consider me a coward?"

"No! I think you're very brave. Amazingly brave, really, since it's highly unlikely that a human could ever defeat a demon in battle. Not without help from the Heavenly Host, and I'm afraid they're not going to respond if I call them. So I won't blame you if you want to go . . ."

He watched her closely. "I'm no' going."

Her breath whooshed out. She hadn't realized she was holding it. She definitely hadn't realized how much she wanted him to stay. "Thank you."

He nodded, then wandered toward the kitchen. "Before we go any further, I need to tell you about myself. The demon referred to me as a parasite, and—"

"Please don't let his insults upset you." She strode toward Connor. "Demons are notorious deceivers. Darafer probably wants to drive a wedge between us, make me doubt you so I'll reject you and lose your protection. He knows we'll be easier to defeat if he can separate us."

"Ye just tried to separate us."

"Yes." She stopped in front of him. "Because I'm worried about your safety. I really should insist you leave." She hung her head. "I'm being selfish to keep you."

"Nay, lass. I stay because I want to."

She lifted her gaze to meet his. "You were willing to fight a demon to keep me safe. You stood by my side and believed in me. You're a good, brave, noble man, Connor Buchanan. You rescued me tonight, and I will always be grateful for your courage and strength of character."

He stood still, watching her with a stunned look. She smiled. Not only was he honorable, but modest, too. She reached up, placed her hands on his temples, and tugged his head down. "God bless you." She kissed his brow, then released him.

She turned away to resume her pacing, but he grabbed her wrist and halted her. She gasped when he shoved her against a wall, her wrist still gripped in his fist and now pinned against the wall close to her ear.

Her heart lurched. "What—what are you doing?"

He planted his other hand on the wall and leaned toward her. His eyes blazed a brilliant blue. "When ye kiss a man, ye should do it properly."

Her pulse raced. "I did give you a proper kiss."

"For a child." He leaned forward till his mouth was close to her ear. His breath feathered against her skin, causing tiny tingles. "I'm a man. I believe ye noticed that."

"*Hardly* noticed it." She shivered when his nose nuzzled her ear. "And I apologized. I didn't mean to offend you."

"Do I seem offended to you?"

"I—I—" Good heavens, was that his tongue? "You were offended earlier when I was uncovered. So it seems . . . logical to assume . . ." She couldn't remember what she was trying to say when his tongue was tickling her ear.

"I was never offended," he whispered. "I've been dying to touch you again."

Her mind swirled, leaving her dizzy. She trembled as his lips moved down her neck.

"Yer pulse is jumping," he murmured.

"I know." She struggled to breathe. "I think this heart must be defective. It's not working right."

He chuckled. "Ye're working perfectly. Ye're so beautiful. So sweet." He kissed a trail to her jaw.

Her heart pounded. Was he headed to her mouth? She should stop him. Angels didn't behave like this. They simply didn't have the desire.

But she did. It had to be this human body. It was so finely tuned to enjoying the nuance of his every touch. The pressure of his lips, the moistness of his tongue. The nibbling. The tickling. The rough scrape of his whiskers made her knees grow weak. And his sweet words made her heart swell with longing.

"Connor," she whispered, her eyes flickering shut.

She felt his breath against her lips. So close. Her heart raced with anticipation.

Good heavens, this had to be lust. No wonder it was a sin. It was so powerful. She opened her mouth to say no, but his lips touched hers. Softly, then he pulled away.

She froze. That was it? Surely there was nothing sinful in that. It had seemed rather . . . sweet.

His mouth met hers again, lingering this time, pressing gently. Yes, definitely sweet. He seemed to be tasting her, sipping from her. He drew her bottom lip into his mouth and suckled gently.

She moaned.

He pulled her into his arms and scattered kisses over her cheeks, her nose, her neck. With her eyes still closed, she wrapped her arms around his neck. It felt so good to be wanted. And by Connor. Such a good, brave, noble man.

He returned to her mouth for another kiss. She tried to return it, mimicking his gentle sucking and nipping motions. A groan rumbled deep in his throat, and the sound reverberated through her, settling between her thighs with a curious sensation.

That was . . . odd. Uncomfortable, somehow, as if she were aching for something. Desperate for something.

Her fingers dug into his shoulders, and she moaned against his mouth.

With a growl, Connor deepened the kiss, molding his mouth more fiercely against her. Warning bells sounded in her head. The sweetness was gone, replaced by something wild and . . . hungry.

Lust. Good heavens, she'd been seduced by sweetness, only to fall headlong into passion. And the most shocking part was she wasn't sure she wanted to stop.

He planted his hands on her bottom and pulled her tight against him. She gasped. Good heavens, he was bigger than before.

"Connor—" She jolted when she saw his eyes. Bright red and glowing.

She jumped back, banging against the wall.

"Careful." He took her by the shoulders, but she scrambled away.

She recalled now that his eyes had turned red earlier. She'd dismissed it at the time, for she'd known all along he wasn't a demon. She would have sensed that immediately. Earlier on the couch, she'd had a glimpse into his soul, and it was human.

It didn't make sense. She'd been so sure he was human. "I don't understand."

He held up a hand as if to reassure her. " 'Tis all right. Ye know I would never harm you."

Her mind raced, zipping through all the possibilities. Was he from another planet? No, he was a Scotsman. A shifter? She didn't think so. What had Darafer called him—a parasite?

With a gasp, it all became clear. And terrifying. For he was the same kind of creature that had killed all those people at the campground. "You're a Cheater!"

He blinked. "A what?"

"A Cheater." Her heart sank. "That's what Zack calls them because they've cheated death. He hates—" *You.* She couldn't bring herself to say it.

Her eyes welled with tears. "You're a vampire."

Chapter Seven

She was disappointed. Appalled. Connor gritted his teeth as he watched a tear slip down her lovely cheek. He was tempted to brush it away, but figured she'd jump back to avoid his touch.

One thing he'd learned in nearly five centuries of existence: everything could change in the blink of an eye. It had taken only a few minutes for him to doom his soul back in 1543. Only a second for Shanna to fall into a death spiral after touching Marielle. Only another second for him to abandon all common sense and surrender to the yearning that had been growing inside him from the instant he'd first heard Marielle's voice. And less than a minute ago, she'd trembled in his arms and moaned with pleasure. He'd thought a miracle had happened. A beautiful angel cared for him, admired him, even desired him.

But seconds later, she backed away in horror.

When would he ever learn? Joy and peace were not meant for him. Love would always be beyond his reach. Whenever he indulged in a glimmer of hope, it was always dashed to pieces. And rightly so.

What a fool he'd been to want Marielle. His black tainted soul wasn't worthy of the lowliest of human beings, and yet, he'd dared to touch an angel?

Her reaction was exactly what he deserved.

"Ye know about vampires," he said quietly.

"Yes." She wiped her cheeks. "I'm a Deliverer—*was* a Deliverer—so I have escorted many souls who were murdered by your kind."

His jaw clenched. It was the Malcontents who went about murdering mortals, but he could hardly claim to be any better.

She took a deep breath, lifted her chin, and looked him squarely in the eyes. Even with despair twisting his gut, he felt awed by Marielle. The poor lass had been wounded and banished from heaven, threatened by a demon, and groped by a vampire, all in one night. And yet, she was still standing, strong and determined.

"Did you kill those people at the campground?" she asked.

"Nay."

She paused, an expectant look on her face as if she were waiting for him to explain. What was he to say? That he was a good man? That he was insulted she would even ask such a question? There was no point in pretending. The demon had verified what Connor had long suspected. He was on the list for hell.

"You were at the campground?" she asked. "Why?"

"I was searching for someone. I was hoping to kill him."

Her eyes widened. "May I ask his name?"

"Casimir."

"Oh." She stared across the room, her eyes unfocused as she pondered something. "Interesting."

Connor shook his head slightly. Being a vampire was one thing, but God forbid he be boring.

She paced toward the fireplace, then skirted the far side of the couch, keeping her distance from him. "We know about Casimir. Zack has been delivering Casimir's victims for centuries, and he hates him with a passion that is unbecoming to an angel. He's been reprimanded several times for it."

She paused in her pacing to glance at Connor. "We're not supposed to interfere in human events. It might disrupt a human's right to free will."

He scoffed. "As if anyone would choose to be murdered by a vampire."

"I questioned that myself." She sighed. "But it only served to anger Zackriel. He was already in trouble for his own complaints and didn't want any of his staff making him look worse."

"God forbid," Connor said dryly. He had no sympathy for the angel who had cruelly abused Marielle.

"But I thought I made a valid point," she continued. "Since vampires are not exactly human, I believe angels should be allowed to interfere. Casimir and his kind are supposed to be dead. Their very existence is unnat—" She stopped with a wince.

"Unnatural?" Connor finished her sentence. "An accursed blight on humanity?"

Her face grew pale. "You are quick to condemn yourself."

She was the one who'd called him *unnatural*. A Cheater. He felt stiff and cold down to the marrow in his bones. "You heard the demon. I'm on the list for hell."

"Did you hear *me*? I told you demons are deceivers. You shouldn't believe anything he told you."

"I knew it long before he told me."

"Why?" She stepped toward him. "What have you done to deserve hell?"

He narrowed his eyes. First the priest had wanted to know, and now an angel, but he would never confess. "I'm a vampire. Is that no' enough?"

"Is it?"

Bloody hell, he didn't know. Father Andrew was always preaching that they were still the children of God. Connor figured there was hope for Vamps like Roman, but not for him. He was doomed, with no one to blame but himself.

And he should never have tainted someone as good and pure as Marielle. "I apologize for . . . touching you. I had no right."

She started pacing again and went around the dinette set before heading back to the couch. She halted and rested her hands on the back of the couch where an Indian blanket rested.

She traced the design with her fingers. "I don't think you need to apologize. You didn't force me."

"Ye're innocent in the ways of the flesh. I took advantage of that."

She glanced his way and arched an eyebrow. "Then I stand corrected. You sorely abused me."

He flinched as if she'd thrust a spear through his heart. He shut his eyes briefly, willing the icy cold inside him to spread out and freeze the pain. "Aye." It was all he could manage to say.

Weariness dragged at him, sapping away his strength. He strode to the refrigerator, pulled out a bottle of synthetic blood, and shoved it into the microwave.

"What is that?" She moved closer.

"Food." He shot her an annoyed look. "Blood. If I doona drink it from a bottle, I might steal it from you."

"Would you?"

He'd rather die. "I've taken blood from others. Thousands of people. I've been around for centuries."

She rested her elbows on the breakfast bar and watched him. "I'm feeling a bit . . . disgusted."

That hurt. "I'm sure ye are." He grabbed the bottle from the microwave and guzzled down some blood.

"When's the last time you bit someone?"

He wiped his mouth with the back of his hand. "What does it matter?"

"Was it last night?"

"Nay."

"Last year?"

He paused, wondering what she was up to. "No." He finished the bottle and set it in the kitchen sink.

She perched on one of the barstools. "As a Deliverer, whenever I touched the dead or dying, their entire lives would unfold before me. I would see everything." She tapped her fingers on the countertop. "Most people spend their lives trying to do right, but not everyone. I have seen some dreadful things."

"Did ye take those people to hell?" Connor asked quietly.

She shook her head. "It was not my place to make that sort of judgment. But I have witnessed enough life stories to recognize the huge difference between a person who chooses evil because he revels in it, or the person who struggles against an evil that has been thrust upon him."

She leaned forward on her elbows, watching him intently. "I may appear innocent in some ways—well, I suppose I am." Her cheeks turned a light shade of pink. "But when it comes to good versus evil, I have millennia of experience. I know evil when I see it. So do you want to know what disgusts me?"

He stepped back, reluctant to hear her answer. "Evil, I suppose."

"There's no evil here."

He blinked. What was she saying?

She frowned at him. "I'm disgusted by your failure to defend yourself."

What the hell? "I was ready to defend myself in battle with Darafer."

"I'm not talking about a physical battle. I accused you of sorely abusing me, and you took it! How could you?"

"I'm a vampire, Marielle. A Cheater. A parasite. I had no right to touch you. And doona tell me otherwise. I saw yer reaction when ye realized the truth. I saw the horror on yer face, the tear that rolled down yer cheek."

"I was shocked, that is true. But it only took me a few minutes to realize you had to be one of the good vampires."

"Ye know—"

"Of course we know." She waved a dismissive hand. "How could we miss the fact that during the Great Vampire War of 1710, thousands of mortals were murdered, drained dry by Casimir and his army, while the opposing vampires managed to feed without killing a single person?"

He stared blankly at her.

She scooted off the barstool and circled the counter. "You're acting like you're no better than Casimir." She motioned toward the empty bottle in the sink. "He would never drink blood that way. He would have attacked and killed me just like he did those other victims at the campground."

Connor's heart pounded in his chest. "Ye canna make me out to be good."

"No?" She stepped closer. "You saved my life tonight. You were willing to fight a demon to protect me. Do you expect me to forget all the brave and noble acts you've committed simply because you're a vampire?"

Could an angel actually consider him good? "Ye doona know the darkness within me."

"Remember what I said about touching the dying and witnessing their lives?" She laid a hand on his cheek. "It doesn't work as well with you, but I can see—"

He moved back out of her reach. "Ye see into my soul?"

"A little. The more I touch you, the more I see."

Bloody hell. That's why she'd wanted to heal him earlier. She'd seen the black torment deep inside him. *Bugger.* The whole time he'd spent kissing her, he'd been opening his soul.

"I know you're a good man, Connor. I saw your strong sense of honor and integrity. I saw a human soul in all its imperfection and glory. That's why it didn't occur to me that you were anything but human. An evil vampire would not have such a black pit of pain and remorse hidden in his heart. He wouldn't know the meaning of remorse."

The pain swelled in his chest, begging to be released. Here was a beautiful woman, an angel, who believed he was still good. Did he dare hope there was anything other than hell awaiting him? "Marielle," he whispered.

"Yes." She placed her hands on his face.

He wanted her so much. He wanted to grab her and never let go. She was everything good and beautiful that he'd ever dreamed of. She was a beacon of light in the darkness where he dwelled. And by some holy miracle, she believed in him. That alone made him want to fall to his knees and lay his heart at her feet.

She gazed intently into his eyes. "Show me what's hurting you."

Let her see what he had done? She would hate him if she knew. He would lose her respect, her belief in him. How could he bear that?

"Nay." He stepped back, breaking contact with her. Dammit to hell. No, damn *him* to hell. He could never confess, never let her know.

She regarded him silently, disappointment causing the corners of her beautiful mouth to tilt downward. He wanted to kiss her again and coax those lips into a sigh of pleasure. But no matter how much he wanted to hold her in his arms, he could never risk touching her and exposing his dark sins.

"You stood by me in my time of need," she told him solemnly. "I hope to return to heaven soon, but in the meantime, if there is anything I can do for you, I will do it gladly."

He didn't dare tell her the first thing that came to mind. Once he pushed aside those lustful thoughts, he recalled her ability to sense death. "There may be something ye can do to help us, but I'll need to discuss it first with my friends."

"You mean other good vampires?"

"We call ourselves Vamps. Together with some shifters and mortals, we're trying to protect mankind and defeat the bad vampires. We call them Malcontents."

She nodded. "I have always been grateful that there are good vampires determined to fight the bad ones, especially since the angels are not allowed to interfere. Whenever Zack complained about the

Malcontents, as you call them, we were told to trust in the Lord, that He had already sown the seeds to resolve the matter. I believe He was referring to you and your friends."

Connor swallowed hard. He'd heard Father Andrew say much the same thing over the last few years, that the Vamps were actually fulfilling some kind of divine purpose in their attempt to protect humanity and destroy the Malcontents. Roman, the former monk, believed it, but Connor had rejected it as a load of psychobabble designed to make them feel good about being Undead. As if it made any sense at all for them to feel warm and fuzzy about being cold and stiff.

"I apologize for the way I reacted to your . . . condition," Marielle continued. "I was upset about those who died at the campground, especially the children, so when I realized you were a vampire, I— for a little while, I feared the worst."

"'Tis all right."

She took a deep breath and extended a hand. "Then I would be honored to call you friend, Connor Buchanan."

"Aye." His heart expanded at the miracle of an angel wanting to befriend him, but he hesitated to take her hand.

She sighed. "I will try to restrain myself from peering past the black wall surrounding your heart."

He reached out, slowly enveloping her delicate hand with his larger, rougher one. The instant his palm pressed against hers, he felt a frisson of awareness sizzle through him. He reacted, folding his calloused fingers over her hand and holding tight.

He looked into her eyes, and he knew then, with a sinking sensation of doom, that he would not be able to resist touching her again. His heart, his soul, his mind, his body—all were screaming at him to pull her close into his arms. Kiss her, cherish her, make love to her, and never let her go.

Her eyes widened and her mouth opened slightly. She glanced down at their hands, then back to his face. "Interesting," she murmured. "I didn't realize handshakes were so—"

A growl emanated from her stomach.

With a gasp, she dropped his hand. "Was that me?" She pressed a hand to her stomach. "Is it normal for a body to make noises?"

Connor smiled. "Ye're probably hungry, that's all."

"Oh." She rubbed her belly. "I was experiencing a curious sensation, as if I were terribly empty and needed something deep inside me. I suppose that is hunger."

Or desire. His smile faded. Had a simple handshake caused her to feel the same pull that he had? Could she possibly long for him? She had moaned with pleasure earlier in his arms. Did he dare hope—

"I don't suppose you have any manna here?" she interrupted his thoughts.

"Manna?"

"It's always been my main source of nourishment." She wrinkled her nose. "I don't think I could stomach any of your bottles of blood."

"Nay, they would probably make you ill." He opened some cabinet doors, searching for mortal food. "Howard and Phil come here often to hunt. There should be something— Here, ye might like this." He handed her a candy bar, then fetched a bottle of water from the refrigerator.

"The food is inside?" She turned the packaged bar over in her hands.

"Aye." He took the bar, ripped open the wrapper, then handed it back. He unscrewed the top off the water bottle, then froze when she let out a startled sound.

She had a bite of the candy bar in her mouth. She chewed slowly, her eyes widening. "Oh my," she mumbled.

She swallowed, then gazed at the bar in wonder. "This is incredible. I've never tasted anything like this." She took another bite and moaned, tilting her head back and closing her eyes.

Bugger. She looked like she was going to climax. He instantly grew hard.

"So good!" She took another bite and her eyes glazed over with pleasure.

He shifted his sporran to hide the expanding problem beneath his kilt. " 'Tis better than manna, then?"

She nodded as she swallowed. "Oh yes. Manna is fairly tasteless, not that it matters, for when we're in our usual spiritual form, we don't experience taste." She stuffed the last of the bar into her mouth, then pressed a hand to her chest and groaned.

He shifted his weight. The lass was certainly attuned to the sensibilities of her new human body. His heart rate sped up at the thought of introducing her to all sorts of sensual pleasure. If she could react this strongly over food, what would she do if he caressed her breasts or kissed the sweet flesh between her thighs? Her soft arms and thighs would hold him tight, her moans would sound like music, and she would shatter in his arms. He could practically hear her scream her release.

She licked her lips. "What is that called?"

Sex. He stopped himself just in time. "Chocolate."

"I love it! Thank you." She smiled. "Do you have anything else I can eat?"

Doona say it. "I'll look." *Under my kilt.* He handed her the bottle of water and turned away to rummage through the cabinets. Holy Christ Almighty, she was going to drive him to ruin. But he was already doomed, so seducing an angel could hardly damage his immortal soul any further.

But he might damage her. She wanted to go back home to heaven. And she believed he was a good, honorable man. If he were, he would do nothing to lessen her chances. He would make sure she remained chaste and pure so she could take her rightful place with the angels.

Besides, touching her could cause her to see why his soul was damned. He could never let that happen. So, it was settled, he decided with a sinking heart. He would not kiss her again. Nor hold her in his arms. Love was always beyond his reach.

His cell phone rang, and he pulled it out of his sporran. The leather pouch was hanging at an odd angle due to the problem beneath his kilt.

"Connor," Angus said. "Ye dinna call back. Are ye done at the doctor's?"

"We dinna have to go to Houston," he answered, glancing at Marielle. "We're still at the cabin, and she's completely healed."

She sipped from the water bottle, watching him curiously.

"How did ye— Never mind," Angus continued. "I'm sending Robby so he can get a full report and ascertain whether she's a threat."

"She's no'—"

"Roman believes she is," Angus interrupted. "I want more information before I decide how to proceed."

Connor gritted his teeth to keep from arguing with his boss. Marielle was not Angus's employee, so her future was not for him to decide.

"Robby will be bringing some clothes that Emma put together," Angus said. "Father Andrew insists on going, and Gregori has offered to teleport him. They should arrive shortly."

"Verra well."

"Do I need to remind you no' to let her anywhere near the Father?"

"Nay." Connor rang off and dropped the phone back into his sporran.

"Your friends are coming," Marielle said quietly.

"Aye. Two Vamps and a mortal priest who is eager to meet you."

She nodded. "It will be good to have someone to pray with. I feel so alone with my own thoughts."

"Ye're no' alone, Marielle."

Her eyes softened and she smiled. He curled his hands into fists to keep from grabbing her.

She shifted her weight back and forth. "I have a strange, urgent feeling like I might . . . leak."

He blinked. Christ, was she really this naïve? "Do ye need to use the restroom?"

She shook her head. "I don't think I need to rest."

"I meant the loo. The W.C.?" When she continued to look at him blankly, he motioned toward the bathroom. "Come, I'll show you."

She followed him into the small room and looked curiously about.

He couldn't believe he was having to do this. "Ye've been watching humans for centuries. Ye've never seen one . . . take a piss?" *Or make love?*

She shook her head. "We never pay attention to bodily functions. As spiritual beings, it's not something we can relate to."

"Well." He felt his cheeks grow warm. "Ye sit there." He motioned to the toilet. "And . . . let it go."

She nodded. "Interesting."

"Then ye dry yerself off and flush it all down." He pointed at the toilet paper and the flushing lever.

"This?" She lightly touched the lever, and the toilet flushed. She jumped back, then laughed. "Look at that! Humans are so clever."

He blinked. He could have sworn she hadn't pushed the lever. He motioned to the sink. "Then ye wash yer hands."

She touched the faucet and water gushed out. "Brilliant!" With a grin, she dangled her fingers in the water.

She hadn't turned the knob. Connor backed out of the room, stunned. "I'll leave you alone, then."

He closed the door and could hear her humming inside, happy with her new toys. The toilet flushed again.

Holy Christ Almighty! What would happen if she accidentally touched a gun or a crossbow? Angus might decide she was indeed a threat.

He grabbed another bottle of blood from the refrigerator and warmed it up in the microwave. He needed to keep up his strength with Marielle around. He never knew what to expect next. How could an angel of death cause things to work? Was there something magical about her touch? He'd certainly enjoyed it whenever she touched him.

He heard another flush, then the sound of water. He retrieved his bottle from the microwave. No matter what, he had to hold to his decision. No kissing. No hugging. He wouldn't even think about sex. Or how wonderfully well her plump breasts had filled his hands.

He glanced ruefully at his bottle of synthetic blood. What he really needed was some Blissky. The added whisky might numb his desire.

The bathroom door creaked open, and he remained by the sink, purposely not looking at her.

"I believe I did it correctly," she announced proudly.

"That's good." He guzzled down some blood. *Doona think about making love.*

"And I discovered something amazing. I have an entire set of female private parts."

He spewed blood into the sink.

"Connor!" She rushed up to him and placed a hand on his back. "Are you all right?"

God help him, she was going to drive him to despair. He wiped his mouth with the back of his hand. "Lass, ye canna say whatever pops into yer mind. There are things we doona talk about."

"What sort of things?"

"Personal things." *Like an entire set of female private parts.* How could he possibly keep that out of his mind?

"I'm accustomed to sharing all my thoughts with the Heavenly Host, and they with me."

"Well, humans doona share everything. We like to keep some things . . . private." *Female private parts. Doona think about it!*

She frowned. "Like the dark secrets you keep hidden in your heart?"

His mouth thinned. "That and other things."

She shook her head. "I'm not sure keeping secrets is a healthy way to live."

" 'Tis the way we are. My friends will be here soon." He changed the subject and rummaged through some kitchen drawers till he found something he could use. "We need to make you more presentable. Lift yer right arm."

She did, and he used a chip clip to fasten the loose sides of the sheet together at her hip. There, that would keep the other guys from seeing more of Marielle than he wanted. Like her entire set of female private parts.

Mine. Finders keepers. But could he really claim Marielle for himself? She didn't want him; she wanted to go back to heaven where it was all beautiful music and perfect angels sharing lovely thoughts. No secrets and sinful creatures like himself.

Three forms wavered close to the couch, then solidified.

He took a deep breath. "We have company."

Chapter Eight

This is Robby MacKay." Connor introduced Angus's great-grandson, who strode toward them, carrying a tote bag. "Robby, this is Marielle."

"How do ye do?" Robby set the bag on the kitchen counter. "We brought you some clothes."

"Thank you." She smiled and extended a hand. "So you're a vampire, too?"

"Aye." Robby eyed her hand. "I hear ye're an angel of death."

"She willna harm you," Connor muttered.

Robby gave her a quick handshake, then slapped Connor on the shoulder. "What happened to yer claymore?"

" 'Tis on top of Mount Rushmore. I'll fetch it later." He noticed Marielle was studying her hand with a perplexed look.

"Wow!" Gregori approached her, smiling. "You are such a babe!"

She glanced over her shoulder.

In spite of an overwhelming urge to throw the nearest object at the womanizing Vamp, Connor's chest filled with warmth. Marielle had no idea how beautiful she was. He leaned over and whispered, "The idiot is referring to you."

"I heard that," Gregori muttered.

"But I have never been a babe," Marielle protested. "I was created as I am, though in a spiritual form. This body is new to me."

Gregori looked her over, his eyes gleaming. "Well, if you need any help getting acquainted with it, just let me know."

"Show some respect, ye bloody pig." Connor glanced at the kitchen counter to see what he could throw. The toaster, perhaps?

"Hey, if she's any indication of what's waiting for us in heaven"—Gregori motioned to her—"then kill me now."

She shook her head. "Oh no! I have no wish to harm you."

Connor leaned close to her. "Doona let him upset you. He's operating under the false perception that he's somehow charming."

Robby chuckled.

Gregori snorted. "At least I'm not an old grouch." He turned to Marielle and winked. "Great outfit. The toga look really suits you."

She glanced down at the sheet. "Thank you. Connor fixed it for me."

"Oh, really?" Gregori's mouth twitched. "I didn't know he was so . . . handy."

"Sod off," Connor grumbled. The toaster wouldn't do. Maybe the big wooden chopping block.

"I am delighted to meet you, my beautiful angel." Gregori took her hand and kissed it, his mouth lingering on her skin.

Connor gritted his teeth. The chopping block wouldn't do. Maybe the meat cleaver.

"Pleased to meet you." She retrieved her hand from Gregori's grasp. Her brow furrowed once again with a perplexed look.

Connor picked up a black rubber coaster. "Why are ye here, Gregori?"

"My mother insisted, so I could give her a full report." He gave Marielle an apologetic look. "She really wanted to come herself. She's dying to meet you, but Roman was afraid there might be some *real* dying after what happened to— Hey!" He narrowly dodged the coaster that zipped past his ear and bounced off the wall behind him. "What the hell was that?"

Connor arched an eyebrow as he reached for a second coaster.

"Why are you throwing things?" Marielle asked.

He shrugged. "Target practice."

Robby's eyes narrowed. "Does she no' know?"

"There's nothing to know." Connor dropped the coaster and led her toward the fireplace where the third person was waiting. The priest had remained silent since their arrival, gazing at the angel with a look of awe and reverence.

"I'd like you to meet Father Andrew," Connor said.

Marielle smiled. "God bless you, dear soul."

The priest pressed a hand to his chest while his eyes glimmered with tears. "I cannot begin to tell you what a joy and honor this is. So many years of relying on faith, struggling with my faith, and here you are—proof that I have not believed in vain, that all the words I have spoken over the years are true."

Her eyes shimmered with moisture. "Son of Man, your Father loves you dearly." She reached out to touch him.

Connor seized her wrist and guided her back to the rocking chair. "Would ye care to sit down?"

The priest hadn't noticed Connor's interference. He was busy retrieving a cotton handkerchief from his coat pocket, then wiping the tears from his face.

But Marielle noticed, and she whispered, "What is going on, Connor?"

He opened his mouth to say "nothing," but found it hard to lie straight to her angelic face.

"She needs to know." Robby moved close to the priest.

"Nay. She's been through enough tonight." Connor wrapped a protective arm around her shoulders and pulled her close. "I willna have you upsetting her."

Robby's eyebrows rose. Father Andrew froze with his handkerchief half tucked into his pocket. And Gregori, blast him, actually grinned.

Connor felt warmth flooding his face, but he kept his arm around her. "She's been through hell tonight—banished from her home, attacked, her back burned and her wings ripped off. She was left in the dirt wounded and bleeding. And she was threatened by a demon—"

"A demon!" Father Andrew's face grew pale. "Oh dear God. Are you all right?"

"Yes," she replied softly. "But I'm afraid there's something you're not telling me."

When the priest nodded, Connor groaned and lowered his arm. Hadn't she been through enough tonight?

"I would consider it a great honor to be touched by an angel," Father Andrew explained. "But my friends are concerned that your touch could harm me."

"Oh. Is that all?" She exhaled wearily. "You need not fear. I have lost most of my angelic gifts. I can no longer fly or communicate with the Heavenly Host. And my touch no longer kills. I have been touching Connor all evening with no effect whatsoever."

Gregori snorted. "Right. No effect at all."

Connor scowled at him. "She would never knowingly harm anyone."

"Tell that to Shanna," Gregori muttered.

"Who?" Marielle asked.

"Stop yer yammering," Connor growled at Gregori. "We can warn her no' to touch mortals and leave it at that."

"Are you saying I'm still dangerous?" Her eyes widened with alarm.

"Only to mortals," Connor grumbled. "Ye can touch us Vamps without a problem. We're already somewhat dead."

"And how do you know this? What happened?" She gave him an annoyed look when he remained silent. "You'd better tell me. You may be centuries old, but I am millennia old, so don't treat me like a child."

He arched a brow at her and whispered, "Have I been treating you like a child?"

Her cheeks turned pink.

"My dear," Father Andrew began. "Perhaps we can help you fill in the blanks if you tell us what you remember from tonight." He motioned to the rocking chair as he sat on the couch. "I, for one, am very eager to hear your story."

"All right." She perched on the rocking chair while Connor remained standing by her side.

Robby and Gregori sat on the couch, sandwiching the priest between them.

She folded her hands in her lap. "Earlier this evening, we were sent to a campground in the area known as South Dakota."

"Who is 'we'?" Robby asked.

"My supervisor Zackriel and I," she explained. "We received orders to deliver seven souls. After we arrived, I took a married couple. They were already dead, but their souls were clinging to each other in great fear and despair over their children."

She shook her head, closing her eyes briefly. "I took them quickly so they could be at peace, but they pleaded for their children, and I . . ." She clenched her hands together tightly. "I could not bear it. Two of the children were still alive, barely, but I thought they could be saved, so I refused to take them."

Connor touched her shoulder. His beautiful, sweet Marielle; she'd lost everything, trying to protect two children. She glanced up at him with tears in her eyes. God help him, he wanted to pull her into his arms and comfort her. But he couldn't do it in front of the others. What he was feeling was far too intense to let anyone else see.

"What happened then?" Father Andrew asked.

She dragged her gaze away from Connor, reluctantly, he thought, and continued, "Zackriel and I argued, but in the end, more Deliverers came to help him take the children. I flew off into the woods to grieve and pray. Then a little while later, Zack found me and told me I was to be banished."

"Damn," Gregori muttered. "That's harsh. All you wanted to do is save a few kids."

She wiped a tear from her cheek. "I disobeyed orders. And it was the third time. I should have known better. Every time I have disobeyed, the consequences have been dire. Tragic events occur in the human world that could have been avoided if I'd only done as I was told."

Robby glanced at Connor, then back at her. "So ye have trouble following orders? Where have I heard that before?"

Connor gave him a wry look.

"So I was punished," she continued, her shoulders sagging. "Zackriel took my wings. I don't remember much after that."

"I heard him attacking you." Connor squeezed her shoulder. "I saw the fireballs and heard yer screams.

He left you in a dirty pit, bleeding and wounded."

She looked up at him, her eyes softening. "I remember someone holding me and a soft, lilting voice that gave me comfort."

"Oh yeah." Gregori smirked. "Our Connor is such a sweetie."

He grabbed a paperback book off a nearby bookshelf and tossed it at Gregori, who managed to dodge it with vampire speed.

"Ye doona remember going anywhere?" Robby asked.

Marielle shook her head. "I remember pain, lots of pain. And darkness. It was very strange, because I've never lost consciousness before. I suppose it happened because of this human body I have now. When I woke up, I was here. With Connor."

She glanced up at him, her blue eyes beseeching. "Please tell me what happened."

He groaned inwardly. "I wanted to spare you the details. 'Twas no' yer fault, lass. Ye kept telling me no' to touch you, but I did anyway, and nothing happened. Emma, Roman, and Laszlo touched you, too—"

"When?" Marielle asked. "Where?"

"At Romatech Industries," Connor explained. "'Tis the place where we manufacture the synthetic blood ye saw me drinking. Roman and Laszlo are brilliant scientists, so I took you there, thinking they could patch you up."

"You were trying to save my life," she said quietly.

"Aye." He didn't want to admit he'd suspected

her of being a Malcontent, or that he'd wanted to keep her alive so he could question her. "Ye warned us several times no' to touch you, but we dinna think much of it . . . ."

She stiffened. "I didn't kill someone, did I?" She jumped to her feet. "Tell me! If he's not scheduled to die, then maybe it's not too late to undo it."

"She's no' dead," Robby said, anger flashing in his eyes. "She's in a coma."

"Oh God." Marielle lifted a trembling hand to her mouth. "I—I'll pray for her to be healed. Bunny could do it."

"A rabbit?" Robby and Gregori both asked.

She shook her head, then bowed her head, clasping her hands together close to her mouth as she murmured quietly.

"Buniel is a healing angel," Connor explained. He touched Marielle's arm. "Shanna is in a vampire coma. Her husband attempted to transform her."

She turned to him, opening her eyes. "Her husband is a vampire?"

"Yes, Roman Draganesti. Shanna already planned on becoming a vampire. It just happened sooner than they expected."

"We're no' sure if she's going to make it," Robby grumbled.

"Then I will pray for Bunny to help her through." Marielle's eyes brimmed with tears. "I'm so sorry. You were trying to save me, and I repaid your kindness with . . . death."

" 'Tis no' yer fault," Connor insisted. "Ye warned us—"

"Of course it's my fault!" A tear rolled down her face. "I disobeyed again. And that always causes terrible things to happen." She gripped Connor's shirt in her fists. "I always mess up! And I hate it!"

"Lass!" He grabbed her hands and squeezed them. Bugger, she was falling apart. He knew she'd been through too much in one night. "Come, let's . . . see what Emma packed for you."

"What?"

"Come." He dragged her back toward the kitchen and grabbed the tote bag off the counter. He glanced back at the three men who were all standing and watching. "She needs a break."

Robby frowned. "I still have a lot of questions."

Father Andrew lifted a hand. "Leave her be for now. Connor's right."

He gave the priest a grateful nod, then escorted Marielle to a nearby bedroom. She stumbled alongside him as if in a daze.

He opened the bedroom door and handed her the tote bag. "Take all the time ye need."

She gazed up at him, her cheeks glistening with tears. "I didn't mean to harm your friend."

"I know, lass." He longed to brush the tears away, even kiss them away, but he didn't want to do it in front of the three guys. "Ye're all that is good and pure—"

She burst into tears.

Damn. He'd thought he was saying the right thing.

"I'm not good," she wailed. "I keep disobeying."

"Disobeying is no' so bad," he grumbled. "I do it all the time."

"But don't you see? Whenever I disobey, I'm questioning the wisdom of the Father. It's rebellion." She shook her head. "Maybe Darafer is right—"

"Nay!" He grabbed her by the shoulders. "Ye willna believe that bastard." He pulled her into the bedroom and shut the door so the guys wouldn't see him fussing at an angel. Unfortunately, Robby and Gregori might still hear him with their heightened vampire senses.

He tossed the tote bag onto the bed and led her toward the door that made a second entrance into the bathroom. "I willna have ye thinking poorly of yerself."

"I killed your friend's wife," she mumbled.

"Ye dinna kill her." He wet a washcloth in the bathroom sink. "She's in a coma, turning into a vampire, which is what she had planned to do eventually."

"If her husband didn't happen to be a vampire, she would have died."

"She'll be all right." He wiped Marielle's face. "'Twas my fault for taking you there."

"You shouldn't blame yourself. You didn't know what I am." She sighed. "I suppose we should be grateful her husband had time to transform her. Usually when I touch a mortal, their death is immediate."

"Ye dinna touch her. She touched you." He set the wet towel down on the counter. "She had on latex gloves, too."

"Oh." Marielle nodded slowly. "Then my power was diminished. Thank God."

"No more talk about believing that damned

demon." He gave her a fierce look. "Ye dinna screw up. I did. I do it often, so I'm quite good at it."

She smiled. "I don't believe that, but thank you. I feel better now. I shall pray that your friend comes through."

"Good. Let's see what Emma packed for you." He strode back into the bedroom.

Marielle followed slowly. "I shouldn't have doubted myself. That's exactly what Darafer is counting on. He knows I'm cut off from the Heavenly Host, so I'm missing the constant stream of praise and confirmation. I never realized how hard it is for humans to stand strong in their faith. You are truly . . . amazing."

She was looking at him with such awe and reverence in her eyes, he couldn't bear it. He turned away, feeling centuries of despair and remorse seeping through him like poison. He'd lost his faith long ago. And his hope.

Actually, there'd been a tiny spark of hope when he'd thought Marielle was going back to heaven. But Buniel had dropped her, and Connor's hopes had fallen along with her. Maybe if he could help her get back to heaven, it would somehow wash away some of his sins. Did he dare have hope?

"What is this?" She had spread a pair of jeans and a T-shirt on the bed, but now she was pulling underwear out of the tote bag.

"That's a bra. Ye wear it over yer . . . breasts." He frowned. It didn't look big enough. "Nay, under yer clothes," he added when she placed it on top of the sheet. "Ye have to take the sheet off."

"Oh." She removed the chip clip and tossed it on the bed.

"No' now!"

She jumped, startled by his shout.

He lowered his voice. "Ye doona dress, or undress, in front of men."

She gave him a frustrated look. "You've seen me before. I thought you might help."

He stepped back. "Nay. I canna."

"Why not?"

He shoved a hand through his hair. "The bra fastens in the back, the jeans in the front."

"All right." She regarded him curiously. "Is it because you feel . . . desire?"

He groaned. "Ye're the most beautiful . . . woman to ever set foot on the planet. Any man would desire you."

She gave him a dubious look. "I don't think so. Father Andrew looks at me like I'm a holy shrine. Robby regards me with suspicion, and Gregori—"

"He's a pig."

She smiled. "He means no harm. He's merely . . . playful."

"A playful *pig*."

Her smile widened. "Will you take my hand?"

In marriage? Connor's heart lurched, then he slapped himself mentally. *Ye fool. Angels doona marry.* She only wanted to hold his hand.

He enveloped her hand in his. When their palms touched, he sucked in a quick breath. His heartbeat quickened, and his grip tightened.

"You felt that?" She sandwiched his hand between both of hers. "At first, I thought there was something odd about handshakes, but I felt nothing when the others held my hand. It is most . . . curious, don't you think?"

"Marielle." He winced when she brought his hand to her chest. Holy Christ Almighty, he could feel the soft fullness of her breasts. His sight darkened, turning red.

She tilted her head, regarding him curiously. "I've been trying to understand this. I thought it might be lust, but I've always considered sin to be ugly and ultimately destructive. This doesn't feel like that. What would you call it?"

He swallowed hard. "Desire. Longing."

Her eyes widened with wonder. "Yes. That's it, exactly."

He grabbed the back of her neck to pull her forward, then halted with his mouth less than an inch from hers. Bloody hell, he had sworn he wouldn't do this. If he kissed her, she would see more of his soul.

She released his hand and wrapped her arms around his neck. "Yes," she repeated, and all restraint was lost.

He kissed her, releasing all the passion that had built up over the night. How he could feel so much, so quickly, he didn't know, but Marielle had fallen out of heaven and straight into his life, awakening his long-dead senses and filling him with purpose.

He would protect her with his life. He would see

her safely back to heaven. And the small seed of hope in his heart would grow because a beautiful angel cared for him. Even desired him.

She pressed against him, kissing him back, tangling her fingers in his hair. How could he be doomed when she desired him?

He invaded her mouth and tasted chocolate on her tongue. She moaned, sinking deeper into the kiss. His hands smoothed down her back, enjoying the indentation of her spine, the narrowing of her waist, the flare of her hips.

He slipped a hand into the side opening of the sheet, and she shivered as his fingers swept across her ribs. He cupped her breast, and she gasped against his mouth.

He planted kisses along her cheek, then nuzzled her ear. He circled her nipple with his thumb, and the skin pebbled. By the time he brushed his thumb across her nipple, it had hardened into a tight bud.

"I've been wanting to touch you again." He kissed a trail down her neck.

She clutched his shoulders. "I—I thought you didn't like my breasts."

He lifted his head and gave her a fierce look. "That was my guilt ye were seeing after I groped an angel. Yer breasts are the most beautiful I've ever seen . . . or touched." He gave her a gentle squeeze.

With a moan, she closed her eyes. "I'm so glad you like them."

"Are ye now? Would ye care to know how much I 'like' them?"

Her eyes opened slowly. "How—"

A knock sounded on the door. He jumped back.

"Is everything all right in there?" Father Andrew asked.

Bugger, the door wasn't even locked. "Just a minute." He grabbed the chip clip and fastened the sheet back together. "Are ye all right?" he whispered.

She nodded.

"I'll leave you to get dressed."

She nodded again, looking a bit dazed.

He touched her cheek. "Ye'll be fine."

She smiled. "Yes. Go ahead."

He eased out the door and shut it behind him. Father Andrew stood nearby, watching him closely.

Robby stood by the couch, his arms folded over his chest, and a scowl on his face. Gregori's eyes twinkled with amusement.

"Is Marielle all right?" Father Andrew asked.

Connor felt his cheeks grow warm. "She's feeling better now."

Gregori snorted, and Robby nudged him with an elbow.

"May I have a word with you in private?" Father Andrew motioned toward the back door.

"As ye wish." A memory flitted through Connor's mind as he walked to the door. The first time he'd stolen a kiss had been in the church belfry. The girl had burst into tears, and the priest had boxed his ears.

Hopefully his kissing had improved. He glanced at the priest's stony face. Some things just never changed.

Chapter Nine

Connor remained silent as he joined the priest in the clearing behind the cabin. Father Andrew was gazing at the stars, murmuring a prayer, his breath frosting in the chilly night air.

The priest crossed himself, then turned to Connor. "I have to thank you. This has been a . . . momentous occasion for me."

Connor hid his surprise. He'd expected the priest to berate him. "Do ye think Shanna will be all right?"

"Yes." The priest gazed at the stars once more. "I have faith she will come through."

Connor nodded. Out of habit, he scanned the woods, looking for danger. "Then maybe Roman will be able to forgive me."

"I believe he will." Father Andrew glanced at Connor. "Can you forgive yourself?"

He winced. "Roman is the one who transformed

me. 'Tis a serious offense in our world to betray one's sire."

The priest's eyebrows rose. "And Roman's sire was Casimir?"

"Yes. Casimir hates all of us Vamps, but he harbors a special hatred for Roman. That betrayal was personal."

"I see." Father Andrew nodded thoughtfully. "Still, I don't think what happened tonight constitutes a betrayal. It was an accident. You had no way of knowing."

"I should have known. The warning signs were there." Just like they were before he'd lost his wife and child. He was always too damned blind, and it was the ones he loved who paid for his mistakes. "I have a long history of screwing up."

"You might feel better if you talked about it."

He gave the priest a wry look. "We've had this conversation before. I confess nothing."

"Stubborn as always." Father Andrew smiled slightly. "That can be a virtue in dangerous times. I'm sure you realize that Marielle needs a protector."

He nodded. "She is wise in spiritual matters, but naïve when it comes to surviving in this world."

"Yes, that, too, but I'm mostly concerned about the demon you mentioned."

"Darafer."

Father Andrew crossed himself. "Do you think he'll come back?"

"I'm sure of it. He considers her a fallen angel."

"She needs protection. Will you do it?" The priest regarded him sternly. "I do not ask it lightly. I will expect you to defend her with your life."

Connor swallowed hard. "I will."

"I'll print out some special prayers I want you to have on hand. And I'll make sure you have some vials of holy water."

Connor snorted. "I would feel better with a few swords."

The priest gripped him on the shoulder. "The demon will attack where you are the weakest. You must be as strong in your faith as you are in physical strength."

Then he was most likely doomed. "I have never found faith to be easy."

"Of course not. That is the nature of faith." The priest squeezed his shoulder. "I have faith in you. And more importantly, Marielle has faith in you. I can see there is a bond between you. She trusts you."

"I am no' worthy—"

"None of us are worthy," Father Andrew snapped, irritation flashing in his eyes. With a sigh, he dropped his hand. "Do you know why I became a priest?"

"To help—"

"That's my reason now. But originally, I took my vows out of guilt. As a young man, I was stupid and selfish. I drove while intoxicated and slammed into a tree. Killed my best friend."

Connor inhaled sharply.

"Appalling, I know." Father Andrew's mouth twisted. "Did you think Vamps have a monopoly on tragic mistakes?"

"I'm sorry."

Father Andrew patted him on the back, then went back to gazing at the stars. "Can you imagine thousands of angels all around us, and we do not see them? There is so much I cannot see, but I have a strong feeling that tonight is important. There is a reason you found Marielle."

"Perhaps." Connor wasn't sure his faith could stretch that far. Still, it was lucky that a Vamp had found her. A mortal would have died trying to help her.

"Be careful."

"I will." He would have to keep his hands off her. Let her remain innocent and angelic. "She wants to go back to heaven."

"Don't we all." Father Andrew headed back to the porch. "Let's see how our angel is doing."

"Say cheese!" Gregori leaned close to her, grinning.

"Why?" Marielle blinked when a bright light flashed.

"It came out well enough, I think." Robby turned the camera to show them.

She had a glimpse of her startled face next to Gregori's before he grabbed the camera for a closer look. "Thanks, Marielle. My mom's gonna love this."

"I'm sorry I wasn't able to meet her." Marielle sighed. "And I'm truly sorry about your friend Shanna. I hope you know I would never purposely harm anyone."

Robby gave her a skeptical look. "Ye're an angel of death. No offense, but I would call that a wee bit of harm."

"We're called Deliverers, actually. And we're not supposed to take someone before their time."

"How does that work?" Gregori lifted his camera, focusing on her. "I mean, do you just go down a line, saying, 'Eenie meenie mynie moe, sorry, dude, you gotta go'?"

"Excuse me?" She squinted her eyes as the camera flashed. Tiny lights sparkled in front of her.

"What the hell are ye doing?" Connor's voice boomed from the back of the cabin.

Her heart warmed at the sound of his voice.

"Oh, now there's a pretty smile." Gregori snapped another photo of her.

She shook her head as she glanced toward Connor. Flickering lights danced around him as he walked through the kitchen followed by the priest.

"Hey, we should make a video," Gregori suggested. "We could put her in a white silk choir robe and call it *Visitation by an Angel*." He turned to her, his eyes bright with excitement. "Can you do any sort of supernatural tricks?"

"Bloody hell, she's no' a circus performer." Connor grabbed something off the kitchen counter.

"It would be the hottest thing ever on the Internet," Gregori announced.

"Ye're no' marketing an angel!" Connor took aim and threw.

"Hey!" Gregori jumped to the side. "Would you stop throwing coasters at me? I'm not talking about making money off her."

"That's a relief," Father Andrew said dryly. "I was about to excommunicate you."

Gregori scoffed. "I'm talking about doing something good for mankind. Imagine how awesome everyone would feel if they knew all that holy stuff was real."

"Stuff?" Father Andrew muttered. "Four years of giving sermons, and that's what I get back? Holy *stuff*?"

Robby chuckled.

Gregori rolled his eyes. "I meant heaven and God stuff. Don't you think it would give people some badly needed comfort and reassurance if they saw Marielle?"

"No!" She shook her head. "Please! You mustn't tell anyone about me."

"What?" Gregori gave her an incredulous look. "Don't you want people to believe?"

"It wouldn't be belief if you make my presence known," Marielle insisted. "That would ruin everything."

"She's right." Father Andrew strode toward them and stopped on the far side of the couch. "People have to believe by faith. If you prove her existence, then everyone would accept her as fact."

Marielle nodded. "And they would lose their free will. Our Father wants us to . . . choose." Her throat constricted with a sudden itchy, desperate feeling. She was the last being on Earth who should lecture about making choices. She'd made the wrong ones, and now she was paying the penalty.

"Are ye all right?" Connor's eyes narrowed.

She opened her mouth to speak, but choked. She coughed, gasped for air, then coughed some more. And more.

She felt a twinge of panic for she no longer had

control over her new body. Tears leaked from her eyes. That was strange. Why did a cough cause her to cry?

Connor pressed a bottle of water into her hand. "Drink."

She sipped some water, then coughed some more, though not as badly. "I don't know what happened." She wiped the tears from her face.

"Don't worry." Father Andrew smiled as he sat on the couch. "It happens to everybody."

She sipped more water. Good heavens, now her nose was leaking.

Connor handed her a white tissue.

She dabbed at her nose, but the leak didn't stop.

Connor stepped in front of her and whispered, "Ye need to blow."

Blow? She took a deep breath and blew air toward her nose.

His mouth twitched. He took the tissue from her hand and placed it over her nose. "Blow out yer nose, lass."

She replaced his hands with her own and blew. Amazed, she wiped her nose. "That was so strange. Coughing and leaking and blowing—these bodies do the oddest things."

"Aye, that they do."

She glanced at his smoky blue eyes and was instantly lost in the intensity of his gaze. He wanted to touch her again, she could feel it.

Warmth spread to her cheeks. What was it about this man that made her react so strongly? She could just look at him, and her heart would squeeze in her chest. If he touched her, her heartbeat raced and her knees grew weak. She'd kissed him twice. In one night!

The desire she felt was so new to her, so obviously nonangelic. It was tempting to put the blame completely on this new body and its ability to make her feel sensations she'd never experienced before, but in her heart, she knew that wasn't entirely true.

There were other men in the room, and she had no desire for them. It was all so strange. For millennia, she'd always loved mankind in general, all equally and from a distance. But now, her heart was yearning to be close to only one. Connor.

And he was feeling the same way. He'd admitted it. *Desire. Longing.* Her skin tingled with goose bumps. She wanted him to touch her again.

When he'd kissed her in the bedroom, she'd caught another glimpse into the darkness that surrounded his heart. An image of a young blond woman had flashed through her mind, a woman named Darcy. Why did she cause Connor so much guilt?

Marielle was impatient to ask him, but she knew it should be done in private. Even then, he might insist it was one of those personal things that humans didn't talk about.

She wanted to do more than talk. She wanted to kiss him again. She wanted to feel his arms around her and his breath against her cheek. Such a human desire. The demon had warned her that the longer she remained on Earth, the more human she would become.

She had to resist getting too involved with him. The Archangels would never let her back into heaven if she couldn't prove herself worthy.

"Thank you." She handed the tissue back.

An odd look passed over his face, then he walked stiffly back past a smirking Gregori to toss the tissue in a trash can.

"My dear, I would love to hear about your life as an angel," Father Andrew said. He glanced pointedly at the other men. "Anything we hear must be kept confidential."

Gregori sprawled on the couch. "My mother will kill me if I don't tell her everything."

"My wife will want to know, too," Robby protested. "And Angus and Emma."

The priest sighed. "Fine. I'll probably need to tell Roman. We'll keep this within our small community. Is that all right with you, Marielle?"

"Yes. I'm grateful that you and your friends are helping me." She knew enough about the current world to know she'd have great difficulty surviving on her own. She had no proof of identity, no birth certificate since she'd never been born, nor any currency to purchase food, shelter, or clothing. Furthermore, it would be nigh impossible to live among humans without inadvertently touching someone and causing a death.

The best place for her was this community of good vampires, and she knew it was more than a coincidence that she'd been found by one of them. Her previous thoughts returned to her. If she could accomplish some sort of noble mission here on Earth, she might be deemed worthy of rejoining the Heavenly Host.

She sat in the rocker and winced at the strange sensation of jeans hugging her thighs and bunching at her knees. Her T-shirt was black with the words *Bite Me* across the chest. An odd shirt to wear among vampires, but apparently, death didn't diminish their sense of humor. In fact, for a group of Undead souls, they were remarkably lively.

She cleared her throat, aware that all four men were watching her expectantly. Robby and Gregori were sharing the couch once again with Father Andrew, while Connor stood behind them, his arms crossed over his bloodstained shirt. Her blood. A wave of grief flooded her once more over the loss of her wings. What if she never flew again?

She swallowed hard. "I want to assure you that I mean no harm to anyone. I believe my powers will fade over time, but for now, I will be very careful not to touch any humans."

"Thank you." Father Andrew smiled. "But to be perfectly honest, it's going to be difficult to know if your power fades away. No mortal is likely to volunteer to test it."

She nodded.

"So how old are you?" Gregori asked.

Robby grunted. "No wonder you doona have a girlfriend."

She smiled. "It's hard to say. We don't view time the same way as you. My full name is Marielle Quadriduum. I was created, along with thousands of other angels, on the Fourth Day."

"Damn," Gregori muttered. "You're like . . . ancient." He winced when Connor cuffed him on the back of the head. "Well, she is. And I thought *you* were old."

Connor arched a brow at him.

"The Fourth Day," Father Andrew murmured. "The same day God created the sun and moon."

"Yes. And millions of other suns and moons." She sighed. "I was assigned to supervise a solar system."

"Wow!" Gregori grinned. "You were like Empress of the Galaxy. Cool."

She gave him a dubious look. "There were only three planets."

Gregori leaned forward. "And one of them had intelligent life?"

"Aye," Connor muttered, "but ye wouldna recognize it."

Gregori shot him an annoyed look while Robby chuckled.

Father Andrew shook his head. "Please continue, my dear."

She leaned back in the rocker. "Each of my planets consisted of a huge, frozen rock surrounded by a thick atmosphere of methane gas."

"Bummer!" Gregori looked offended on her behalf. "Out of all the planets in the universe, you got stuck with some duds."

She laughed. "I hate to tell you this, but most of them are duds. Or they appear to be. Many of them still serve an important purpose."

"Like Jupiter attracting meteors to protect the Earth?" Connor asked quietly.

She nodded, smiling. "Yes." Leave it to Connor to know about planets that served as protectors.

Gregori glanced over his shoulder at Connor. "You know about astronomy?"

He scowled back. "I've been looking at the night sky for almost five hundred years. Why would I no' learn about it?"

"By the Sixth Day, I was so bored, I asked for a transfer," she continued. "The Father had created mankind and all sorts of animals on Earth, and He was exceedingly pleased. In fact, we were all fascinated, and the Father wanted to protect His new creations, so many angels were reassigned. Some became Guardians and God Warriors. Others became Healers and Deliverers."

"Like you?" Robby asked.

She frowned. "I was originally a Healer. Buniel was my supervisor, and we became close friends. I loved healing."

"What happened?" Gregori asked.

"I . . . disobeyed. The first time, it was in Eastern Europe, toward the end of what the humans call the medieval period. I was reprimanded, and I managed to behave myself for several of your centuries. But the second time I disobeyed—" She shuddered. "It was really bad."

"You needn't tell us if you don't want to," Father Andrew said quietly.

She didn't like talking about it, but when she looked at Connor, she felt a sudden urge to confess. She wanted him to know. "I was told to heal a woman in a hospital in Missouri. I did, but as I was leaving, I heard the desperate prayers of another woman, who was crying over a dying child. The little boy was only a year old, and I couldn't understand why he wasn't on my list. The woman and child were in so much pain, I couldn't bear it, so I touched her to give her comfort, and then I touched the boy. When Zackriel arrived to deliver the boy, he was furious that I had healed him. He wanted to take the boy but received orders not to interfere. I would have to watch the result of my wrongdoing."

"What could be wrong with saving a young child?" Connor asked.

She winced. "The mother came to believe that her son was special, incapable of being harmed, and therefore, superior to all others. She raised him with that belief, and he . . . he became warped."

"What did he do?" Father Andrew asked.

Her throat constricted, but she forced the words out. "He murdered. Over and over. And he enjoyed it." She closed her eyes. "It was my fault. I should have let him die."

"Ye had no way of knowing," Connor said.

She opened her eyes to see the compassion on Connor's face. He wasn't judging her, and that touched her heart. "It was still wrong of me. I should have trusted in the Father's wisdom."

"I guess faith is hard for all of us," Father Andrew said with tears in his eyes.

She nodded. "My healing powers were stripped, and I was made into a Deliverer. My punishment was to deliver all the women who were raped and murdered by the monster I had allowed to live."

"He killed women?" Robby asked, his face pale. "What was his name?"

"Otis Crump."

All four men flinched.

"Bloody hell!" Robby jumped to his feet.

Marielle stiffened at the furious look Robby shot at her before he stalked away. Her mind raced, seeking an explanation for their reaction. Otis had been human all the years she had delivered his victims. She'd been so relieved when he'd finally been imprisoned that she'd immediately put in a request to become a Healer once again. While her request was being considered, she'd been assigned to delivering the elderly. She hadn't found the work objectionable until tonight when Zackriel had told her to deliver the children who had been attacked by Cheaters.

The order had infuriated her. It was the Cheaters who should be delivered, not the innocent children.

"I've heard enough," Robby growled as he paced around the dinette set. "Angus will have my report. We will have nothing to do with her."

Connor strode toward him. "Wait—"

"Nay!" Robby glared at Marielle. "She may have killed Shanna, and she came damned close to killing my wife!"

Marielle gasped.

Father Andrew and Gregori stood, so she rose to her feet, also. Her heart pounded as she tried to understand what was happening.

"This proves how dangerous she is to us," Robby announced.

"Nay," Connor protested. "It proves how important she is. Her fate has already been linked to ours."

"I have to agree with Connor," Father Andrew added, then turned to Marielle. "Robby's wife, Olivia, worked for the FBI. She was the one who put Otis Crump in jail."

Marielle's skin pebbled with goose bumps.

"Aye, but the bastard still tormented her for years!" Robby yelled. "And then Casimir teleported him out of prison and transformed him. He nearly killed Olivia!"

Marielle stumbled back and knocked against the rocking chair. "I—I didn't know."

"Ye're a bloody angel. Ye're supposed to know everything!" Robby shouted.

She shook her head. "I don't. Humans, even vampires, have free will. I can't predict what they'll do."

"Ye can predict I want nothing to do with you," Robby growled. "And I'm telling Angus to do the same."

"Then ye're a fool," Connor said quietly.

Robby spun to face him, his face darkening. His hands curled into fists. "Ye care to repeat that, Connor?"

"Enough!" Father Andrew strode toward them. "Robby, your wife is all right, and Otis Crump is dead. Marielle had nothing to do with him being transformed."

Robby shot an angry look at her. "She was supposed to let him die."

"Aye, she disobeyed," Connor said. "And she was punished for it."

Marielle's vision blurred as tears threatened to fall. "I am aware that my mistakes have caused others to suffer. I am truly sorry." Her gaze met Connor's, and the fierce determination in his eyes gave her comfort.

"Robby," Gregori began. He ran a hand through his thick hair. "Dude, we can't just . . . drop her. What would happen to her?"

Robby folded his arms across his chest, scowling.

"She can sense death," Connor announced.

Robby glowered at him.

"The next time Casimir and his minions feed and the victims start dying, Marielle will know," Connor explained before glancing at her. "Ye know exactly where death is happening, aye?"

She nodded.

"Wow," Gregori whispered.

"We've always followed Casimir's trail of dead bodies," Connor continued. "But then we arrive after the fact, after Casimir and his minions have escaped. Imagine how it will be if we can arrive while they're still feeding and we catch them by surprise?"

Robby's eyes lit up. "I could finally kill Casimir."

Marielle's heart expanded in her chest. This was it—the noble mission she needed to accomplish so she could return to heaven. It was perfect! All those arguments with Zackriel where she'd insisted that the evil vampires be stopped—she could now use her powers to make it happen.

Connor looked at her, his eyes gleaming. "We need her. She's our secret weapon."

"I agree that Marielle was sent to us for a purpose," Father Andrew said. He turned to her with a worried frown. "But we must be upfront with you, my dear. Battling Casimir is dangerous. Are you willing to help us?"

She nodded. "Yes. I am." Her gaze drifted back to Connor, and her heart filled with joy. The Heavenly Father had not abandoned her. He'd sent Connor to rescue her and protect her. But more than that—Connor and his friends were presenting her with a wonderful opportunity to make the world a safer place and, by doing so, prove she was worthy to return to heaven.

She was eager to spend more time with Connor. And she was still curious about the darkness he hid in his heart. Perhaps at some point, she would get up the nerve to ask him about Darcy.

Chapter Ten

*M*arielle's plan wasn't working out.

Connor teleported to Romatech with Robby to discuss strategy with Angus and Emma MacKay. Before leaving, he explained that Angus had served as the general of the Vamp army, and now, he and his wife were head of MacKay Security and Investigation, the modern-day company that fought against Casimir and his Malcontents.

"I canna guard you when the sun is up," Connor told her.

"You won't be here?" she asked, bewildered by how disappointed she was. How quickly she'd learned to depend on him. But there was no depending on him when he would be dead in about two hours.

"What about the demon?" Father Andrew asked before Connor could respond to her question. "Would he come here during the day?"

"It's possible," she murmured. Somehow, the thought of Connor actually being dead during the day was more disturbing than the possibility of seeing Darafer again. No wonder Connor seemed enveloped in sadness. She couldn't imagine never watching a sunrise or catching sight of a rainbow.

"I'll find someone to guard you," Connor said, then vanished.

She missed him immediately.

Father Andrew busied himself in the kitchen, making them each a cup of tea. It tasted all right, but not nearly as good as the chocolate Connor had given her. The priest had many questions, but Gregori soon declared she needed a break, and he knew exactly what would cheer her up.

It was called disco dancing. And it did make her laugh. Father Andrew watched them, smiling, but eventually, slumped over on the couch fast asleep.

"Poor guy." Gregori turned the volume down on the CD player. "It's gotta be way past his bedtime."

Soon afterward, three forms wavered, then solidified.

"Hello, ladies." Gregori greeted them with a charming smile. "May I present our resident angel, Marielle?"

They all stared at her as if stunned.

She smiled a welcome, even though she felt a stab of disappointment that Connor hadn't returned. The three women looked interesting, though. One had purple spiky hair and was dressed in a clingy black outfit with high-heeled black boots and a black whip around her waist. She was holding on to another woman who wore blue jeans, a flannel shirt, and cowboy boots. Her thick, long hair was a beautiful mixture of brown, gold, and red. As soon as she materialized, she stepped away from the woman with purple hair.

The third woman looked very young, although her ability to teleport indicated she was a vampire and could be any age. She had brown hair, severely pulled back into a ponytail, and she wore blue jeans and a plain cream-colored sweater. Her arms were filled with tote bags.

"Vanda, good to see you." Gregori grinned as he gave the purple-haired woman a hug. "I see married life hasn't crimped your style. Hey, Marta, how ya doin'?"

The young vampire smiled shyly in his direction as she headed into the kitchen. "I'm fine." She set her tote bags down on the counter. "We brought some things for the . . ." Her gaze darted nervously back to Marielle.

"God bless you." Marielle smiled, and Marta's face reddened before she turned away.

"So you're an angel?" The woman in cowboy boots asked as she hooked her thumbs into her belt loops.

"Have we met?" Gregori asked. "You look familiar."

The woman gave him an impatient look. "We might have. I fought in the battle at South Dakota, but I was in wolf form for most of that."

Marielle stiffened. The woman was a werewolf? She had nothing against shifters, but the wolf form tended to make her uneasy since it was a guise so many demons enjoyed adopting.

"This is Brynley," Vanda introduced her. "Phil's twin sister." She glanced at Marielle and clarified, "Phil is my husband. And Marta over there is my sister."

"I see." Marielle tried not to look confused. Vampire sisters? And one of them was married to a werewolf? And had purple hair?

"Delighted to meet you." Gregori smiled as he approached Brynley. "Phil and I are good friends."

"Oh yeah?" Brynley cast a wry look at Vanda. "Well, he has weird taste."

Vanda snorted. "I think she's including you in that insult, Gregori."

"Surely not." Gregori pressed a hand to his chest, affecting an injured look. "I'm one of the nicest guys you'll ever meet."

Brynley looked unimpressed.

"Well dressed, too." Gregori adjusted his cuff links.

Brynley arched an eyebrow. "Can you bring down an elk in sixty seconds?" When Gregori hesitated, she shrugged. "I didn't think so." She turned to Marielle and regarded her curiously. "Are you really an angel of death? You don't look very scary to me."

"She could bring *you* down in sixty seconds," Gregori muttered.

Brynley paled a bit, but lifted her chin. "I'm not afraid."

Marielle could tell that the female werewolf wasn't as tough as she pretended. "Did you volunteer to guard me during the day?"

Brynley shrugged. "Someone had to do it. The

Vamps are completely useless in daytime, and the mortal women were too nervous. I figured why not? It's not every day you get to meet a real, live angel."

"I appreciate your bravery," Marielle said. "And I can assure you that I mean no harm."

Brynley nodded. "That's good to know."

Vanda gave her sister-in-law a fond look. "Brynley came to live with us about a week ago. Phil and I are delighted."

Brynley looked embarrassed. "Well, I got sick and tired of my dad telling me what to do. He had the gall to throw me a big birthday party and announce my surprise engagement in front of a hundred pack members."

"You're getting married?" Marta asked as she unloaded the tote bags in the kitchen.

"No," Brynley snapped. "I'd never even met the guy before. Some Alpha wolf from Alaska. Anyway, I packed my bags and left. I knew Phil would welcome me at his school."

"We all welcomed you," Vanda said quietly.

"You're from a school?" Marielle asked.

"Dragon Nest Academy," Vanda explained. "I teach art there. Brynley's planning to teach English, and Marta works in the office." She ran a hand through her purple spiky hair. "To tell you the truth, I'm glad to get away for a little while."

"Me, too," Marta mumbled from the kitchen.

"Why?" Gregori asked. "What's wrong?"

Vanda snorted. "Ten teenage werewolf boys all learning to become Alpha? We'll be lucky if they don't kill each other."

Brynley winced. "There's a reason why a pack only has one Alpha."

"And then you throw in five were-panther orphans, plus the new were-tiger from Thailand—" Vanda shook her head. "Cats and dogs do not mix well."

"We need more girls there." Marta set a plate of food in the microwave. "The werewolf boys keep trying to hit on me."

Brynley laughed. "Well, you do look about fourteen."

With a groan, Marta punched some buttons. "I was fifteen when I was transformed, but that was back in 1939."

"So it is a school for shifter children?" Marielle asked.

Vanda nodded. "We have some mortal kids, too, who know too much to go to a regular school. And then there are the hybrids—half mortal, half vampire."

"Roman figured out a way for the Vamp guys to father children," Gregori explained. "He and Shanna have two."

The woman she'd almost killed had children? Marielle sent up a prayer that Shanna would pull through. Silence. Her shoulders slumped.

"So I gather Connor caught you up to speed?" Gregori asked Vanda.

"Yes. He seemed really . . . concerned." She eyed Marielle curiously. "It's an honor to meet you."

"Connor thought you might be hungry," Marta

said as she removed the plate from the microwave. "We brought some food from the cafeteria."

"And we brought other stuff, too," Vanda added. "Shampoo and lotion and all sorts of girly things. Connor said you'd never had a body before, so you might need a little female . . . advice."

"Sounds like time for me to leave," Gregori muttered. He walked over to the couch and gathered the priest up in his arms.

"Thank you for coming, Gregori." Marielle inclined her head.

Gregori grinned. "See you later, angel." He disappeared, taking Father Andrew with him.

"Well, come and eat while it's still hot." Marta set a bowl and plate at the end of the table.

"She needs silverware." Vanda hurried into the kitchen.

Marielle walked slowly to the table, then sat in the chair that Marta indicated. A real human meal. The smell drifted up to her nose, spicy and enticing. Hunger grew in her belly, but a small fear accompanied it. What if she enjoyed being human too much? She'd certainly enjoyed feeling Connor's arms around her and his lips against hers.

"This is salad." Marta motioned to the bowl, then to the plate. "And that's lasagna and a breadstick."

It all looked so foreign. And colorful. Marielle didn't know where to begin.

"And here's your knife and fork." Vanda set some utensils on the table along with a smaller plate. "And that's your dessert. Chocolate cake."

Marielle sat up. Chocolate? She took the fork and poked at the cake.

"Oh no," Marta whispered. "You're supposed to eat the cake last."

"Why?" Marielle put a bite of cake in her mouth.

Brynley laughed as she took a seat at the opposite end of the table. "I've always wondered that myself."

Vanda set a glass of water and a napkin on the table. "After all you've been through tonight, I'd say to hell with the rules."

Marielle nodded as the chocolate melted in her mouth. So delicious. "I'm not good at following orders."

Brynley sighed. "I'm going through a rebellious period myself right now."

"You don't want to get married?" Marta brought two bottles of synthetic blood to the table and handed one to her sister. She and Vanda sat in the side chairs.

"I could live for hundreds of years." Brynley slouched in her chair. "Why would I want to chain myself to one person?"

"Your brother did." Marta sipped from her bottle.

Brynley shrugged. "Phil's in love." She gave Vanda an annoyed look, then grumbled, "But he seems to be happy."

Vanda smiled. "He is." She took a drink from her bottle.

Marielle continued to eat the cake while she watched the women.

"You might change your mind about marriage when you meet the right man," Marta suggested.

Brynley scoffed. "No such thing as the *right* man.

They're all alike. Mortals or shifters—they're all interested in the same thing." She drummed her fingers on the table. "Not that I have anything against sex. I really like sex. A lot."

Marta winced and glanced at Marielle. "I don't know if that's an appropriate topic."

"Please don't feel that you have to censor yourself on my account." Marielle took another bite of cake.

"Exactly. If we're supposed to give her advice on being a woman, then she needs to know about men." Brynley jumped up and headed into the kitchen. "Is there any more of that cake?"

Vanda looked at Marielle curiously. "What do you think? Are all men alike?"

"No. I believe each human is unique." A vision of Connor drifted across her mind.

"I'll admit that they can look and act a little differently," Brynley called from the kitchen. "But they still have only one thing on their mind."

Marta shook her head. "Not all the time."

Brynley walked back to the table, a plate of cake in one hand and a fork in the other. "You haven't heard of the Three-Step Rule?"

"The what?" Marta asked.

Brynley set her plate on the table and took a seat. "This is how it works. At any given time, sex is only three steps away in a man's thoughts."

Vanda grinned. "All the time? What if I ask Phil to take out the garbage?"

Brynley counted the steps off on her fingers. "One: sure, I'll take out the garbage for her. Two: what could she do for me? Three: blow job."

Vanda burst out laughing while Marta turned pink and gave Marielle an apologetic look. "It's not funny," she hissed at her sister.

Vanda covered her mouth to hide her grin. "It's just that two nights ago I asked Phil to take out the garbage and then afterward—"

"Don't want to hear it." Brynley lifted her hands to stop Vanda.

"Certainly not." Marta took a sip from her bottle.

"What's a blow job?" Marielle asked.

Marta choked.

Vanda and Brynley laughed, then looked at each other.

"Are you going to tell her?" Brynley asked.

"You tell her," Vanda muttered. "You brought it up."

Brynley stabbed at her cake. "It's oral sex, somebody's mouth on somebody's private parts." She stuffed a big bite into her mouth.

"So it's similar to kissing?" Marielle asked.

"Mmm." Brynley nodded with her mouth full. She pointed down with her fork. "But farther down."

Marielle recalled the image of Connor flat on his back with his kilt thrown up to his chest. Her cheeks grew warm as the full meaning became clear.

"No offense, Brynley, but I'm not convinced about your Three-Step Rule," Marta announced. "There are times, dangerous times, when men have to think about more important things than sex."

Marielle nodded. That made sense to her. She'd been in the company of men tonight, and they hadn't discussed sex.

"I have to agree," Vanda said. "I've been around

Vamps for years, and if the guys were always thinking about sex, then their eyes would be glowing all the time."

"Vampire eyes glow?" Brynley asked.

Marielle stiffened, and her heart began to race.

"Yes," Vanda replied. "You can always tell when a Vamp's in the mood for sex. Our eyes glow red."

The fork tumbled from Marielle's hand.

"Are you all right?" Marta asked.

"Yes." She quickly picked up the fork. "It's just that this is all new to me." Connor had wanted to have sex with her? *Three times?* Her cheeks blazed with heat.

"No need to feel embarrassed," Marta assured her. "You'll get used to being human."

"I—I think I'm full." She set the fork down.

Marta wrapped up the food and stashed it in the fridge while Vanda bustled Marielle into the bathroom and showed her all the products they'd brought. After Marielle was done, Vanda helped her into a blue silk nightgown.

"Any questions?" Vanda asked, sitting on the bed next to Marielle.

"I don't think so." She combed her damp hair, enjoying the flowery scent of the shampoo she'd used. The silk material felt good against her skin. "I must seem like a helpless child."

Vanda smiled. "You don't look like a child. You're really beautiful, you know. I'm sure the men noticed."

Her cheeks warmed, thinking about Connor. When was she going to see him again?

Vanda patted her on the shoulder, then stood. "It's

almost sunrise. My sister and I need to go. But we'll come back tomorrow night, if you like."

"That would be lovely. Thank you." Marielle followed Vanda back into the main room to say goodbye to Marta.

The two Vamp women disappeared.

Brynley lifted a shotgun off the gun rack on the wall. "I'll just get this ready in case we need it."

Marielle nodded, though she wasn't sure how well the human weapon would work on a demon.

A form materialized in the kitchen, and Marielle's heart lurched when she realized it was Connor.

She grinned. "You're back!"

His eyes widened as he looked her over. She noticed he'd changed into a clean kilt and shirt. His hair was damp and tied back neatly. In his arms, he carried three sheathed swords.

"Hello!" Brynley called from the kitchen table where she was loading the shotgun. "You must be Connor."

"Aye. Ye must be Brynley, Phil's sister." He inclined his head. "Thank you for coming."

"Not a problem," Brynley said. "You came well armed."

"Aye." He set two of the swords on the kitchen counter, but kept one. "Feel free to use these, if ye need to." He gave Marielle a worried look. "The sun is about to rise. I doona have time to teach you tonight."

"I'll be fine," she assured him. "I still have some of my own skills."

"Aye. Ye knocked me out twice with that blast of air."

She tried not to think about how she'd discovered him flat on his back with his kilt up. *Don't think about it.*

He opened the door to a walk-in closet, then went inside and placed the third sword on the floor. He took a blanket off the shelf and spread it beside the sword.

She peered inside. "What are you doing?"

"I'll be falling into my death-sleep soon."

"I . . . don't like thinking about you being dead."

His mouth twisted. "Usually, I welcome it."

"How can you say that?"

He shrugged. "Ye canna feel anything when ye're dead." He gave her a worried look. "Tonight I hate it. I hate no' being here for you, no' knowing if ye'll be all right."

"I'll be fine." She glanced at the floor. "Wouldn't you be more comfortable in the bed?"

"The bedroom has windows. The sunlight would fry me." He tilted his head, studying her. "You should use the bed. It has been a long night. Ye must be verra tired."

She nodded. She was beginning to feel weary. And sad.

"Ye need to go now, lass," he whispered. "I'm about to keel over."

She stepped back, then froze when he touched her cheek.

"Be safe."

She smiled slightly. "You, too." She shut the door. Why did she feel like crying?

Instead of going into the bedroom, she went out the front door and stood on the porch. The sun broke the horizon in the east, shooting glorious rays through the trees and painting the sky with gold and pink.

"'The way of the righteous is like the first gleam of dawn,'" she whispered. Her vision blurred with tears, and she blinked them away. She'd always loved sunrises in the past. But now, she could only think of Connor dying in the closet.

A few hours later, she could barely keep her eyes open. Brynley encouraged her to go to bed and get some sleep.

As she brought the sheet up to her chin, she thought of Connor in the closet. Still dead. Her eyes flickered shut.

A moment of panic flared when she felt a dragging sensation on her consciousness. She opened her eyes, staring at the ceiling. She'd never slept before. She'd always rested on the Seventh Day, but she'd never slipped away into a real sleep. It was an odd sensation, so peaceful and comforting, yet terrifying as all her control withered away.

Her eyes burned as she tried to keep them open, but in the end, weariness overcame her, and she drifted into sleep.

She awoke with a jerk, then smiled slowly as she realized how refreshed she felt. After using the bathroom, she washed her face and brushed her teeth, grateful that Vanda had shown her how. Then she dressed and went into the main room.

Glorious scents filled the kitchen, and her stomach rumbled.

"There you are." Brynley backed away to keep a safe distance. She motioned to the counter. "I made some bacon and eggs. And there's toast and jelly."

"Thank you." She prepared herself a plate. "Did anything happen while I was asleep?"

"Nope." Brynley settled on the couch with a paperback book. "It's been real quiet. The sun's already going down."

Marielle smiled at the thought of seeing Connor soon and starting her new mission to help the Vamps. After eating, she went out onto the front porch to watch the sun descending in the west.

A new adventure awaited her. She would help the Vamps destroy the Malcontents. The world would be a safer place. The Archangels would be so pleased, they would vote her back into the Heavenly Host.

She strode back into the cabin and headed for the closet.

"Are you sure that's a good idea?" Brynley asked from the couch.

"I'll be fine." She let herself into the closet, turned on the light, then closed the door.

Connor was stretched out on his back with his hands resting on his flat stomach. She knelt beside him, admiring his handsome face. Even though his hair was a bright golden red, his eyebrows were a reddish brown. His eyelashes looked thick and dark against his pale skin. He must have shaved, for the stubble along his chin was gone.

He wore a dark green shirt that hugged broad shoulders and went well with his red and green plaid kilt. Even his knee socks were green. She smiled at the dagger hidden beneath his right knee sock. He'd tried to take on a demon with that weapon.

His chest suddenly expanded as if a burst of energy had struck his heart. His hands jerked, and his eyes opened.

"Good morning." She grinned. "Or rather, evening. It's confusing—agh!" She gasped when he seized her by the arms and shoved her onto the floor.

"Connor, what are you—" She gasped again when he leaned over her, his eyes glowing red. *Good heavens!* He'd been awake for only two seconds. Was he already thinking about sex?

His hand slid up to her neck. "Lass, ye should never wake a sleeping vampire."

"You woke yourself." She shoved at his chest. "And I don't care about the Three-Step Rule. I'm not giving you a blow job."

Chapter Eleven

*C*onnor reeled back. "What the—" Had he actually heard those words come from the mouth of his innocent angel?

He stared at Marielle, so stunned that he forgot for a moment how hungry he was. Or how much the sight of her had instantly incited a hunger for her body as well as her sweet-smelling blood. "Ye dinna— What did ye—?"

"There's no need to act so surprised. Vanda told me what the glowing red eyes mean." Marielle scrambled to her feet and gave him an indignant look. "You're thinking about sex. Again!"

Bloody hell. He jumped to his feet. "And what were ye thinking? Ye never close yerself up with a waking vampire! I could have bitten you!"

She crossed her arms. "I don't think it was food

that was on your mind. I know about the Three-Step Rule now."

"The *what*?" His stomach twinged as a hunger pain jabbed at him, demanding blood. "Never mind. I have to eat." He threw the door open and rushed straight to the fridge.

He shot her an annoyed look as she exited the closet. "Doona ever do that again." He grabbed a bottle of blood, wrenched the top off, and stuffed the bottle into the microwave. His gums ached with the strain of keeping his fangs from springing out.

"Why are you fussing at me?" she asked. "You were the one with the glowing eyes who shoved me onto the floor."

He heard a gasp from the couch. *Bugger.* Now Phil's sister knew what was happening. He seized the bottle from the microwave and guzzled down some blood.

Relief poured through him. The pain in his gums melted away, and his vision returned to normal.

Marielle stepped closer, peering at him. "Your eyes stopped glowing."

He groaned inwardly. "Lass, a Vamp's hunger is verra powerful when he first awakens. It has a way of triggering lust." And thanks to Vanda's interference, Marielle now knew that he'd lusted for her last night. There was no point in denying it. "I find you verra tempting and . . . beautiful."

When she smiled, he gritted his teeth. "'Twas no' meant as a compliment, lass. I'm giving you a serious warning. Ye must stay away from me until I've had my first bottle of blood. I could be dangerous."

Her smile lingered. "I've never thought of you as dangerous."

"Vampire." He gave her a wry look and drank some more.

She shrugged. "I don't believe you would harm me. Even in the closet, with all your hunger and lust, you didn't bite me or demand sex."

He choked on the last swallow of blood. He glanced toward the couch where he could hear some smothered giggles. *Bugger*. Had he made a big mistake asking Vanda to bring along a few women so they could give Marielle some female guidance?

He set the bottle in the sink. "What did ye talk about with the ladies?"

"Lots of things," she replied. "The Three-Step Rule, oral sex—"

"Holy Christ Almighty." He pressed a hand to his brow. "They were supposed to teach you how to shampoo yer hair, no' give you instructions on oral sex!" His heart lurched at the thought. "Did they?"

"Did they what?" she asked.

Laughter erupted from the couch, and he shot an angry look at Brynley. He turned to Marielle, and as usual, her beauty took his breath away. He lowered his voice, hoping the female shifter couldn't hear. "Did they give you . . . instructions?"

She nodded. "Yes."

His groin tightened. "Really?" He blinked, trying to keep his eyes from turning red.

"Yes. I learned how to shower and brush my teeth. All sorts of useful things." She smiled at Brynley. "And I was well guarded all day. Thank you."

Brynley grinned back, her eyes twinkling. "You're welcome."

"Excuse me." Connor slipped into the bathroom to relieve himself and get a grip. He needed to stop thinking about sex and focus on business. After he washed his hands and face and brushed his teeth, he returned to the kitchen.

Marielle was still there, drinking a glass of water.

"The demon dinna return?" he asked. Just as she shook her head, the phone in his sporran rang. He quickly answered it. "Aye?"

"Good news," Emma reported. "Shanna woke up and she's drinking her first bottle of blood."

He exhaled in relief. "Thank God."

"You'll start with the training today as planned?" Emma asked.

"Yes." Connor looked at Marielle. He'd have to explain what was decided at the strategy meeting last night.

"I'll let you get to work then," Emma said. "I just wanted you to know that Shanna's doing well, and she's eager to see the children."

"I'm sure she is."

"She expressed a desire to meet the angel, but Roman said no, not with the children about. I'll call back if she manages to change Roman's mind." Emma chuckled. "She usually can."

"Aye." Connor rang off and dropped the phone into his sporran.

Marielle was watching with a hopeful expression. "Shanna's all right?"

"Aye, if ye call being a vampire all right."

"I'm sure her husband and children are happy she's still with them." Marielle sighed. "I would have felt awful if I'd killed her."

"It wasna yer fault," he insisted. "I was the one who took you there."

She gave him a wistful smile. "I missed you during the day."

He wished he could say the same, but he didn't feel anything in his death-sleep. That had always been a blessing before, but he suspected nothing would ever be the same now that he'd met Marielle. "Ye look well. Ye rested?"

She nodded. "I slept for the first time."

"Good. Ye need yer strength tonight." He was just about to explain when a form materialized close by.

Ian MacPhie set two tote bags on the kitchen counter. "Vanda thought ye could use some more supplies," he told Connor, though his attention quickly shifted to Marielle.

"Greetings." She inclined her head at Ian.

His eyes widened. He looked at Connor, then back at Marielle. He opened his mouth to speak, then changed his mind and bowed.

"This is Ian," Connor explained. "He's no' usually speechless. Or so well dressed." He hid a smile. Ian had worn his dress kilt, black jacket with brass buttons, and white shirt with ruffled cuffs and cravat.

Ian gave him an annoyed look. "I shouldna wear my best clothes to meet an angel from heaven?"

"You look very nice," Marielle said. "I love your shirt."

Ian blushed. "Thank you."

Connor crossed his arms and muttered, "I have a shirt like that, too."

Marielle ignored him and continued to talk to Ian. "The colors on your kilt are lovely."

Ian shot a triumphant look at Connor. "Aye, I've always thought the MacPhie tartan was one of the best."

Connor snorted, although he wondered if she liked the Buchanan plaid.

"Have ye heard the good news?" Ian asked. "Shanna woke up and she's doing fine."

Marielle nodded. "I am greatly relieved."

"Me, too." Ian hesitated, shifting his weight. "If it is no' too forward of me, I would ask a boon from you. My wife is expecting our first child, and if ye could remember them in yer prayers, I would be eternally grateful."

When Marielle smiled, Connor's breath hitched. It was the closest he'd come to seeing a ray of sunshine in hundreds of years.

"That's wonderful! Congratulations." Marielle touched Ian on the shoulder. "God bless you and your family."

Ian bowed his head. "Thank you. If there's anything I can do for you, I would be honored." He stepped back. "But I shouldna take up any more of yer time. Ye have a great deal to do tonight."

"I do?" she asked.

Ian looked surprised. "Connor dinna tell you?"

"I was just about to," Connor growled. "But we were interrupted."

Ian's mouth twitched. "Try no' to be such a grouch. She's an angel, ye ken."

Connor arched an eyebrow.

Ian's eyes glittered with amusement as he turned to Brynley. "Do ye need a lift back to school?"

"Yes." She jumped off the couch and waved at Marielle. "See you tomorrow."

"Yes, thank you." Marielle waved back.

Ian walked over to Brynley and wrapped an arm around her shoulders. " 'Twas an honor to meet you, angel." He vanished, taking Brynley with him.

Alone at last. Connor watched as Marielle shoved her long blond hair behind her shoulders. She seemed deep in thought and momentarily oblivious to him. He took advantage, letting his gaze wander slowly down her body. Her clothes, borrowed from Emma, were better suited to a slimmer, more athletic build.

The T-shirt was a sky-blue like Marielle's eyes and stretched tight across her chest. Those soft, full breasts had filled his hands to overflowing when he'd fallen on top of her on the couch. *Doona think about it.* He shifted his gaze lower. Her jeans hugged nicely rounded hips and, as she would say, a complete set of female private parts.

Doona think about it! He lifted his gaze to her face, so lovely and angelic that surely his thoughts would become more chaste. She chewed on her bottom lip, drawing his attention to her mouth. Her words in the closet came rushing back. *I'm not giving you a blow job.*

Bloody hell, he was pathetic. He grabbed another bottle of blood from the fridge and stuck it in the microwave. How could he lust so badly for such an innocent? He was unworthy to touch her toes, and yet he longed to take her in his arms and worship her with his mouth. He must have been out of his mind when he'd told Angus at the meeting last night that he would take charge of her safety and training. The poor angel was not safe around him.

"Ian's wife is pregnant." She frowned, still deep in thought. "Then she must be mortal?"

"Aye."

She turned toward him. "And their child will be another hybrid like Shanna's children?"

"Aye. And there are others on the way. Jean-Luc and his wife had twins."

"Do they have both human and vampire characteristics?"

Connor nodded. "They appear like normal children, awake during the day and eating real food. But they have other . . . gifts, like levitation, teleportation, an ability to heal."

Her eyes widened. "How fascinating. I would love to meet some of these children." She sighed. "But I'm afraid it would be too dangerous."

Connor shrugged as he removed his bottle from the microwave. "Our community is always dealing with some kind of danger. Casimir and his Malcontents would like to destroy us all. And if the mortal world ever learned of our existence, they would want to kill us, too."

She frowned. "Maybe humans would accept you

once they learn you've been protecting them from the Malcontents."

He lifted his bottle. "Before Roman invented this stuff, we were feeding off humans. We dinna kill them, but I canna imagine they would be pleased. They'll see us for what we are: bloodsucking parasites. Unholy creatures of the night."

She winced. "I won't have you talking that way about yourself. You're a good, noble man. And all of your friends seem perfectly lovely."

He snorted. "Ye're still thinking like ye're in heaven. This is Earth, and humans will believe it is their sacred duty to kill us. That's why nothing is more important than keeping our existence a secret."

"Then we're in the same boat. I need my existence kept secret, too." She sighed. "Until I can get back to heaven. *If* I can get back."

"Ye will get back. We'll make sure of it."

Her eyes softened and the tips of her mouth curled up. "Thank you."

His heart squeezed in his chest. Bugger, how would he survive being alone with her? He gulped down some blood, then headed toward the couch. "We need to talk."

He took a seat and set his bottle on the coffee table, noting the shotgun and sword that Brynley had left nearby. What would happen if Marielle touched the shotgun? He didn't want to find out, so he quickly removed the shells.

She sat at the other end of the couch.

He stashed the empty shotgun under the coffee

table. "You should stay away from weapons you doona know how to use."

"That won't be problem." She turned sideways on the couch to face him, curling her bare feet beneath her. "I don't want anything to do with them."

He'd suspected she would feel this way. He'd even told Angus that, but it had only led to another argument. Whereas they both agreed that she needed to be kept safe, they had disagreed on how to go about it.

He set the shells on the table and picked up his bottle. "As soon as we find Casimir, we'll try to defeat him in battle. And since ye'll be helping us locate him, ye could find yerself in the middle of a verra dangerous situation."

"I understand."

He sipped from his bottle. "Angus wanted me to train you in self-defense. I . . . said no."

He heard her quick intake of air, so he turned toward her. "Doona misunderstand. I do want you to be safe and protected. But I doona want you arriving at a battle scene with a sword in yer hand. The Malcontents have had years, some of them centuries, for their training. A few nights of training would no' be enough. 'Twould be suicidal for ye to engage in battle."

She grimaced. "I don't think I could, even if you wanted me to."

He swallowed down more blood. "Ye're putting yerself at great risk in order to help us. Can I ask why?"

"I think the world would be a much safer place

without Casimir and his evil companions." She sighed. "But I can't pretend that I'm doing this only to protect humans. I'm hoping I'll be able to prove my worthiness, so the Archangels will let me back into heaven."

"I see." It seemed like a good plan, but he needed to keep her alive till she could accomplish her ultimate goal. "What do ye usually do if ye're in danger?"

"I'm not usually in danger." She turned her head to gaze out the window. "Before I could always fly away."

"What about the way ye knocked me down with a blast of air?"

Her gaze remained on the window, and her eyes glistened with unshed tears. "I'm only allowed to do that in a case of extreme emergency."

"Staying alive counts as an emergency."

She looked at him and blinked away her tears. "You're right. I used it to try to stop Zackriel. And again when I thought Darafer would kill you."

"So ye can control air?"

"All angels can control the elements to a certain degree. And some are more skilled than others. For instance, water. I can make it boil or freeze. I can even make it rain. Some angels can cause the current in a river to flow backwards or—"

"They can part the Red Sea?"

She nodded with the hint of a smile. "Yes. Although something that big requires prior approval and a large coordinated effort. We don't do that sort of thing very often since it tends to get noticed."

He snorted. "And fire? Can ye control that?"

She shrugged. "A little. You should see the God Warriors. They're magnificent. They can wield huge swords of fire and drive chariots of fire."

They did sound impressive. "Are they likely to help you if ye're in danger?"

"I—I don't know." Her shoulders slumped. "They would have before."

"The lightning I saw in the woods—that was Zackriel manipulating fire?"

She made a face. "He's very talented at throwing fireballs."

"He was throwing them at *you*! I saw the burn marks on yer back."

She rubbed her forehead. "He was trying to cut my wings off. I refused to stand still, so that's how I ended up burned—"

"Doona make excuses for him," Connor growled. "If I ever get my hands on him, he'll rue the day he was born . . . or created . . . or hatched from a damned egg, I doona know. I only know he's a bastard."

Her mouth twitched.

" 'Tis no' amusing."

She smiled. "I can't help it. There's something very appealing about you when you get all fierce and gruff."

He shrugged that off even though he felt some warmth in his face. "So can ye protect yerself with fire?"

She winced. "I was never very good at that."

"Show me."

She hesitated.

"Do we need to go outside? I suppose if ye start a forest fire, ye can make it rain to put it out?"

She groaned. "That won't be necessary." She extended an arm, her hand reaching toward the fireplace.

Connor felt a slight frisson of energy zip across the room. A small flame ignited on the log in the fireplace, then died away.

He blinked. "Ye—ye were just warming up?"

Her face reddened as she lowered her hand. "That was it."

He glanced back at the fireplace where only a tendril of smoke was curling over the log. "I've seen more fire on top of a birthday cake."

She sighed. "I never developed the skill. I didn't want to. It seemed destructive, and all I've ever wanted to do was help people. I loved being a Healer."

She looked so dejected, he tried to think of something comforting to say. "I . . . like you the way ye are."

Her mouth curled up and her eyes softened again with that tender look that made his heart squeeze in his chest. He guzzled down the rest of the blood and set the bottle on the table. "Which elements are left? Earth?"

"I could cause the earth to tremble. It might stop someone from attacking me."

He winced. "It would affect everyone. Just like the thing ye do with air. It would knock everyone down. Hard to win a battle that way . . . unless . . . Do ye think ye could learn to narrow yer focus?"

"I suppose I could. I've seen God Warriors do it."

"Then that is how ye will defend yerself." Connor stood and extended a hand. She accepted it, and he pulled her to her feet. He started to release her, but her fingers curled around his hand.

"Thank you for helping me, Connor Buchanan."

He swallowed hard. Holy Christ Almighty, how he wanted to pull her into his arms and kiss her. Would she object? Or would she melt against him? Would she use some of those instructions the ladies had given her?

He blinked and looked away. He couldn't afford for his vision to turn red. She would know what it meant. And if he kissed her, she might see into his black soul. Right now, she labored under the false impression that he was good and noble, and God help him, he liked it. He couldn't bear to lose her trust and respect.

Besides, there was no point in getting too close to her. She wanted to go back to heaven. The last thing he needed in his life was more heartache.

He released her and stepped back. "Do ye have any shoes?"

"Yes."

"Put them on and meet me outside." He headed for the front door. "We have work to do."

Chapter Twelve

*W*hen Marielle stepped outside, the cool mountain air instantly lifted her spirits. A bird sang in the forest, and the scent of pine wafted toward her on a breeze. *Glory to God in the Highest!*

There was no answer, but she refused to let that get her down. She had a plan now for getting back to heaven, and even though she was stuck on Earth for a short time, she had to admit she was enjoying it. Especially her time with Connor.

The porch light was on, making it easier to see the clearing in front of the cabin. Connor was moving quickly back and forth from a woodpile to the clearing. The moon, over three-quarters full, gleamed off his red hair. His kilt swished about his knees as he stood cut logs on end in a large circle.

While digging through the clothes from Emma, she'd found socks and shoes and a hooded jacket.

She was glad now that she'd put them all on. The night air was chilly, and apparently, she was going to be outside for a while.

"Come." Connor motioned for her to join him.

She descended the steps, mindful of the odd strings dangling off her shoes. She glanced at his shoes. "Oh, I need to tie myself up like you."

"Excuse me?"

She pointed at her shoes.

"Och, yer laces are untied. Sit and I'll show you."

She sat on the porch step. When he knelt in front of her, her heart rate quickened. His head was bowed so close to hers, she could see how fine and shiny his hair was. His gaze was focused downward at her shoes, and the thick fringe of his eyelashes cast shadows across his cheekbones. There was something about the shape of his face, his cheekbones and jawline that made her feel strange inside, as if her innards were quivering. It was hard to breathe, too, and she wondered if he could feel her shaky breaths against his face.

"Watch carefully so ye'll learn how." He glanced up and his smoky blue eyes widened.

Her heart lurched. She'd been caught admiring his face. Heat crept up to her cheeks.

His jaw shifted. "I'll start again. Watch."

She focused on her shoe as he tied the lace and described the act, but her heart kept pounding. What was wrong with her? She shouldn't exacerbate her situation by developing strong feelings toward Connor. She was hoping to return to heaven as soon as possible. She couldn't fall prey to human desire and longing.

"There." He finished. "Ye want to try?"

"Yes." She leaned over to mimic his movements. Her hair fell forward obscuring her view. She pushed it back and was halfway through tying the second shoelace when her hair fell forward again. She made a small sound of frustration. She couldn't see, and if she let go to shove her hair back, she'd have to start over.

He gently gathered her hair and held it back. Her heart leaped up her throat. With trembling fingers, she completed the bow.

He released her hair. "Ye did it. Ye learn quickly."

"You gave good instructions."

He jerked to a standing position. "Och, well, that was the sort of instruction ye were supposed to receive." He walked stiffly away.

She wondered what was bothering him as she joined him in the middle of the clearing. Maybe Brynley was right about men and the Three-Step Rule.

"I've set twelve logs around us like the numbers on a clock," he began.

"It reminds me of a stone henge." She pivoted in a circle. "I've always loved those."

" 'Tis no' like a henge."

"I think it is."

He gave her an impatient look. "Nay. I know what a henge looks like. I have one at home."

"You do? Can I see it?"

A pained look flitted over his face before he turned cold as stone. "I never go there. Forget I said it."

Her mouth fell open. Why would a man refuse

to go home? It must have something to do with the black pit of pain in his soul. Now that she was alone with him, maybe she should ask him about the blond woman Darcy. Or she could discover more about him by embracing him. That strategy made her heart race.

"Stand here in the center." He clasped her shoulders from behind and moved her into position. He pointed over her shoulder at the large log straight in front of her. "That one represents twelve o'clock, yer target. Our goal is for ye to learn to knock down yer target and only yer target. Agreed?"

"Yes." She nodded, frowning. She would have to be careful to conserve her energy if she was going to do this over and over.

"All right," Connor said, standing behind her. "For yer first attempt, try to narrow yer blast to half the circle, nine o'clock to three o'clock. Can ye do that?"

"I'll try." She looked from side to side, concentrating on the logs. Could she actually control the scope of the blast? And the intensity? "Maybe you shouldn't stand right behind me."

"Why? Are ye planning to fail?"

She glared at him over her shoulder. "I've never tried this before." And if she didn't manage to turn down the volume, she'd run out of energy in just a few attempts.

"Verra well." He moved back till he was standing between two logs. "Have a go then."

With a groan, she extended her hands. She wasn't sure how to do this other than using her thoughts.

Less power. Half the circle. She squeezed her eyes shut, and let loose what she hoped was a small spurt of energy.

She heard some thudding noises and a muffled curse behind her. She opened her eyes. The logs in front of her had moved about twenty feet, crashing into the forest, but she usually averaged forty to fifty feet, so she had managed to decrease her energy output. Not bad, she thought with a grin. She turned and winced.

The logs behind her had flown twenty feet, too. And so had Connor.

She ran to where he had landed on a snowy patch beneath a tree. He was flat on his back with a stunned look on his face and his kilt blown up.

She looked away, but the image was still seared into her mind. Somehow, he looked even larger tonight than he had last night. Brynley's description of oral sex came rushing back, and her cheeks blazed with heat.

"What the hell was that?" He sat up, glaring at her as he pushed his kilt down. "Ye were supposed to knock down only half the circle."

"I . . . missed."

His eyes narrowed and his mouth thinned. "If ye want to see my privates, lass, just say so. There's no need to keep knocking me down."

"I didn't do that just to look at your—" She grabbed one of the fallen logs and returned it to the clearing. "These logs only moved about twenty feet, and that's half the distance I usually move things, so I actually did have some success."

He hefted himself to his feet. "Verra well. I believe you." He went along the forest edge, locating the logs and returning them to the clock formation, his actions speeding up until she could see only a blur.

She returned to the center of the circle. "You move so quickly. Is that one of your skills as a vampire?"

"Aye, we have super strength and speed. Heightened senses." He walked toward her. "I can hear it when yer heartbeat quickens."

She stiffened.

He gave her a knowing look. "Like it is now."

Her heart lurched. "I'm excited about helping you locate and defeat the Malcontents. It will make the world a safer place."

His mouth twitched. "We'd better not achieve world peace. Ye could have a heart attack." He stopped beside her. "So do ye plan on knocking me down again?"

"I'll try to do better, but I can't guarantee it. You might be safer on the porch."

One end of his mouth curled up in a half smile. "Doona fash. 'Tis my choice to stay close to you. I know it comes with a risk."

Once again, he positioned himself next to the logs behind her. She concentrated on the half circle in front of her and released a small burst.

This time the logs moved only about five feet before toppling over. She glanced over her shoulder, and four logs were still standing, along with Connor.

"Ye're doing it!" He strode toward her. "Excellent, lass."

Her heart swelled with his praise. She turned to face him, and he grinned. Her breath caught. He looked so young and handsome when he smiled like that, as if a few centuries of despair had rolled off him. His smile faded and his eyes narrowed.

Good heavens! She faced front. He must be able to hear her heart racing. She pressed a hand to her chest. How could she stop it? She didn't seem to have any control over it.

He dashed around the circle to stand up the fallen logs. She took a deep breath to steady her nerves.

Again and again she practiced. After about a dozen attempts she was knocking down only three logs—the target and a log on each side of it.

She swayed. "I—I'm sorry. I'm out of energy."

"Come and rest." He led her onto the porch and settled her into a rocking chair.

She rested her head back and closed her eyes. A few minutes later, she heard his footsteps approach.

"Here." He pressed a bottle of water into her hand.

"Thank you." She took a sip. "Are we done for the night?"

"Nay." He leaned against a wooden post and crossed his arms. "When ye sense death, will ye be able to tell which ones are caused by Casimir and his minions?"

She drank some water. "Not directly. I can tell how many are dying, and if there is a lot of fear and terror involved, I can sense that."

He nodded slowly. "They'll feed right after they awaken at sunset, so the timing will give us a clue, too. How well can ye pinpoint the location? Can ye give us coordinates like GPS?"

She frowned. "It doesn't work like that. Normally, I just feel where to go and my wings take me there." She sighed. "I may not be of any use to you without my wings."

"Ye can feel it in yer mind?" When she nodded, he pushed away from the post and stepped toward her. "Then I will be your wings."

"How? Can you fly?"

"I'll teleport you. I have a tracking device embedded in my arm, so the other Vamps can follow me."

"How will you know where to go? I don't know how to tell you."

"Vampires have some psychic ability, so I should be able to slip inside yer mind."

Her eyes widened as she gazed at him, stunned. She'd felt so empty and lonesome without the constant voices of the Heavenly Host filling her mind with song and praise. She missed them sorely, yet somehow the thought of Connor being in her mind was . . . troubling. His thoughts would not be angelic. And having only one other person in her mind made it seem too . . . intimate.

She swallowed hard. "That works both ways. If we make a connection, I'll see into your mind, too."

His jaw shifted. " 'Tis a risk I'll have to take." He glowered at her. "I'll expect you to cooperate. When I enter yer mind, focus all yer concentration on the location ye wish to go to. As soon as we've teleported, I'll break the connection. The whole procedure should only take a few seconds."

"I see." He was hoping it would happen so fast she wouldn't have time to peek into his black pit of pain and remorse.

"We need to practice," he continued. "Every night that Casimir and his Malcontents are allowed to roam free, they will feed and kill."

She set the bottle down and stood. "All right. Let's do it."

He nodded. "We should start off with something easy."

She gave him a wry look. "An easy death? Tell that to the person who's dying."

"I meant a nonviolent death. And one close enough that there'll be no risk of me teleporting into daylight and getting fried."

"I understand." She closed her eyes to slowly access her sense of death. She'd learned years ago not to fling the door open, otherwise she could be overwhelmed by the amount of death that occurred worldwide at any given moment. She reached out gently to the nearest town where a death was occurring.

"I found one." She opened her eyes and for half a second caught Connor watching her intently before he shifted his gaze. "There's a town nearby where an elderly man is dying in a nursing home."

"Can ye focus on a place close by? If we teleport straight into the nursing home, we'll cause a fright. Or ye might end up accidentally brushing against someone and causing more death. Some place outdoors and isolated would be best."

She nodded, frowning. She'd never purposely missed the mark before. "I'll try."

He checked the dagger in his sock. "We shouldna run into any trouble, but I like to be prepared." He looked her over and grabbed the hem of her hooded jacket. "'Tis a wee bit chilly out here." He connected the zipper and zipped it up to her chin.

"Oh, I was wondering how that worked." She smiled sheepishly. "I knew it looked like the fastener on my pants, but I didn't how to get it started." She moved the zipper up and down. "I love this. Humans are so clever."

"Lass." He covered her hand with his own to stop her. "Are ye ready?"

To let him inside her mind? She swallowed hard. She'd always been an open book before, sharing everything with the Heavenly Host. But she'd never had these quivery feelings of desire before. She didn't want Connor to know that he was causing them, that even now she wanted him to pull her into his arms and kiss her.

She took a deep breath. She would focus all her thoughts on a place in the vicinity of the nursing home. That would be all he would sense. "I'm ready."

He grabbed her by the upper arms and pulled her close.

She gasped. *Good heavens!*

"Ye need to hold on to me," he said softly. "So I can teleport with you."

"Oh, right." She slipped her arms around his neck. Her heart thundered in her chest. *Concentrate. Think about the location. Not about being in his arms.*

His arms enveloped her and his cheek pressed

against her temple. "Open yer mind," he whispered. "Let me in."

She shuddered when she felt a cold stab at her brow.

Marielle. His voice echoed in her mind.

He was with her, his presence strong and determined. So masculine. And bold, as if he were staking a claim on her soul. *Marielle*, he repeated, and she wanted to melt around his voice.

She rallied her thoughts and focused on the location.

I have it, his voice said, then everything went black.

Connor scanned their surroundings quickly to see if anyone had witnessed their arrival. Marielle had stumbled a bit when they materialized, so he continued to hold her. They appeared to be in a dark alley.

"Good. No one saw us." He glanced down at her pale face, and his heart squeezed like it always did when he looked at her. Only now, it was stronger. He'd been inside her mind, and it was a beautiful place filled with love and compassion, so much so that he wondered if she could ever forgive the monstrous things he'd done in the past.

Doona even think about it. He was a condemned man, already on the list for hell. An angel could never care for him, not one as beautiful as Marielle. At least he suspected his secrets were safe. She'd been too busy protecting her own thoughts to even attempt to breach the thick wall he'd taken five centuries to build.

He led her toward the street. "Are ye all right?"

"Yes." She peered to the right. "The nursing home is that way."

Apparently, they'd arrived at one of the main streets in this town for it was fairly busy. Cars drove by in a steady stream. Other cars were parked along the street. The sidewalk was wide, and street lamps illuminated a long line of shops with colorful signs and awnings.

Pedestrians walked by in small groups, chatting and laughing. Horns blared in the distance. The scent of grilled meat drifted from a nearby restaurant.

Across the street, a wrought-iron fence separated the sidewalk from a garden. A large arch spanned an opening in the fence with the words *Hudson Park* painted across it. A man in a security uniform was closing and locking the gate.

"Let's find the nursing home," Connor said. "I want to see how close you managed to get us."

"There are too many humans here," she whispered. "I'm afraid I'll hurt someone."

"Stay close to the storefronts. I'll make sure no one touches you." *Except me.* He hooked her hand around his elbow and led her down the street.

She clung to his arm, her shoulders hunched with tension as she watched mortals pass by.

He recalled the way her touch had activated the toilet and bathroom sink. It seemed like an odd gift for an angel of death to possess. "Does yer touch always kill?"

She frowned. "My touch used to heal, but now . . ."

She shook her head. "It was hard for me to adjust to being a Deliverer. The job isn't meant to be destructive, although humans tend to see it that way. We deliver souls, giving them comfort and companionship as they cross over."

"But when ye touch someone, they die."

She sighed. "The touch itself doesn't destroy. It releases energy, enough energy to set the soul free. And when all the energy is gone, the body ceases to be."

"I see." So when it came to mechanical objects, her touch released energy, making things work until the energy ran out.

After a few blocks, she relaxed and looked curiously about. "This is amazing. I've never done this before."

"Walk down a street?"

She smiled. "I like the way you say *down*." Her smile widened when he rolled his eyes. "And no, I've never walked *dune* a street. We usually come to complete an assignment, and then leave. Oh, look." She stopped to peer into the window of a gift shop.

Connor checked to see what was catching her eye. It was a sun catcher in the shape of an angel with crystal wings and a golden halo.

He smiled. "Och, will ye look at that. Ye're famous."

She laughed, and the sound warmed his heart.

Her head turned when a young woman walked past them eating an ice cream cone. "What is that?"

"Ice cream." He slapped himself mentally. She

was probably hungry. He'd made her work for several hours, and he hadn't even thought about feeding her. "Ye should try some."

He spotted the ice cream parlor two shops down and led her inside. Two human customers were at the counter, and she tugged at his arm.

"Doona fash," he whispered. He positioned himself between her and the customers. They received their orders and wandered off to a table in the corner.

He stepped up to the counter. "A cone, please."

The lad behind the counter took one look at his kilt and smirked. "Whatever you say, man. What flavor?"

Connor ignored the pimply-faced youth and turned to Marielle. "What kind would ye like?"

"There are so many to choose from." She wandered down the freezer, peering through the window, then jerked upright with a smile. "Chocolate."

Connor smiled back. "One scoop of chocolate for the lady."

"The one wearing the pants in the family?" the lad muttered as he scooped up a ball of chocolate ice cream.

Connor narrowed his eyes. He was sorely tempted to cuff the young whelp on his head, but he wanted to get the ice cream for Marielle.

She edged closer to him and whispered loudly, "Did I ever tell you how much I love your kilt?"

"Nay." He wondered if she was telling the truth or putting on a show for the rude employee. "Do ye really?"

"Oh yes." She nodded seriously. "It makes me think about . . . giving you a blow job."

The lad squeaked and dropped the scoop of ice cream on the floor. "Don't worry! I'll get you another one." He hunched over, digging furiously at the ice cream, his face bright red.

Connor arched a brow at Marielle, and she looked away, her cheeks blushing. He bit his lip to keep from laughing out loud.

The lad completed the cone and reached toward Marielle.

"I got it." Connor grabbed the cone, then passed it on to Marielle. "How much do I owe you?"

The lad told him, then lowered his voice. "That's an awesome kilt, dude. Where did you get it?"

"In Edinburgh." Connor retrieved some money from his sporran and handed it to the lad, who looked perplexed. "That's in Scotland."

"Oh, right. That's like . . . far away, huh?"

"Ye could probably order one online," Connor muttered as he dropped the change into his sporran.

"That's right!" The lad grinned. "Thanks, dude." He glanced at Marielle, then gave Connor two thumbs up.

He found himself grinning as he led Marielle from the store and down the sidewalk. "I appreciate what ye did, lass, but there are certain things ye doona talk about in public. For instance, blow—" He glanced at her and jerked to a stop.

Holy Christ Almighty, she was running her tongue all over the scoop of ice cream. A bead of chocolate drizzled down the cone. She caught it with the tip of her tongue, then dragged her tongue up the side of the cone.

His groin tightened. "Good Lord," he whispered.

She licked her lips. "Would you like some of this?"

God, yes. "Nay." He frowned at the cone she was extending toward him. "It would probably make me ill."

"Oh, that's a shame 'cause it's really good. Though I'm not quite sure how to eat it." She opened her mouth, molded her lips around the entire scoop, and sucked on it.

He groaned.

She gave him a worried look. "Are you all right?"

He looked away. "I will be. Where is the nursing home?" *And do they have ice packs?*

"It's on the other side of the street. Just past the park."

"All right." He walked slowly down the sidewalk, trying his best to ignore the sucking and slurping noises she was making. The ladies didn't need to give her any instructions. She was a natural.

In spite of the growing discomfort in his kilt, he found himself smiling again. She had purposely embarrassed herself in the ice cream shop in order to lend him support.

A loud noise drew his attention. Someone was having trouble starting a car that was parked half a block up the street. The engine made a whirring sound, then died. He caught the words of the distraught woman inside the car.

"Please, please start! Don't die on me now. Please, just get me home," she wailed. "Oh God, help me!"

He took Marielle by the elbow and maneuvered her over to the car. "Let's cross the street here."

"Okay." She took a bite out of the cone, then stepped off the curb.

He pretended to bump into her, causing her to stumble against the car's rear bumper. "Sorry."

The car started, and the woman inside squealed with joy.

He bit his lip to keep from laughing as he pulled Marielle back onto the sidewalk. "Are ye all right?"

She nodded and took another bite into the cone. "This is really good. I'm sorry you can't have any."

He grinned. "I'm fine."

She studied him as she chewed. "Are you usually this happy?"

"Nay." He watched the car drive off. "I havena been this happy in centuries."

"You look very handsome when you smile."

The tenderness in her eyes nearly melted his heart. "Come." He took her hand in his and led her across the street.

By the time she finished her ice cream cone, they were standing in front of the nursing home.

"We arrived too far away," he said. "We'll try again tomorrow night."

She tilted her head back to gaze at the stars. "It was a good passing. His family and friends were by his side."

"Ye can sense that?"

She nodded, still gazing at the night sky. "He's very happy to be with his wife again. He lost her to cancer a few years ago and missed her sorely. That sort of love is amazing, don't you think?"

His chest grew tight.

She closed her eyes and breathed deeply. "Can you feel it?"

"Feel what?"

"So much love. He's surrounded with it." A tear rolled down her cheek. "Glory to God in the Highest."

Something jabbed at his chest, causing a crack in his defenses. He lifted a hand to wipe the tear from her face, but stopped. How could he even touch her? She was so perfect, and he was so flawed. And yet, he wanted her so much. He lowered his hand.

She opened her eyes and smiled at him.

Christ Almighty, he was falling for her. "We should teleport back." He looked around. The parking lot was too visible from the busy street. The park. It looked empty and dark. "Come." He motioned for her to follow.

The side gate was locked with a chain, but with a quick jerk, the chain broke. He led her inside.

They walked down a brick path, flanked by brilliant yellow and red flowers. In the distance, he could see fruit trees bursting with spring flowers. He breathed deeply of the scented air. This was a night he would cherish for centuries.

She sighed. "It's lovely."

"Aye." He stopped by a water fountain. "Are ye thirsty?" He pushed the button, and a spray of water arched into a basin.

She took a drink, then rinsed her hands, and they resumed their leisurely walk.

When they reached a crossroads, she halted with a gasp. "Is that a carousel?"

She ran up to the low fence that surrounded it. "Look at all the different animals. I love it."

"Would ye like to ride on it?"

She waved a dismissive hand. "It's closed."

He leaped over the low fence. "Come on." He grabbed her by the waist, lifted her over the fence, and deposited her next to him.

"Connor, it's not working."

He jumped onto the carousel platform and extended a hand to her. "Trust me."

She placed her hand in his. He pulled her onto the platform, and it lurched into motion.

She gasped, stumbling to the side, but he steadied her. Music blared around them, a waltz played by a pipe organ. All the twinkling white lights came on.

"Good heavens." Her eyes widened with astonishment. "It's so beautiful."

"Come." He led her to a white unicorn with a golden horn and saddle.

It was moving up and down, making it difficult for her to mount, so he levitated her up and placed her on the saddle. She tilted her head back and laughed.

When he climbed onto the horse next to her, she looked at him and laughed some more. "Connor, you're riding a pink horse with a garland of flowers."

He glanced down and frowned. "Bugger."

She laughed again, and his frown turned into a

smile. When had he ever smiled this much in one evening? Never, not even as a human. Life had been too harsh back then, and survival had been a constant challenge.

He watched Marielle, marveling over the expression of pure joy on her face. What was really amazing was he'd had a part in causing her joy. After centuries of misery and remorse, he hadn't even thought himself capable of joy.

Or love. His heart squeezed. Christ, he was falling hard.

"Hey!" a voice yelled over the music. "What the hell are you doing here? The park is closed."

As the carousel swung around, he spotted the security guard taking out a cell phone.

"I'm calling the police!"

Marielle gasped. "Are we in trouble?"

He jumped down from his horse and grabbed her. "Trust me." He teleported, taking her with him.

They materialized eighty yards away. The carousel instantly went dark. The music and motion ground to a stop.

The security guard stared. "What the hell?"

Connor shot a surge of vampire mind control at him. *Nothing happened. Ye'll go home, remembering nothing.*

The guard wandered off toward the front gate. Connor smiled at Marielle and led her farther into the park. His heightened senses had picked up the scent of roses. Sure enough, they were soon in the midst of a rose garden.

Marielle pivoted to look around. "It's a piece of

heaven." She faced him and grinned. "Thank you. I'll always remember this night."

"So will I." He plucked a budding rose and handed it to her.

With a laugh, she accepted it. The bud unfurled into a large, beautiful blossom. But then it withered and turned brown. She dropped it with a horrified gasp.

Bugger. He should have known that would happen.

She stepped back. "I killed it. I'm sorry."

"Nay, I killed it the minute I picked it."

She shook her head. "I hate being a Deliverer. I hate it." Tears glimmered in her eyes. "All I ever wanted was to be a Healer."

"Ye are a Healer." He stepped toward her. "Ye're healing me."

Her eyes widened.

He moved closer. And closer. Her gaze held steady, never wavering from his face.

Holy Christ Almighty, he shouldn't do this. It would give her a chance to see into the black pit in his soul. She might learn what a rotten, coldhearted bastard he really was.

He touched her cheek. She didn't pull away.

Doona do it! He slid his hand around the back of her neck. "Are ye going to stop me?"

"No," she whispered, and touched his chest.

And he was lost.

Chapter Thirteen

*M*arielle's heart was pounding and melting at the same time. Her mind considered that unlikely, but she couldn't deny something was happening to her. Something different from last night.

Those kisses had been demanding, and Connor's passion had left her weak in the knees and hardly able to think. She'd been instantly swept into a storm of glorious sensations, making her intensely aware of her new human body.

Now, somewhere in her bedazzled mind, she knew this kiss was different. He was tender. Hesitant. Almost . . . fearful. And in every gentle movement of his lips, she could sense why. *He cares for you.*

With a moan, she wrapped her arms around his neck. She wanted him to know how much she cared, too. When he deepened the kiss, she melted into it.

When he ran the tip of his tongue against her lips, she opened and let him inside.

Her intent had been to give, but with a small shock, she realized she was receiving, too. With each invasion of his tongue, she felt a spark sizzle down her body. It made her tremble. It made her want more.

She dug her fingers into his shoulders and pressed against him.

"Marielle," he whispered, and trailed kisses down her neck.

More sparks tingled down her body. With another small shock, she realized all the sizzles were gathering between her legs, and a desperate need was building inside her. An empty ache that begged to be filled.

His hands cupped her rear end, and he pulled her against him.

She gasped. His groin was hard. And large. The empty ache inside her could only mean her human body wanted to join with his. *And the two shall become one.*

Good heavens! She pulled away. "What am I doing?"

Connor blinked, his eyes red and glowing. "I— 'Tis called making love."

She stepped back. "Do these things really happen so quickly? We only met last night."

He frowned. "I thought ye were beautiful the minute I saw you. And we've been through a hell of a lot together. Are ye denying there is something between us?"

"No. I—" Her emotions were all jumbled up, but there were a few things she knew for certain. She squared her shoulders. "I care deeply for you, Connor Buchanan."

The red glow in his eyes intensified.

"But I intend to go back to heaven. I need to stay . . ."

His mouth twisted. "Unsoiled?"

She winced. "I was going to say focused."

His eyes turned back to their normal smoky blue. "I'm a distraction."

"No! You saved my life. I will always be grateful."

"Is that what ye were doing? Showing gratitude? Next time, send me a card."

"That's not it! I was dangerously close to wanting sex!" She grimaced and covered her mouth, but the words had already come out.

He looked shocked for a few seconds, but then he scoffed. "A fate worse than death."

She curled her hand into a fist, ready to jam it down her own throat if she said anything else embarrassingly honest. She'd always been able to share any thoughts she had with the Heavenly Host, but the rules in the human world were confusingly different. And the emotions involved were more powerful than she'd ever imagined. "I don't think you understand."

"I understand verra well." His face turned cold and blank. "Ye need to stay pure and innocent. I doona resent that. 'Tis part of who ye are, and I doona wish to destroy yer chances of returning to heaven."

She lowered her hand. "I do wish to retain my angelic nature."

"Of course." He bowed his head. "I apologize for molesting you."

"You didn't molest me!" She glared at him. "You are a good and noble man, and I will not have you speak ill of yourself."

He snorted. "What do ye expect from me, Marielle? I know damned well I'm no' good enough for you."

She made a noise of sheer frustration. "You still don't understand. I *do* want you, Connor. I am . . . shocked by how much I want you."

His eyes widened. "Ye want me?"

"Yes! But if the two become one, then you would be a part of me. How would I ever be able to leave you?"

"Ye—ye would have trouble leaving me?"

"Of course, you dolt! I told you I care deeply for you. Words have meaning, you know." She groaned inwardly. She'd done it again and said more than she should.

He continued to look stunned for a moment, then a twinkle lit up his eyes. "Did ye just call me a dolt?"

She winced.

"That wasna verra angelic of you." He assumed a wounded expression. "Words have meaning, ye know."

She narrowed her eyes. "Careful. I can still knock you down with a blast of air."

A corner of his mouth tilted up. "Still wanting a peek under my kilt, lass?"

She couldn't help but smile. "You're incorrigible."

"Aye. That's why ye love me." He winced. "I shouldna have said . . . 'tis merely an expression, I dinna mean to imply . . ." He ran a hand through his hair.

It was almost a relief. She wasn't the only one saying more than she should. Still, the word *love* seemed to hang in the air between them. It was strange. She'd lived her entire existence surrounded by love. The Father was love, and she'd always basked in its glow. But now, it had become a fearful, awkward thing that neither she nor Connor could admit to.

"I will do everything in my power to help you get back to heaven," he said quietly. "Ye have my word on that."

"Thank you."

"I should return you to the cabin." He stepped toward her. "And then I need to drop by Romatech to give Angus a progress report."

She held up a hand to stop him. "Before we go, can I ask you something? It's . . . personal."

He shifted his weight with a wary expression. "What is it?"

"I was wondering . . ." She took a deep breath. "Who is Darcy Newhart?"

He flinched. "What? How?" His eyes narrowed. "While I was pouring my heart out to you just now in a kiss, ye were playing the busybody, snooping around in my soul?"

She scowled at him. "I didn't see anything then. I was too . . . overwhelmed."

He arched a brow at her. "No' overwhelmed enough. Ye were able to stop."

"If I hadn't stopped you, you would have kept going?"

"Aye." He folded his arms across his chest. "A man doesna start something he canna finish."

She recalled how hard his groin had felt. He really had been prepared to have intercourse with her. Heat rose to her cheeks.

"Then ye spied on me when I entered yer mind to see where to teleport?" he asked.

She shook her head. "It happened last night. It wasn't intentional. Her name and face flashed through my mind while we were kissing. The second time."

"In the bedroom?"

"Yes."

"When I touched yer breast?"

She gave him an annoyed look. "Not at that precise moment, no."

He nodded slowly with a glint in his eyes. "So I can safely fondle yer breasts without revealing more information?"

"Excuse me?" When he chuckled, she realized he was teasing her, and she slapped at his shoulder. "Brynley must be right about the Three-Step Rule."

"What is that?"

She narrowed her eyes. "I know what you're doing. You're trying to distract me from the main topic of conversation."

"Nay, our main topics are merely different. I want

to talk about yer breasts. Actually, I'd like to see yer breasts. And then I'd like to kiss them."

She huffed. "Three steps. Brynley *was* right."

The phone rang in his sporran and he pulled it out. "Aye?" He listened for a while. "Verra well. I'll see if she'll come." He dropped the phone back into his sporran.

"What is it?" she asked.

"Shanna wants to meet you. Will ye come to Romatech with me?"

She nodded. "Yes, of course." She owed the poor woman an apology. And Connor was sadly mistaken if he thought she would forget to question him about Darcy Newhart again.

When Connor teleported with Marielle to the side entrance of Romatech, Phineas was there to greet them.

Connor introduced the young black Vamp. "This is Phineas McKinney. He works for Angus, too, and he's in charge of security here."

"God bless you, dear soul." She gave him one of her dazzling smiles.

"Wow." Phineas's eyes widened. "Robby just said she was dangerous. He didn't mention she was smokin' *hot*!"

Connor glowered at him. "Her hearing works well, too."

"It's not her ears I'm worried about," Phineas muttered. He turned to Marielle. "We have a few mortal and shape-shifter employees here tonight.

They have been warned to remain in their offices until you leave the premises."

She nodded, her face growing sad. "I understand."

"She wouldna purposely harm anyone," Connor grumbled.

"I know." Phineas gave Marielle an apologetic look. "I don't mean to insult you, but as head of security here, I would feel personally responsible for any . . . accidents."

She stuffed her hands into the pockets of her hooded jacket. "I'll be careful."

Phineas opened the side door and motioned for them to enter. "Shanna's waiting for you in the cafeteria. Roman is outside with the children. Radinka and Father Andrew are with them."

"Radinka is Gregori's mother," Connor explained as they walked down the corridor, followed by Phineas. "She's mortal and helps Shanna with the children." He winced. Radinka would have to watch over the children all day now.

"Gregori has a mortal mother who is still alive?" Marielle asked.

"Aye, he's a young Vamp. Transformed in the parking lot here after Casimir attacked him. Radinka found him barely alive and begged Roman to save him."

Marielle nodded. "I thought he was younger. Not as . . . heavily burdened as others." She gave Connor a worried look.

She was obviously referring to him and the black pit of remorse she kept trying to dig into. He didn't want to talk about it or even think about it. Tonight had been a magical night, buying her first ice cream cone and sharing her first ride on a carousel. And hearing her admit that she cared deeply for him.

Tonight had filled his heart with joy. It would be a memory he would treasure long after she returned to heaven. He flinched inwardly with a pang to his heart. He didn't want to think about that, either. It would hurt like hell when she left.

But of course, he was on the list for hell, so it was exactly what he deserved.

They reached the main foyer, and Connor turned left, motioning for Marielle to follow.

"I guess an angel like you has to be really old," Phineas said as he walked behind them.

Connor glanced back with an irritated look.

Phineas smirked. "I bet you're even older than grouchy old Connor."

Marielle smiled. "I am." She looked at Connor. "How old are you?"

His jaw shifted. "I doona discuss my private life."

"I can translate that for you," Phineas offered. "It means he's embarrassed he was a caveman and ate brontosaurus burgers for lunch."

Connor arched an eyebrow at him. "The correct translation is 'sod off.'"

"Dude, that's no way to talk in front of an angel. Just because you're having a mid-life crisis, it doesn't mean you can be rude."

Connor scoffed. "I'm no' having a bloody mid-life crisis. And I'm no' rude, so bugger off."

Phineas leaned close. "I can give you some pointers on how to sweeten her up."

"She can hear you," Connor muttered.

"Right. And she heard you, too, bro. You're in desperate need of some professional help from the Love Doctor."

"You're a doctor?" Marielle asked.

"Of love," Phineas clarified, then puffed out his chest. "You'll never find so many happily married couples as there are around here. Is it a coincidence that all this romance occurs when the Love Doctor is around? I think not!"

Connor shook his head and led them down a glass-lined hallway to the cafeteria. Through the glass, he could see Roman playing with his children on the basketball court. Radinka and Father Andrew sat on a bench nearby.

"Now let me tell you how to set up the perfect date with your lovely lady," Phineas continued. "You gotta take her somewhere romantic."

"Like a park?" Marielle asked.

"Yeah, that would work," Phineas agreed.

Connor slanted a glance at Marielle, and she was watching him, her eyes twinkling with humor.

"And then, bro, you gotta buy her something sweet to eat," Phineas said.

"Like ice cream?" Marielle asked.

"Yeah, that's it." Phineas slapped Connor on the back. "You just do whatever your angel here wants. She'll tell you what's romantic."

She smiled at Connor, and his heart did its usual

squeeze. "My goal is no' to date her, but to get her back to heaven."

"Oh." Phineas looked disappointed as he turned to Marielle. "You don't want to stay here with us?"

Her smile faded. "I don't belong here. I live in constant fear of brushing up against humans and causing their death."

Phineas nodded. "That's a bummer. Roman's still kinda pissed about what happened."

Marielle sighed. "I've come to apologize, but I know that's woefully inadequate."

Connor's jaw clenched. "'Twas my fault." He stopped outside the cafeteria doors. "Shanna's in here. I can leave you alone a few minutes while I report to Angus."

"Angus isn't here, bro," Phineas said. "He and Emma went to Nebraska. Robby and Olivia went with them."

Connor stiffened. "Dead bodies?"

"Yeah. Sean Whelan called to let us know that a local sheriff discovered ten bodies in a small town. They went to see if Casimir was behind it."

Marielle hung her head. "I'm so sorry. I should have sensed that."

"'Tis no' yer fault," Connor said. "I asked ye to find a peaceful death close by. We'll try again tomorrow night."

"You were able to teleport to a death scene?" Phineas asked.

"Aye." Connor nodded. "When ye see Angus, tell him the training is going well. We should be ready in a few nights."

Phineas nodded. "Will do." He turned back to Marielle. "I need to get back to the office to keep an eye on everything. Thank you for helping us."

"You're welcome." She touched Phineas's shoulder. "Bless you."

As Phineas headed back to the security office, Connor opened the cafeteria door and escorted Marielle inside.

Shanna was across the large room, standing by the window and gazing out at her children. When the door banged shut behind them, she turned.

Connor kept his face blank, but a sharp jab speared his heart. Shanna had always seemed so vibrant and full of life, but now she had joined the ranks of the Undead. There was a new fragile paleness to her skin, and something a little different about her eyes. The blue irises were more intense.

"Thank you for coming," she said softly and smiled.

Connor flinched inwardly. Shanna's fangs were retracted, but he could still see the sharp points. *Bugger.* He didn't understand it. How could so many of his friends marry mortal women, knowing full well this would be their future?

Shanna's eyes widened as she looked Marielle over. "You're really an angel."

Marielle knelt and bowed her head. "Dear soul, I have caused you terrible wrong. I pray you will forgive me."

Shanna approached her. "Father Andrew told me how upset you were when you learned about the accident." She leaned over. "It *was* an accident. There's nothing to forgive."

Marielle looked up at her with tears in her eyes. "I'm so relieved you're all right. God bless you and your family."

Shanna's eyes glimmered with tears, too, and she extended a hand. "Thank you."

Marielle took her hand and stood.

Connor looked away. They were probably able to forgive so easily because neither one had been at fault. He was the one who had brought Marielle here, ignoring all her protests that she mustn't be touched.

He sat at one of the tables, giving the ladies some distance so they could chat. Still, with his heightened senses, he could hear everything they said. As always with Shanna, the conversation soon turned to her children.

She led Marielle over to the window to point out Constantine and Sofia, who were still playing on the basketball court with their father.

"They're beautiful," Marielle murmured. "You and your husband are truly blessed."

Shanna nodded, tears shimmering once again in her eyes.

"How are they doing?" Marielle asked.

Shanna sighed. "It's not easy for them. Since they were born, they grew up knowing their father was unavailable during the day, so they just accepted it. And they always had me." A tear slipped down her cheek. "Now they don't."

Connor noted the pink tint to Shanna's tear and turned away. Tears crowded his own eyes. Guilt bore down on him.

"We'll adjust," Shanna continued. "They'll learn to sleep more during the day so they can be awake more at night. And they can spend more time at the school. Thank God I have Radinka. She's like a grandmother to them. And my sister, Caitlyn, is a big help."

"I'm glad your family is here for you," Marielle said.

Shanna sighed. "Not all my family. My father is the head of the CIA Stake-Out team. He hates vampires. And shifters. I—I don't know how I'm going to tell him."

Marielle touched her shoulder. "What is his name? I will pray for him."

"Sean Whelan." Shanna smiled sadly. "It'll take a lot of prayers to sway him. He's still furious that Caitlyn turned into a were-panther."

Marielle's eyes widened. "How did that happen? Was she attacked?"

"She married a were-panther," Shanna replied. "She risked her life to be with the man she loved."

"Good heavens," Marielle whispered. "She was very brave." She turned toward Connor and their eyes met.

His chest tightened. God help him, he was falling for her. He looked away. What a bloody fool he was. Always berating the other guys for falling in love, and here he was falling faster than any of them had. It was pathetic.

"Caitlyn's expecting twins in a few months," Shanna continued. "We're all very excited about it."

Marielle smiled. "That's wonderful."

A tap on the nearby window snagged Connor's

attention. He glanced up to find Father Andrew motioning for him to join them outside.

He trudged toward the glass door and nodded at the ladies. "Excuse me." He let himself out onto the patio.

Radinka was still seated on the bench, but she was staring at the window with an expression of awe. "I can't believe I'm seeing a real angel. She's so beautiful."

"Aye." Connor glanced toward Roman.

A glint of anger flashed in Roman's eyes, then he turned back to his children.

"He'll come around in time," Father Andrew said quietly, then gestured toward a cement bench farther away.

"He has every right to be angry," Connor muttered as he followed the priest.

Father Andrew withdrew three vials from his coat pocket. "These contain holy water. To help you fight the demon. Has he returned?"

"Nay, no' yet." Connor dropped the vials into his sporran.

"Thank you for agreeing to protect Marielle." Father Andrew sat on the bench. "I've been pondering how we can return her to heaven."

Connor sat beside him. "She hopes that helping us defeat Casimir and the Malcontents will prove her worthiness, and the Archangels will take her back."

"She believes she can earn forgiveness?" Father Andrew frowned. "In my experience, it doesn't usually work that way. The Lord honors a truly penitent heart."

Connor scoffed. "She is truly penitent, and look where it got her. Wounded and left bleeding in the dirt."

The priest sighed. "I cannot presume to understand everything that is going on, but I do feel that we are witnessing divine providence. Perhaps the Lord has loaned her to us for the express purpose of defeating Casimir."

"And then afterward, He intends to take her back?" Connor glanced toward the windows where she was standing next to Shanna.

"I believe so," Father Andrew said. "Can I count on your assistance in getting her home?"

He continued to watch her. "I gave her my word I would do everything in my power to get her back."

The priest was silent for a moment. "Perhaps your assistance will help prove your own worthiness."

He snorted. "I am past redemption, Father. Even the demon knows my name and said I was on his list."

"There's a word for a man who believes what a demon tells him." Father Andrew gave him a wry look. "He's called a fool."

Connor scoffed. "I'm a realist."

"God is real."

"So is the demon. I've seen him."

Father Andrew sighed. "Does she understand how dangerous this mission could be?"

"Aye. We worked tonight on a way for her to

defend herself. And we successfully teleported close to a place where she sensed death."

"How did you know where to teleport?"

Connor shifted on the bench. "I had to . . . slip inside her mind for a few seconds."

The priest sat back. "You were inside the mind of an angel?"

"For a few seconds."

"That must have been incredible. What—what did you see, if you don't mind my asking?"

He leaned forward, resting his forearms on his thighs. "It was . . . a beautiful, peaceful place full of love and compassion."

"I bet it was." Father Andrew sat silently for a moment. "I've never met a man whom the Father couldn't forgive. If you confess—"

"Nay. I confess nothing." Connor stood. "I'm a lost cause, Father. That's why I'm the perfect choice to protect Marielle. I have nothing to lose."

"And everything to gain," the priest muttered, then rose to his feet. "Come. Let's see if we can convince Roman to talk to Marielle."

"So he can forgive her?" Connor asked dryly. *Or forgive me?*

Father Andrew walked toward the glass door to let himself into the cafeteria.

"Father, no!" Roman strode toward him. "It's not safe."

The priest gave him a bland look. "I talked to her last night without any problems."

"You had several Vamps to protect you," Roman argued.

"Then come in with me." Father Andrew opened the door and walked inside.

"God's blood," Roman muttered, then glared at Connor. "Aren't you going in?"

"After you."

Roman's eyes narrowed, then he glanced back at the children. "Stay here with Radinka. I'll be right back."

"I want to meet the angel," Constantine said.

"Me, too!" Sofia skipped toward him.

"*No!*" Roman winced, then softened his tone. "I need you to stay here. You can watch her through the glass."

"Come, my darlings." Radinka gathered the children in her arms. "We'll have a lovely view right here."

Roman shot Connor an annoyed look as he entered the cafeteria.

Connor followed and saw that the priest was talking to Marielle, but keeping a safe distance.

Shanna grabbed Roman's hand and led him toward Marielle. "You would think a former monk would be eager to meet an angel."

Roman looked properly chastised as he stopped in front of Marielle. "It is an honor to meet you."

Marielle inclined her head. "I am so very sorry for the pain and grief I caused. I will remember your children in my prayers each day."

"Thank you." Roman extended a hand.

She took it, then flinched and looked more closely at him. "I have encountered your soul before."

"Yes." Roman nodded. "I met you last night, though you were mostly unconscious."

"No, it was . . ." She tilted her head, studying him. Then with a gasp, she released his hand and stepped back. "Good heavens! It can't be."

Connor moved to her side. "What's wrong?"

She shook her head. "It was so long ago. How can . . ." She looked at Roman, her expression a mixture of shock and horror. "You were my first mistake."

Chapter Fourteen

*R*oman stiffened. "You're calling me a mistake? After nearly killing my wife? That's what I would call a *mistake*!"

Marielle winced. She still needed to learn not to say everything that came to mind.

Roman strode toward the door. "This meeting is over."

"Give her a chance to explain," Connor said.

Roman whirled around and glared at him. "What has gotten into you? Have you forgotten where your loyalty lies?"

Marielle saw Connor's hands curl into fists, and she grabbed his arm to stop him. "Please don't blame Connor for my mistakes," she told Roman.

He scoffed. "And your mistakes include me?"

Connor shot her an angry look. "Release me. I fight my own battles."

She let go, surprised that his angry lash stung her more than Roman's. Why shouldn't she seek to protect him? He always protected her.

"Enough!" Father Andrew scowled at them all. "Let's all sit down and let Marielle explain."

She took a seat and glanced warily at Roman.

He sat with an impatient huff. Shanna sat next to him, took his hand in hers, and leaned close to whisper something in his ear. His tense expression relaxed.

They had a good marriage, Marielle realized, one filled with understanding and tenderness. Roman's sour mood stemmed from the fear he had endured, the fear of losing his beloved wife.

She glanced at Connor who was sitting nearby, his arms crossed, his face frowning. She sighed. He'd been so happy earlier in the evening, but now he seemed downright grouchy. *He knows he is losing me.* She'd go back to heaven as soon as she could. And he would be left behind, still lonely and still full of pain and remorse.

His words came back to her. *Ye're healing me.* Dear Lord, she hoped so. She couldn't bear the thought of him existing for centuries with so much sorrow and despair.

"Please begin when you are ready," Father Andrew said, interrupting her thoughts.

She took a deep breath. "Father Andrew and Connor heard some of my story last night. I have been banished from heaven for disobeying orders. Last night was my third time."

"Her second time was when she healed a baby

who was supposed to die," Father Andrew explained. "The boy grew up to be a serial killer."

Roman nodded. "Otis Crump. Robby told us about that."

Marielle shifted on the hard chair. "That's when the Archangels decided to strip away my healing abilities. As a punishment, I became a Deliverer, and I had to deliver the souls of all the women who were murdered by Otis."

"That must have been heartbreaking for you," Shanna said.

Roman snorted. "I'm sure it was a lot tougher on the women."

"Yes," Marielle conceded. "You are correct."

"What does this have to do with me?" Roman asked.

"I think I know." Father Andrew leaned forward. "You mentioned the first time you disobeyed. Eastern Europe in the Middle Ages?"

"Yes, in 1461." She noticed Roman's stunned reaction. "I was a Healer then. I was sent to a small village in Romania where a farmer's wife had given birth to their third son."

Roman jumped to his feet. "You witnessed my birth?"

Marielle gave him a sad look. "You and your mother were dying. I was given orders to heal your mother. But not you."

He flinched. "I was supposed to die?"

"I touched your mother to heal her, and your father broke into tears, praising God. Then he vowed that if God would heal you, too, he would dedicate you to the Church."

Roman paled. "My father made a vow?"

"Yes. He pledged to give you to the local monastery."

Roman walked away slowly till he came to a wall of glass windows overlooking the garden.

"I couldn't see any harm in healing you," Marielle continued. "The world was full of poverty and disease. I thought you could do some good as a monk."

Roman leaned a forearm against the window and gazed outside. "I never knew. My father took me to the monastery when I turned five and left me there. I thought he didn't want me."

"He loved you greatly from the moment you were born," Marielle said quietly. "He cried and pleaded for you until my heart could no longer bear it. So I healed you."

"You saved his life," Shanna whispered, tears glimmering in her eyes.

Roman rested his brow against his forearm. "When my father left me, the monks gave him a sack of flour. I thought he had sold me for food."

Shanna rushed toward him and hugged him from behind. "It was probably a gift since they knew how poor your family was."

"I'm sure that's all it was," Father Andrew agreed. "But as an abandoned child in pain, Roman misinterpreted it."

"Were ye punished for healing him?" Connor asked her.

"I was reprimanded." She sighed. "But I didn't learn my lesson very well. I still have trouble following orders."

"Well, thank God you disobeyed." Shanna turned toward her. "I wouldn't have Roman now if you had let him die. Or my children."

"I wouldna be here, either," Connor said. "Neither would Angus or Jean-Luc or Gregori or any of the others who were sired by Roman."

Roman turned and wrapped an arm around his wife's shoulders. His eyes glinted with unshed tears. "I can't help but wonder why I was supposed to die. Ever since I was transformed by Casimir, I have believed it was my destiny to bring about his defeat."

"You've done a lot to protect mortals and encourage Vamps to live in a good way," Shanna told him. "I've always been proud of you."

He smiled and kissed her brow. Then he looked at Marielle. "Do you really consider me a mistake?"

She shook her head. "The mistake was mine, but I cannot regret it. You have led a good and noble life. I have always been grateful that there are good vampires who are willing to fight the evil ones. And I am thankful that I can offer you my assistance."

"The Lord works in mysterious ways." Father Andrew smiled at her. "I believe your destiny has long been linked to these Vamps."

She took a deep breath. Could it be true? Could she somehow be exactly where she was supposed to be?

She glanced at Connor and found him watching her intently. Her heart lurched with a burst of emotion. No, this couldn't be what the Father intended.

An angel didn't succumb to human emotions like desire and longing.

No angel was supposed to fall in love.

It was over an hour later before Connor was able to teleport Marielle back to the cabin. Shanna insisted on fixing her a meal in the cafeteria, which turned into a cooking lesson. Meanwhile, Angus and Emma returned from Nebraska, along with Robby and Olivia.

Connor spent some time in the MacKay security office, describing the progress he was making with Marielle. Angus was eager for a final showdown with the Malcontents. The dead bodies in Nebraska had indeed been Casimir's victims. Shanna's father, Sean Whelan, had given them the tip about the bodies, and now, in return, he was demanding to be included in their battle.

"The man is crazy if he thinks he can fight a vampire," Robby muttered.

Angus shrugged. "I told him as much, but he insists. He claims he can weaken them with silver bullets before they ever get close to him."

Connor snorted. "All it takes is one Malcontent to teleport behind his back and snap his neck. He'd never see it coming." He glanced at Robby's wife. As a former FBI psychologist, she'd received some training in self-defense, but he didn't think it was enough. As far as he was concerned, no mortal who was susceptible to mind control should ever attempt to fight a vampire. "I hope ye're no' allowing the mortal women to take part in the battle."

"I'm discouraging it," Angus said. "Ian's wife can

defend herself well, but now that she's expecting, she's agreed to stay out of it."

Emma smiled. "Lots of babies on the way. Caitlyn's twins are due in June. Toni's baby in September. And Darcy's having her second one in October."

Connor sat back. He hadn't known Darcy was pregnant again. He stayed out of her life now that she was married to Austin Erickson. In truth, she had never welcomed his interference, but at least he knew now that she no longer hated him. She and Austin had named their son Matthew Connor. After the baby's birth, nearly two years ago, she'd sent him a note saying she'd never be alive to have a child if he hadn't saved her.

Olivia reached over to take her husband's hand. "Shall we break the news?"

Robby grinned. "Sure. Go ahead."

She grinned back. "We're expecting."

"What?" Angus jumped to his feet.

Emma leaped to her feet with a squeal. "You're pregnant?"

After Olivia nodded, Emma squealed again and lunged toward her for a big hug.

"Hot damn!" Phineas gave Robby a high five, then slapped him on the back. "You da man!"

Emma bounced over to Angus and threw her arms around him. "We're going to have a grand-baby!"

Angus patted her on the back with a stunned expression. "I'm going to be a great-great grandfather?"

Connor suspected he was missing a few *greats.* "Congratulations." He shook hands with Angus and Robby, then sat down and waited for the celebration to end.

The laughter and hugging went on for a good five minutes, then the questioning began. How was Olivia feeling? When was the baby due?

Connor shifted in his seat. First all the Vamp men were getting married. Now they were having children. It was damned depressing.

"Can we get back to business?" he grumbled. "We were discussing the upcoming battle and Sean Whelan's foolish desire to fight. Do ye think he'll try to make the mortals on his team fight, too?"

Emma gave him a wry look. "Funny you should ask. Sean has been especially pissed with you lately. Turns out Alyssa has a crush on you."

Connor blinked. "Who?"

"The woman on the Stake-Out team," Emma explained. "Apparently, you told her she was pretty."

Connor thought back, trying to remember, then became aware that everyone in the room was watching him with expressions of amusement.

"Whoa, Connor." Phineas waggled his eyebrows. "I didn't know you were such a ladies' man."

"I doona remember her," he muttered.

"It was a few years ago," Emma said. "Austin told me about it. He and Alyssa were holding Shanna prisoner in a hotel room when you teleported in to rescue her. That's when you told Alyssa she was pretty."

Connor shrugged. "Then it was merely a strategic maneuver aimed to distract them while I escaped with Shanna." His face grew warm. Had such an offhand remark really caused a woman to develop a crush on him?

"Hot damn, bro." Phineas gave him a thumbs-up. "You've got a fan club."

Connor stood. "'Twas no' my intent." He headed to the door. "I need to take Marielle home—I mean, back to the cabin." His face grew hotter, and he exited quickly.

Bugger. He needed to be more careful. If one silly remark had caused a woman to develop a crush, what would happen to Marielle if he kept touching her? And kissing her? The poor lass wanted to go back to heaven. That was her home. Not the cabin. If he somehow made her feel too much affection for him, it would only be harder for her to leave.

The problem was he wanted her affection. Hell, he wanted her, period. What kind of fool was he to think he could compete with heaven? He was setting himself up for severe heartache. And worse, he could end up causing Marielle heartache, too.

He had to back off, put distance between them. And yet, he had to keep training her and slipping into her mind to know where to teleport.

Damn. What a tangled mess.

He found Marielle in the cafeteria discussing theology with Roman and Father Andrew. Shanna had gone outside to play with the children.

As he approached, Marielle glanced up and smiled. His heart constricted as usual. "I'm ready to take you back to the cabin, whenever ye wish."

"I'm ready." She stood and gathered up her dishes. "I enjoyed talking to you again, Father. And meeting you, Roman."

He stood. "Thank you . . . for saving my life."

Father Andrew moved out of her way. "I look forward to seeing you again, my dear."

Connor picked up her glass and salad bowl. "I'll help you."

"Connor." Roman paused with an uncomfortable look. "I judged you too harshly."

"'Tis my job to protect you and yer family. Ye had every right to be angry."

"I'm convinced now that we need Marielle," Roman said. "Please take good care of her."

"I will." He accompanied her into the kitchen where they set her dishes in the sink. "Ready to go?" He took her gently by the arms.

"Don't you need to hold on tighter?" She wrapped her arms around his neck. "I don't want you to lose me on the way."

He would have to lose her eventually. He enveloped her in his arms. "I have you." *For now.*

The black void sucked them in, then they materialized in the cabin next to the couch. As soon as she was steady on her feet, he released her.

She gave him a shy smile. "It's been another long night."

"Aye."

She sat on the couch. "Now that we're alone, I'd like to talk." She motioned to the space beside her.

He didn't sit. He knew where she was headed. "I have some errands to run before the sun rises."

"You're going to leave me here unprotected? Darafer might show up."

Connor winced. She had him there.

She patted the sofa cushion. "I want to talk."

"There's no point."

"Yes, there is. You're suffering from too much pain and remorse—"

" 'Tis none of yer business."

"You said I was healing you. How can I if you won't let me?"

He shifted his weight. "I've done fine for centuries. I doona need yer help."

"But I want to help. I can't stand the thought of you suffering all alone—"

"I doona want yer pity!"

She stood. "Then take pity on me. Because I will be miserable in heaven if I know you're here suffering and feeling lonely."

He took a deep breath to ease his frustration. "Once ye're back in heaven, ye'll forget about—"

"Don't tell me that!" Her eyes flashed with anger. "I will always remember tonight, and I will always treasure it."

But ye'll still leave me. He turned away and rubbed a hand against his brow. "I doona think it is a good idea for us to get any closer. It would make it . . . harder to say good-bye."

"If I have to leave you knowing I didn't help you, that would be the hardest blow to endure. I told you, Connor Buchanan, that I care deeply for you."

He looked at her, and the tears in her eyes ripped at his heart.

"I told you about my mistakes," she continued. "It was my fault that a serial killer was let loose on Earth. Those women died because of me. Doesn't it make you angry? Do you want to hate me because—"

"Nay! I doona think ill of you. Ye took mercy on a dying child."

She lifted her chin. "So you didn't judge me. Give me credit for being as understanding as you are. Tell me about yourself. I won't think poorly of you."

She would, if she knew everything he'd done. She had erred out of mercy, believing she was doing the right thing. He had acted out of rage, knowing full well it was wrong.

She sat on the couch.

He waited for her to say something, but she simply waited, watching him with a hopeful look.

He sat stiffly beside her.

Still she said nothing. Why couldn't she nag him? It would be easier to refuse her then.

He sighed. What good could come of this? "I was born in 1512."

"So young," she murmured, her eyes glinting with humor. "Practically a baby."

He frowned at her. "I thought ye wouldna judge."

She smiled. "How old were you when you were transformed?"

"Thirty." He slanted a nervous glance her way. "Ye couldna guess? Do I look much older?"

She looked indignant. "I wouldn't presume to judge."

His jaw shifted. He was sorely tempted to poke her or tickle her. Then kiss her senseless. Actually, he could skip the tickling and go straight to the kissing.

"Were you always this handsome?"

His eyebrows shot up. "Aye."

She laughed.

His mouth twitched. "Of course ye might think that was immodest of me, but thankfully, ye're no' judging me."

"I wouldn't dream of it." Her eyes grew tender. "So how did it happen? Roman was the one who changed you?"

"Yes. Ian MacPhie and I were fighting in the Battle of Solway Moss, just south of the Scottish border. The lands there were always under dispute, the English and Scottish kings snarling at each other, and puir sods like Ian and me paying the price." He sighed. " 'Twas a humiliating defeat, even more humiliating when I realized I was going to die."

She touched his arm. "I'm so sorry."

He shrugged. "That night, Roman and Angus found us and asked if we wanted to keep on living and fighting for a just cause. We both said yes, no' quite realizing what lay in store for us, but neither of us wanting to die."

"Of course not."

"Roman changed me, and Angus changed Ian. The puir lad was only fifteen."

"He looks older now."

Connor nodded. "Roman invented a drug that can keep a Vamp awake during the day, but it also ages him a year for each day. Ian took the drug so he could look older."

"How interesting. And now he's married, and

they're expecting their first child." Marielle smiled. "I'm glad it worked out so well for him."

"Aye."

"Why did Phineas say you were in a mid-life crisis?"

He scoffed. "'Tis a ridiculous theory that a vampire will develop some . . . emotional issues after he's lived half a millennium."

She tilted her head, considering. "Five hundred years doesn't seem long to me. But I would agree that you are overly burdened with remorse."

He crossed his arms over his chest. "I've lived with it for centuries. I'm used to it."

"And who is Darcy Newhart?"

He winced. "A mistake."

"She was on the fringe of your remorse, not well hidden."

"Aye, I suppose that's true. Things have worked out well for her, so I doona feel as bad as I once did."

"What happened?"

"Gregori dragged me to a bar where mortal youngsters like to pretend they're vampires. Darcy was a television reporter, doing a feature on the place, and when she tried to interview us as make-believe vampires, we thought it was great fun. But then she was attacked in the alley by some Malcontents, and by the time we found her, she was close to death."

"How terrible."

"I couldna bear to see her die like that, so I transformed her." Connor sighed. "I thought I was giving her life, but I was actually taking her life away. She lost everything that was important to her. Her job, her family and friends."

"She didn't like being a vampire?"

"Nay. She hated me for changing her and no' giving her any choice in the matter."

Marielle nodded. "And that's why you feel guilt and remorse. But you said everything worked out for her?"

"Aye. Roman discovered a way to make her mortal again, and now she's happily married to another mortal. They have a wee bairn and another one on the way. She and Austin work for MacKay S and I, too."

Marielle smiled. "That's wonderful. I love happy endings." She lounged back against the sofa. "Thank you for telling me. It wasn't too painful, was it?"

"I may be traumatized for a few centuries."

She scoffed. "I let you off easy. I know there's a lot more you're hiding in there." She touched his chest.

He squeezed her hand, grateful that she wasn't going to push any further. It was surprising, though, how easy she had been to talk to.

She scooted closer to him on the couch and leaned her head against his shoulder. When he glanced at her, his chin rubbed against her hair, so silky and soft. The scent of her shampoo filled his nostrils.

He looked away. "We should be careful no' to get too close."

"But I consider you a close friend, Connor. Surely two friends can embrace without it causing problems." She wrapped an arm around his torso and rested her head on his chest.

He swallowed hard. "I suppose an occasional hug would be all right." He extended his arm around her shoulders.

She snuggled closer. "I do like being able to touch you. For so long I couldn't touch anyone without making them shrivel up and die."

He certainly didn't shrivel up when she touched him.

She skimmed her fingers along his jaw. "I like the way your whiskers feel. A little ticklish."

A vision popped into his head of him tickling her bare breasts with his whiskers.

"Thank you for a wonderful evening." She kissed his cheek.

"Lass." He touched her face. "We shouldna kiss."

"It was just a tiny one on your cheek."

He pressed his lips against her brow. "Then we willna kiss . . . on the mouth." He kissed her temple.

"That's probably wise." Her hand slipped around his neck.

He trailed kisses down her jaw. "We shouldna get too involved."

"Exactly." She tilted her head so he could more easily nuzzle her neck. "Did you mean what you said earlier about my breasts?"

"That I wanted to touch and kiss them?"

"Yes."

"Aye, I do," he whispered in her ear. "But we should be careful." He planted kisses across her cheek.

With a moan, she leaned closer.

"We should practice . . . restraint." He kissed the corner of her mouth.

"Yes."

He paused, his mouth only a fraction away from hers. Her lips were open, full and moist. Her breath stirred gently against his lips.

Stop it, ye fool! Before it was too late, he turned his head and kissed the other corner of her mouth.

Someone cleared a throat across the room, and he jumped back. *Bugger.*

Vanda, Marta, and Brynley were back, and by the looks on their faces, they were enjoying the show.

Chapter Fifteen

*M*arielle gasped. Heat rushed to her face. She didn't know which was worse—the way the women looked amused or the way Connor looked appalled. Mortified, even.

She rose to her feet. Connor did the same, standing stiffly a few feet away from her.

"Hi, guys," Vanda greeted them, her eyes twinkling. "How's the training going?"

"All right," Marielle mumbled at the same time that Connor grumbled, "Good."

"Looked real good to me," Brynley said with a smirk.

Marta shook her head, smiling, as she deposited two tote bags on the kitchen counter. "We didn't realize we were going to interrupt your . . . workout."

"Well, it could have been worse." Vanda's mouth twitched. "They were practicing restraint, you know."

Marielle winced. Just how long had the women watched?

Connor muttered something in Gaelic that sounded like a curse. "I would appreciate it if ye would use some restraint yerselves and no' repeat what ye saw."

"I didn't see anything." Vanda turned to Brynley. "Did you see anything?"

"Nope, but I have a strange craving for raw oysters."

While the women laughed, Marielle stole a glance at Connor. Anger simmered in his smoky blue eyes when he met her gaze.

"I apologize for the . . . embarrassment." His jaw shifted. "It willna happen again."

A pang jabbed at her heart. Did he mean he would never kiss her again?

"I have a few errands to run." He raised his voice. "I'll return shortly before dawn."

"Connor, you don't have to . . ." Vanda paused when he teleported away. "Sheesh, we didn't mean to chase him away."

"Party pooper," Brynley muttered.

Marielle frowned at the empty spot where Connor had stood. He hadn't said good-bye.

"Are you all right?" Marta asked from the kitchen as she unloaded the tote bags.

Marielle nodded. "Yes."

Vanda perched on the back of the couch. "I don't mean to be nosy, but what the heck is going on? I thought you wanted to go back to heaven."

"I do." Marielle stuffed her hands into the pockets of her hooded jacket. "Connor's helping me."

"Is that what he calls it?" Vanda's eyes narrowed. "He had better not be taking advantage of you."

"He's not," Marielle protested. "I wanted to—" Her blush returned.

"Holy moley," Brynley whispered. "Have you fallen for him?"

"I . . ." Marielle hesitated. "I don't know. Maybe."

"You don't know?" Brynley planted her fists on her hips. "The guy is legally dead. And he wears a skirt!"

"I like his kilt," Marielle said quietly. "And he's not really dead."

"He talks weird. And he's got red hair!" Brynley wrinkled her nose in disgust. "You can't possibly think he's good-looking."

Marielle stiffened. "Connor is very handsome. And I won't have you insult him further."

"Busted!" Brynley pointed a finger at her. "Don't tell us you don't know. You are seriously into him."

Marielle swallowed hard.

"Oh, that was clever of you," Marta said to Brynley. "You made her reveal her true feelings."

Brynley shrugged. "I've been around the block a few times."

Marielle fiddled with the zipper on her jacket, recalling how Connor had zipped it up earlier that night. "I believe your Three-Step Rule may also be accurate."

Brynley chuckled. "I know it is."

Vanda held up a hand. "I don't think this is a laughing matter." She regarded Marielle with a worried look. "Have you ever been in love before?"

She started to say she loved all mankind, but she knew that wasn't what Vanda meant. She was referring to the way her heart lurched whenever she looked at Connor. And the way desire and longing filled her up to the point she feared she might burst. "I've never felt like this before."

"And Connor?" Vanda asked. "How does he feel?"

With a sudden pang in her chest, Marielle realized she wanted him to love her.

She winced. How could she be so selfish? Did she really want to leave him brokenhearted when she returned to heaven? He was already burdened with so much pain. How could she add to it? "I don't want to hurt him. What should I do?"

Vanda exhaled slowly. "Well, if you're really planning to leave . . ."

"You gotta dump him," Brynley finished.

Marielle flinched. "But . . . he's my protector. He guards me at night."

"We can find someone else to protect you," Brynley suggested.

Vanda nodded. "I'm sure Ian would do it. And Phil would help, too. You wouldn't have to worry about either of them making a move on you."

Marielle's chest tightened. "Connor's training me to protect myself, and he can enter my mind to tell where to teleport to—"

"Any Vamp can do that," Vanda interrupted. "Look. I know you want to keep Connor around. That's natural when you have feelings for him. But the more involved you get with him, the more it's going to hurt when you leave."

"Then it's settled," Brynley announced. "You gotta dump him."

Marielle nodded as tears filled her eyes. God help her. There was no way to avoid hurting Connor. She could hurt him now . . . or later.

"And the sooner you dump him, the better," Brynley added.

"That seems harsh," Marta said as she walked toward the couch.

"Yeah, but that's the way it goes." Brynley slouched in a kitchen chair. "Life sucks and then you die." Her eyes narrowed on Marielle. "And that's when you show up, right?"

A tear rolled down her cheek. "Yes."

"Don't be so rough," Vanda snapped at Brynley. "This sort of thing is new to her."

Marta touched Marielle's shoulder. "Please don't cry."

Marielle wiped her cheek. "I never knew how difficult it was to be human."

Brynley sighed and propped her cowboy boots up on the neighboring chair. "I'm just saying love isn't for wimps. If you don't have the courage to take it to the end zone, then don't get in the game." She crossed her arms, frowning. "I learned that the hard way."

"Well, don't take your misery out on the rest of us," Vanda grumbled. She walked over to Marielle and patted her shoulder. "It'll be all right. Things have a way of working out in the end."

Marielle blinked away her tears. "You're right. I have to stay strong." She had to keep believing, no matter what.

Vanda smiled. "We brought a surprise for you tonight."

Marielle took a deep breath to ease her nerves. "What kind of surprise?"

"Homemade chocolate chip cookies and milk," Brynley said. "Guaranteed to make you feel better."

"And I packed a bag of spa stuff," Vanda added. "Since we can't take you to a spa, we brought the spa to you."

"Spa?" Marielle asked.

Vanda nodded. "It'll be fun!"

It was torture. At least in the beginning when Vanda showed her how to wax her legs. It did help, though, to take her mind off Connor. But when they left her soaking in the bathtub, her thoughts slipped right back to him.

"Time for your pedicure." Vanda hustled her out of the tub and wrapped her in a thick robe.

"You'd better move," Vanda warned Brynley as she led Marielle back into the main room.

Brynley jumped up from the couch. "I'll fix her some milk and cookies." She headed to the kitchen, steering clear of Marielle.

Vanda set Marielle down on the couch, then perched on the coffee table across from her. She placed one of Marielle's feet in her lap. "You have such new skin, like a baby."

"Here." Marta brought over a plastic bin, filled with a variety of nail polish. "Pick a color."

Marielle chose a luminous pink that reminded her of sunsets, and Vanda started with her toes.

"Is this supposed to make me more attractive?" Marielle asked.

"Mmm-hmm." Vanda concentrated on her work.

"Is that wise? I mean—you don't think Connor and I should—"

"I don't know what to think." Vanda started on her other foot. "But I do know that Connor has been miserable for a long time, and . . . I want him to be happy. You, too."

Marielle sighed. She wasn't sure how to accomplish that, but she did know one thing. She wanted Connor to be happy, too.

Brynley set a plate of cookies and glass of milk on the coffee table, then retreated back to the kitchen table.

Marielle enjoyed the cookies until it was time to paint her fingernails. While the polish dried, Vanda and Marta settled on the couch next to her, each enjoying a glass of synthetic blood. Brynley sat across from them on the rocking chair, munching on cookies and milk.

"I can see why Connor likes you." Vanda sipped from her glass. "You're not just beautiful. You're very loving, and . . . I think he needs that."

Marielle leaned back. "I'm trying not to think about it right now." *He needs you. He needs love.*

"Then let's talk about things we hate about men," Brynley suggested. "Like what big babies they can be when they're in pain."

Vanda chuckled.

Marielle didn't think Connor would be that way.

"Sometimes I wake up from my death-sleep,"

Vanda said, "and Phil is lying next to me snoring something awful. So I punch him and tell him he snores loud enough to wake the dead."

Brynley laughed.

"I don't think Connor snores," Marielle said.

"Of course he doesn't! He's dead!" Brynley winced. "Speak of the devil."

Marielle sat up and looked over her shoulder. Her heart did its usual jolt. Connor had returned. He was wearing new clothes, his hair was damp, and he was as handsome as ever.

"The sun rises in fifteen minutes," he announced.

"All right." Vanda stood. "Marta and I will be going."

Marta finished the last of her blood and set down her glass. "It was good to see you again, Marielle. Take care."

Marielle gave her and Vanda hugs. "Thank you. For everything."

Vanda smiled. "It was fun." She set her empty glass on the coffee table next to the tray of nail polish. "Good luck with your . . . problem." She glanced at Connor, then lowered her voice. "I'll talk to Ian."

Marielle nodded.

"Don't worry about the mess," Brynley said. "I'll clean up. I don't have much to do all day."

Vanda and Marta teleported away.

Connor inclined his head. "I'll be preparing for my death-sleep now." He turned and walked into Marielle's bedroom.

"Whoa," Brynley whispered. "Is he going to sleep in your bed?"

"I—I don't think he can." Hadn't he said that the light coming through the window would fry him?

"Weird," Brynley muttered. She gathered things off the coffee table and took them to the kitchen.

Marielle wished she could help, but she needed to keep her distance from Brynley.

The door to her bedroom opened, and Connor emerged. His gaze sought out Marielle, then he looked away. "Good night." He went into the closet next to the kitchen, closing the door firmly behind him.

"Connor's in the closet," Brynley whispered in a singsong voice, then laughed.

Marielle yawned. It had been another long night. "I think I'll go to bed, too." She trudged toward the bedroom. "Thank you for guarding us during the day."

"No problem." Brynley smiled as she washed dishes. "If that nasty demon shows up, I'll blast him full of shotgun shells."

Marielle paused at the bedroom door. "I hate to leave you alone all day, but I've been up all night."

"It's okay. Get some sleep."

Marielle nodded. "God bless you."

A hint of pain flickered in Brynley's eyes before she smiled back. "Good night."

Marielle shut the door behind her and wandered over to the window. The night sky was growing lighter, taking on that luminous glow just before the sun shattered the horizon with glorious light and color.

Daybreak had always been her favorite time, a time filled with the hope and promise of a new day.

But now, she could only think of Connor lying in the closet so near to her. Dying. All alone.

With a sigh, she turned toward her bed. A ray of morning sun shot through the window and landed on her pillow. Something sparkled.

She stepped closer, then gasped. There on her pillow was the angel sun catcher she'd admired earlier in a shop window. Connor must have gone back to get it. That sweet, adorable man.

She picked it up and ran her fingers over the smooth golden glass of the angel's body and the carved facets of the angel's crystal wings.

How she missed her wings! Tears filled her eyes, and she sat on the edge of the bed. She held the angel in her lap and skimmed her fingers over its wings. A tear fell onto the angel, and she used the edge of her bathrobe to dry it. She'd lost her wings. And the longer she stayed here on Earth, the more human she would become.

She'd lost her wings. But she'd found Connor.

With a sob, she pressed the angel to her chest. There was no point in denying the truth that was in her heart.

She was falling in love with him.

It was late afternoon when she awoke. She showered and dressed, then peeked out the bedroom door. She preferred to know exactly where Brynley was so she wouldn't accidentally bump into her.

A delicious smell wafted toward her. Brynley must have cooked something, but she was no longer in the kitchen.

"Hello?" Marielle stepped into the main room.

"In here," Brynley called from the walk-in closet.

Marielle gasped. What on earth was Brynley doing in there? She rushed to the open door and gasped again.

Brynley had removed Connor's shoes and knee socks, and she was busy painting his toenails hot pink.

"Good heavens!" Marielle watched in horror. "What are you doing?"

"What does it look like?" Brynley smirked, then motioned toward his kilt. "Hey, should we lift it up and take a peek?"

"No!" Marielle's face flushed with heat. She didn't want to admit she'd already seen his private parts. Twice.

"You just proved my point." Brynley went back to painting the toenails on his right foot. "You don't have a mean bone in your body."

"What do my bones have to do with you painting his toenails? It's going to make him very angry."

"I'm counting on it." Brynley started on his left foot. "I was thinking about it all day, and I don't think you'll be able to dump him. You're too nice. So, the only option left is to piss him off and chase him away."

Marielle grimaced. "Chase him away?" She glanced at his handsome face. Could she really do that?

Brynley looked up at her. "If you try to reason with him, he'll just argue with you until you cave in. So the best strategy is to make him so angry, he wants to leave."

Marielle swallowed hard.

"Listen carefully," Brynley continued. "When he comes after you, furious and demanding why you did this to him, you tell him, 'I felt like it. And if you don't like it, you can leave and never come back.'"

"That sounds terrible."

"Yeah, but it works." Brynley's mouth twisted. "I should know." She started on Connor's fingernails.

"Oh no!" Marielle protested. "Not those, too."

Brynley gave her a stern look. "It's your only hope. Now let me hear you say it."

Marielle winced, then quietly said, "I felt like it. And if you don't like it, you can leave and never come back."

"Again. With more strength. He has to believe you mean it."

She repeated it, although each word felt like it was being wrenched from her soul.

She trudged outside and sat in a rocking chair on the front porch. How had she come to this in just a few days?

A while later, Brynley came out with a plate of food and a glass of water. She set them on the small wooden table next to Marielle. "You must be hungry. And you need to keep your strength up."

"Thank you." She ate a little, but her appetite worsened as she watched the sun descend in the sky. Could she do it? Could she chase Connor away?

As the sun hovered over the horizon, the temperature dropped. She shivered and took her dishes into the cabin.

Brynley had turned on the lights. "Almost time." She picked up the shotgun. "I'm ready for him."

Marielle dropped her plate with a clatter into the kitchen sink. "How angry do you think he's going to get?"

A thumping noise came from the closet, and Marielle jumped. He was awake. He would notice right away that his shoes and socks had been taken off.

"What the bloody hell?"

"Remember your lines," Brynley whispered as she headed out the front door, carrying the shotgun. "I'll be out here if you need me."

The closet door crashed open. Connor stood barefoot in the opening, his eyes a brilliant, gleaming blue, his red hair wild and loose about his shoulders.

Marielle gulped.

His gaze zeroed in on her. "Woman," he growled.

She stepped back. "Your eyes are glowing blue."

"Rage." His fangs sprang out.

With a gasp, she stepped back again.

He wrenched the refrigerator door open, grabbed a bottle of blood, then stuffed it into the microwave. He pressed the buttons, then stopped to glare at his hot pink fingernails. His hand curled into a fist.

His head turned toward her. *"You."* His eyes burned into her. He grabbed the bottle from the microwave, still cold, and guzzled some down.

He slammed the bottle down on the kitchen counter, then advanced toward her. His fangs were still out and stained red with blood. "Why did ye do it?"

She lifted her chin. "I felt like it." Her voice trembled. "And if you don't like it, you can . . ."

He arched a brow as he continued to move toward her. "I can what?"

Tears stung her eyes. "You can leave and never come back."

Chapter Sixteen

Leave? Connor halted his advance on Marielle. His vision turned a more intense blue as his rage surged to a dangerous level.

What were those crazy women doing to his angel? The first night they'd taught her about blow jobs, and now they had obviously embroiled her in some sort of stupid drama that was supposed to make him leave.

Leave? Over his dead body.

His hands curled into fists. "What about yer training? Do ye intend to go into battle unable to defend yerself?"

She stiffened her spine in a gesture of strength, but the tears in her eyes told another story. "I can train myself."

"Can ye teleport yerself?"

"Ian will take me. And he and Phil can protect me."

"Ye're planning to replace me?" She might as well

have stabbed him in the chest. "Am I suddenly *un-trustworthy*?" he bellowed.

When she flinched, he made an effort to tamp down on his rage.

He grabbed the bottle off the counter and drank the rest of the blood. It tasted awful this cold, but it helped cool his rage a little. His fangs retracted, but his vision remained tinted blue, a sure sign he was still on the verge of losing control.

He set the empty bottle down. "Do ye know what infuriates me the most? 'Tis no' the damned nail polish. Nor the fact that those women have lured you into some sort of childish plot."

When she didn't respond, he turned his head to glare at her. "I gave you my word that I would help you, that I would get you back to heaven no matter what."

Her face paled.

He advanced toward her once again. "And ye ask, nay; ye *tell* me to leave? Does my word mean nothing to you?" His voice rose to a shout. "Do ye expect me break my pledge?"

Her eyes shimmered with unshed tears. "I expect you to leave."

His jaw shifted. "Ye're forgetting something." He stepped closer. "Angels make terrible liars."

Her mouth opened to protest, but before she could say a word, he clamped his hand around the back of her neck and pulled her against his chest. She gasped.

"Yer heart is pounding something fierce." He touched her cheek. "Yer heart doesna lie."

A tear slipped down her cheek and he caught it with his thumb.

"Yer tears doona lie." He dragged his hand down her throat, then farther down to cup her breast. "Ye tremble at my touch. Yer body doesna lie."

He gently squeezed her breast, and she moaned. "At last, some truth coming from yer lips." He kissed her lightly. "Now tell me if—"

The front door slammed open.

"She told you to leave, so go!" Brynley stormed inside, leveling a shotgun.

Bloody fool! If she pulled the trigger, she might kill Marielle. Connor teleported behind Brynley, ripped the shotgun from her grasp with one hand, and shoved her against the wall with the other.

She gasped, no doubt surprised by his vampire speed and strength. She attempted to move, but he kept her pinned.

"It was you, aye? Ye're the one who painted my nails."

Brynley grabbed his arm and tried to shake him lose. "Let me go, you undead creep!"

He slid his hand up to circle her neck, then leaned closer. "Doona ever mess with me while I'm in my death-sleep."

"Fine!" Her eyes blazed with anger. "And you stop pawing the angel."

He released her and stepped back. Holy Christ Almighty, was that what this was about? The women didn't want him touching Marielle? He glanced at her. She looked miserable, with red-rimmed eyes. She'd gone along with their ridiculous plan. That could only mean she wanted him to stop touching her, too.

An icy cold wave swept through him, chilling him to the bone. "Agreed." He walked outside.

Pain expanded in his chest, so sudden and so sharp it stole his breath away. *Bugger*. He'd thought he was too much of a coldhearted bastard to ever get hurt like this. Marielle had certainly proved him wrong.

He removed the shells from the shotgun and laid the weapon on the porch next to the house. The blue tint to his vision was completely gone now. No more rage. Just pain. And sadness.

He retrieved his cell phone from his sporran and called Ian. "Are ye coming to pick up Brynley?"

"Aye, in just a few minutes," Ian replied. "I—uh, Vanda asked me to spend the night there as Marielle's protector."

"Nay. The job is mine. Just come and take Brynley. And . . . bring me some nail polish remover."

Ian paused. "Some what?"

"Nail polish remover! I assume yer wife has some."

"Aye. I'll be there soon."

Connor rang off and dropped the phone back in his sporran. *Bugger*. Ian was going to get a big laugh out of this.

"Connor?" Marielle's voice sounded soft and hesitant behind him.

His heart squeezed in his chest. He didn't turn around, didn't want her to see the pain on his face. "Go back inside."

"Are—are you still going to train me?"

"Aye. We'll continue yer training and practice teleporting. We should be ready to face the Malcontents in a few more days." He gritted his teeth. "Ye willna have to put up with me for much longer."

There was a long pause, and he wondered if she'd gone back inside.

"Thank you for the glass angel," she whispered. "I'll treasure it . . . for as long as I'm here."

Dammit, she made his heart ache. "I guess ye canna take it with you to heaven?"

"No." She made a sad noise that sounded like a cross between a sob and a sniffle. "I'm sorry."

The door closed, leaving him alone on the porch. "I'm sorry, too."

For the next few hours, Marielle remained determined not to cry. Connor stayed true to his word and continued her training, but he was cold and distant, barking out orders and never making eye contact.

He set up the wooden clock in front of the cabin. When she teased him that it looked more like a henge, he didn't respond.

She worked hard for several hours and learned to knock down only one log. Her efforts were rewarded with a grumbled "Good." No smiles. No pats on the shoulder. No twinkle in his eyes.

He held her stiffly when they teleported close to a hospital in Cleveland where a woman was dying in surgery. When he encouraged her to widen her scope and search out multiple deaths accompanied by horror, she led them to what turned out to be a violent shoot-out between two drug cartels along the southern border. With bullets flying around them and innocent bystanders falling in the street, he'd teleported them quickly back to the cabin.

She was visibly shaken, so he set her on the couch, brought her a glass of water, and told her to rest. She tried closing her eyes, but each time she did, the violent scene replayed in her mind. The screams of the innocent echoed in her head. The human world could be so cruel.

Dear God, how she wanted to go back to heaven! She missed the peace and love that had permeated her soul, the constant stream of praise and support that had always filled her mind. She missed her friend Buniel and her beautiful white wings. What if she never heard the singing of the Heavenly Host again? What if she could never fly again, feel the wind rush against her face, and see the stars twinkling around her as she soared through the heavens?

She blinked away the tears. She didn't want Connor to see her falling apart. Ever since their return to the cabin, he had paced about like a caged animal. A few times, she glanced his way and discovered him looking at her. He always turned away, but not quickly enough that she didn't catch the glint of pain in his eyes. His pacing continued until he retrieved his claymore from the closet and went outside.

After a while, she wandered over to the window to look outside. The nearly full moon shone down on the clearing in front of the cabin. Connor had erected make-believe enemies out of logs and bales of hay, and he was practicing with his sword.

No, he was more than practicing. He was slaughtering his pretend enemies. The force of his blows was frightening. The rage in his shouts pierced her heart.

"Connor," she whispered, pressing a hand against the window. "I don't belong here. I'm sorry."

As soon as the women arrived, he teleported away.

"He looks so sad," Marta murmured as she brought Marielle a plate of food.

"Of course he's sad." Brynley grabbed a beer from the refrigerator and popped the can open. "He got dumped."

"Brynley told us about the pink fingernails." Vanda sat on the couch close to Marielle and gave her a worried look. "I hear he was really pissed."

"Yes." Marielle set her plate of food on the coffee table. "But it wasn't so much the polish. It was the way I rejected him and his word." The tears she had held back for hours escaped and ran down her cheeks. "I didn't want to hurt him."

"He hurt himself when he fell for you." Brynley walked over to the kitchen table.

"Shh," Vanda hushed her. "He's not the only one hurting."

"Don't make me out to be the bad guy," Brynley grumbled as she sprawled onto a kitchen chair. "We all know she had to dump him. I'm sorry that it hurt, Marielle, but it would have hurt a lot worse if you had gotten more involved with him."

Marielle sighed. "I suppose you're right."

Marta handed her a box of tissues, then sat across from her in the rocking chair. "You're not eating. You need to keep your strength up."

"I'm not hungry."

"Are you in love with him?" Vanda asked quietly.

"Yes." She wiped her face with a tissue. "A part of me wonders how it could have happened so quickly. But then I see him, and my heart feels like it will burst, and I think how could I possibly not love him?"

Vanda's eyes narrowed. "How much do you love him? What's it worth to you?"

She set the tissue box on the coffee table. "All love that comes from the Father is deemed worthy."

"This is Earth," Vanda said. "Everything we do here has a price. Even love."

"I would never seek love for financial or personal benefit."

"I'm not talking about money." Vanda gave her a stern look. "How much are you willing to sacrifice for your love?"

Marielle swallowed hard as she finally understood Vanda's question. How much did she love Connor?

To Marielle's dismay, Connor continued to remain cold and distant on their fourth night together. He set up the clock, then yelled different times from the front porch. Three o'clock. Seven o'clock. She was supposed to react by knocking down only the log that corresponded to his order. Sometimes she succeeded, sometimes not. With a frown, he announced she wasn't ready yet.

A small voice inside her celebrated, and it occurred to her that if she was slow with her training, she would have more time with Connor. But then she chastised herself for being selfish. The Malcontents were feeding and killing every night. They needed to be stopped.

When she sensed a number of deaths in Colorado, Connor linked minds with her for a few seconds to go there. The last reported location of the Malcontents had been in Kansas, so it was close enough that he wanted to check it out.

But the deaths were the result of a collapsed mine shaft, and the area was swarming with media. Connor didn't want them to be noticed, so he quickly teleported them back to the cabin.

Was it just her imagination or did he hold her longer than necessary when they arrived? She stood very still, hoping the few seconds could stretch into an eternity, but he eventually let go.

On their fifth night of training, she worked hard to improve, and with a sad, hollow voice he claimed she was ready. She didn't feel like celebrating, either.

She sensed multiple deaths coupled with fear and horror in a mountainous area in Arkansas, so they teleported a short distance away from the incident.

They landed beside a two-lane road that wound through the mountains. Gravel shifted under her feet, and Connor grabbed her arm to steady her as she bumped against a metal guardrail.

"Careful. There's a precipice there." He motioned to the other side of the flimsy metal railing.

They were standing on a narrow shoulder beside the road. Marielle winced at how close they'd come to missing the road altogether. It was dark, the only illumination caused by the nearly full moon and stars. All she could see was the black-topped road, a steep tree-covered incline on one side and the rocky precipice on the other.

"This way." Connor started down the road, staying on the narrow shoulder. "I can hear the cries."

She walked behind him as the road made a big curve around the mountainside. Then she heard the cries, too. She stepped onto the pavement, so she could see around Connor. Down the road, where it twisted in a dangerous horseshoe curve, a car had crashed through the guardrail and careened down the precipice.

"Two are dead. But three are still alive." She tugged on Connor's arm, pulling him onto the road. "Come on! We have to help them."

"Ye canna touch them."

"You can. You have super strength and speed."

"Verra well." He reached into his sporran. "I'll give you my phone, so—"

Lights suddenly brightened the road. Marielle spun around to see a huge eighteen-wheeler truck zooming around the bend and hurtling straight for them.

A horn blared. Brakes screeched.

Connor shoved her out of the way, and she fell onto the next lane.

"No!" she screamed. Connor was still in danger of being hit.

"No!" She scrambled to her feet, then realized why Connor was still standing in the truck's path.

He was frozen.

The truck was frozen.

Time had come to an abrupt halt.

No sound. No horns or screeching brakes or cries from the car accident down the road.

No movement. Silhouetted against the nearly full moon, a bird was frozen in mid-flight. The expression on Connor's face was frozen, his eyes blank and not seeing. His arms were still extended from tossing her out of the way.

A chill skittered down her spine, and she pivoted, searching for the one who had manipulated time. As far as she knew, only a few beings could accomplish such a tremendous feat. The Heavenly Father and a few of His most trusted Archangels.

Or a very powerful demon.

Chapter Seventeen

*M*arielle stiffened when she heard footsteps on the pavement. She whirled around to face the end of the truck. A tall, dark form stepped into the moonlight. A long black coat. Black shirt and tie. Black leather pants. Black wings that folded with a snap and disappeared.

Darafer.

She took a deep breath to steady her nerves. *Keep your wits about you. He can't take you to hell unless you agree.* But of course he would try all manner of trickery to make her agree.

He strolled toward her, his expensive leather boots tapping on the black asphalt. Moonlight gleamed off his raven-black hair and luminous pale skin. A corner of his wide mouth curled up in a humorless smile.

She glanced at Connor. He couldn't help her. He

was, in fact, in danger of being mowed over by the eighteen-wheeler whenever Darafer decided to release time.

The demon circled her, studying her intently with his emerald-green eyes. "Why have they dressed you so shabbily? Don't they realize what a beauty you are?" He stepped forward and hooked a finger under her chin.

She eased back.

He smiled, a genuine smile that actually made him appear handsome. "I would treat you like a rare princess. You would wear the finest silks and jewels."

She started to tell him, *Begone,* but snapped her mouth shut. If he left, time would unfreeze. The truck was so close to Connor. He would have only a few seconds to react. He could teleport or jump out of the way at vampire speed, but what if he was disoriented for a second? Would he have enough time to escape, or would he be crushed by a massive truck?

Darafer frowned when she glanced nervously toward Connor. "Still hanging out with the parasite, I see." He walked toward Connor and studied him with a disdainful look.

"Not much of a protector, is he?" Darafer snapped his fingers in front of Connor's face. "I don't know what you see in him." He flicked a finger against Connor's nose.

"Don't." Marielle stepped forward, then halted when Darafer's eyes gleamed. She winced inwardly. She'd revealed a weakness.

"You like him." Darafer gave her a smug smile. "Has he slept with you yet? Has he nestled between your lily-white thighs and popped your angelic cherry?"

She lifted her chin, determined not to be pulled into any more traps. "He is an honorable man."

Darafer laughed. "Right. Tell that to all his victims with bite marks on their necks." He leaned against the front grille of the truck, crossing his legs at the ankles and his arms over his chest. "He's at my mercy, you know."

"Leave him be."

"Say you'll come with me, and I'll save him."

"I don't believe you."

Darafer smiled. "You're right. He's on my list for hell, so I might as well take him with me." He arched an eyebrow at her. "Why don't you come with him? Then the two of you could live happily ever after."

She scoffed. "No one's happy in hell."

"You'd be surprised." A look of disgust flitted over his face, then faded away.

She watched him carefully. At the slightest indication that he was going to unfreeze time, she would need to act quickly.

He glanced up at the stars and sighed. "They're using you, you know."

"The Vamps? I agreed to help them."

"Not the Vamps." Darafer pointed up toward heaven. "The Big Kahuna. Don't you think it was odd that you saved Roman Draganesti as a baby, and now he's a leader among the Vamps?"

She shrugged. "I disobeyed. You know that. That's why we're both here."

He snorted. "Disobeyed? Do you really believe that?" He pushed away from the truck. "You've been played, Marielle. All along. From the very beginning."

She stepped back. "That's not true."

"Doesn't it piss you off? You're just a damned pawn, and they don't have the courage to let you know."

She swallowed hard.

He walked toward her. "They ripped your wings off, made you suffer, just so you could play your role in their stupid game."

"It's not a game!"

"But you could fool them all." Darafer extended a hand toward her. "Stop being their pawn and come with me."

"Never." It couldn't be true. This was just another trick. "Glory to God in the Highest," she whispered.

"And on earth, war, pestilence, and despair toward men."

She flinched. "Stop it."

"Why should I? It's all part of the big game. Good and evil, yin and yang, you and me. We need each other." He stepped closer. "You know what, Marielle? I'm sick of being a pawn, too."

He stroked a finger down her cheek. "We could pluck a few people off this rock and start our own planet. No war, no pestilence. We could make it perfect." He touched her lips. "Just say the word, and we could be gods."

She turned her head. *Don't listen to him. It's all lies.*

He leaned forward to whisper in her ear. "Come away with me."

Fear coiled in her belly over the consequences of her next word. "Begone."

With a frown, he stepped back. "Are you sure? Your precious little parasite will be crushed. Not exactly the traditional stake through the heart, but still, I seriously doubt he can survive having his brains and guts splattered all over the—"

"In the name of Jesus Christ, begone!"

Anger flashed in Darafer's green eyes, then they turned black. His massive black wings unfurled.

Quickly, Marielle directed a narrow blast of air at Connor. He flew backward just as Darafer vanished and time whooshed back into motion.

The horn blared as the truck zoomed past her. For a few endless seconds, all she could see was the silver side of the truck. She couldn't see Connor, didn't know if he had survived.

The truck passed, but he was nowhere in sight. She gasped at the crumpled guardrail. In her desperation to keep him from getting hit, she'd used too much force.

She'd blown him over the cliff.

"Connor!" She ran to the shoulder and peered down into the dark precipice.

Good heavens, had she killed him? How could he survive such a fall?

She stepped over the railing. "Connor!" She worked her way down the incline, hanging on to bushes to keep from falling.

She spotted some broken branches. He must have hit them on his way down. She used them as a trail, hoping it would lead her to him.

"Connor, can you hear me?" She paused to listen, but heard nothing.

Panic caused her heart to race and her hands to shake. It was so hard to see in the dark. Branches scratched at her arms and slapped at her face. A few times, her feet slipped out from underneath her and she fell back onto her rump, skidding a few feet before she managed to grab another limb.

"Connor!" Her feet slipped again, and she cried out as a sharp rock jabbed her in the back.

If only she had her wings! She could fly straight to him and take him somewhere for help.

She gritted her teeth and kept going. Her feet skidded to a stop on level ground.

She'd made it to the bottom.

"Connor?" She squinted, trying to see. The moon was close to full, but there were too many trees obstructing the light.

Was that him? She dashed toward a dark shape on the ground, but it was just a fallen log.

She pivoted, breathing heavily. "Where are you?"

She heard a moan and ran toward the sound.

Tears filled her eyes when she saw him. "Thank God I found you."

He was lying in the dark shadow beneath a tree. Actually, she realized, he must have hit the tree after falling down the last of the incline.

She knelt beside him. "Connor, I'm here." She reached for him, then remembered how dirty her hands were, so she wiped them on her thighs.

"Can you hear me?" She rolled him onto his back.

He moaned. "Are ye safe, lass? The truck dinna . . ."

"I'm fine." A tear slipped down her cheek. How like Connor to worry more about her safety than his own.

"Good." His eyes flickered shut.

"Connor?" Her heart lurched. Had he died? No, she would have sensed it. She was panicking, fearing the worst. Because she loved him so much.

More tears escaped. She had to help him somehow. He'd saved her life, pushing her out of the way of the truck. Now she had to save him.

If only she had her wings! Connor was unconscious, so he couldn't teleport them. But other Vamps could teleport.

She opened his sporran and dug around till she found his cell phone. "It'll be all right, Connor. I'll call your friends, and they'll take you to Romatech and patch you up."

The phone lit up in her hand, and she frantically studied the odd pictures, trying to figure out how to call Roman.

"How quickly you're becoming human," a voice said behind her.

She spun around, dropping the phone and falling on her rump. A white light shimmered in the distance. White wings pulled in and vanished, leaving the form of a tall man. He wore a long white tunic over white pants, topped with a long, hooded white robe. He pushed the hood back, revealing a handsome face and blond wavy hair.

"Bunny!" She scrambled to her feet and ran toward him.

He grinned and enveloped her in his arms. Instantly, she felt all her scrapes and bruises disappear.

He moved her back, grasping her by the shoulders while he searched her eyes. "Why did you seek a human solution? Why didn't you call me?"

She bowed her head with embarrassment. "I—I didn't think of it. It seems like a long time that I've been cut off from you."

"I have always been close by." Frowning, he smoothed a thumb over her damp cheek. "It seems like every time I check on you, you're crying."

"It's been hard." She glanced over her shoulder at Connor. "Can you help him?"

"Let me see." Buniel accompanied her back and regarded Connor curiously. "This is the man who rescued you that first night."

"Yes."

"And he has been watching over you and protecting you."

"Yes."

"And yet for all the good he has done for you, he makes you cry."

She wiped her cheeks. "I'm in love with him."

Buniel tilted his head, watching her. "Should love be so painful?"

"I have to leave him when I go back to heaven." She winced. "If I can go back."

Buniel nodded. "I have put in many requests for leniency on your behalf." He squatted down beside Connor. "We love all humanity from a distance. Is it not enough to love this man in the same manner?"

"I—" She didn't want to admit she wanted more. She knelt down. "Can you help him?"

"He's badly injured." Bunny laid a hand on Connor's brow. "Skull fracture, concussion, internal bleeding, cracked ribs, multiple contusions. But nothing I can't fix." He closed his eyes and prayed. A white glow surrounded his hand.

"There, it's done." The glow disappeared, and he rose to his feet. "He will sleep for a short time."

Marielle took a deep breath. "Glory to God in the Highest."

Buniel smiled at her. "And on earth, peace, good-will toward men." He removed his thick white robe and laid it on top of Connor. "This will keep him warm till he awakens."

She stood. "Thank you."

"What's going on?" a male voice asked sharply.

She turned to see Zackriel striding toward them.

"Marielle. I'm glad to see you're surviving as a human." He nodded at Buniel. "They could use you at the car accident."

"I'll be there shortly," Buniel replied.

Zack regarded him suspiciously. "Two of my Deliverers were working the accident when they reported a time anomaly. Was it you?"

"No." Buniel motioned toward Connor. "I was healing this man."

Zack glanced down at Connor and scoffed. "That's not a man. He's a Cheater. Why would you heal a Cheater?"

"I asked him to," Marielle said quietly.

Zack gave her a curious look. "You're keeping company with Cheaters now?"

"He's one of the good Vamps," she explained. "I'm going to help him and his friends defeat Casimir and his evil gang of Malcontents."

"Sounds dangerous," Buniel murmured.

"It will be worth it if we can be rid of the evil vampires and make the world a safer place for humans," she continued. "And maybe . . . I can be forgiven."

"Ah." Zack nodded. "The hidden agenda. You want back into heaven."

"She needs to go back," Buniel insisted. "The human world is too dangerous for her."

"And the time anomaly?" Zack asked her. "What do you know about that?"

"It was caused by Darafer," she said quietly.

Buniel stiffened. "The demon? What does he want with you?"

She sighed. "He considers me a fallen angel."

"Maybe you are," Zack whispered.

Buniel raised a hand toward Zackriel, his eyes a fierce glowing blue. "She is not."

Zackriel stepped back, stunned. "Are you threatening me, Healer?"

"Bunny, please." She touched him. "I'm all right. Darafer tries to trick me into going to hell with him, but I always send him away." She turned to Zackriel. "I know you don't believe in me, but I will prove myself worthy."

Zack gave her a worried look, then frowned at Connor. "Watch your neck." He vanished.

Buniel smiled at her and drew her into an embrace. "Be strong, Marielle. Be careful."

"You be careful." She hugged him back. "I don't want you to get in trouble for helping me."

With a chuckle, he stepped back. "I can take care of myself." He glanced at Connor, then back at her. "You have a good heart. If you follow it, you will not regret it." His wings unfurled, and he disappeared.

"Bye," she whispered, missing him already. Missing her own wings.

She hurried back to Connor and knelt beside him. "How are you?" She rested a hand on his chest and felt it moving slowly and steadily as he breathed.

She tucked Bunny's thick white robe around his shoulders. "Don't want you getting cold."

She smoothed his hair away from his brow. "Skull fracture and concussion. I guess your head's not quite as thick as I thought."

She touched his cheek. "I'll just say this while you're asleep, so it won't complicate matters. I love you, Connor Buchanan."

His mouth curled up.

She sat back with a gasp. "You're awake."

His eyes flickered open. "Now why would ye want to waste such words on a sleeping man?"

Chapter Eighteen

*S*he loved him.

Connor's heart filled with joy. It was not a feeling he'd felt very often in his four hundred and ninety-nine years of existence, so it came coupled with fear. Fear that it wouldn't last. It couldn't last. She would eventually return to heaven where she belonged. But for now, he would try to savor the moment.

She loved him.

He smiled, recalling the night they'd walked in the park and ridden the carousel. He'd bought her ice cream and gotten hard, watching her eat it. He needed to stop distancing himself from her. Instead, they should create more beautiful memories that he could cherish after she was gone.

She loved him.

He chuckled. Marielle looked so embarrassed.

She should be embarrassed. A beautiful angel like her falling for a coldhearted old undead bastard like him. How could he be so fortunate? Better not question it, and just enjoy the moment. Here he was, lying beneath a tree with—

His smile faded. Where the hell was he? He struggled to remember, but his thoughts were fuzzy.

A memory flashed through his mind. A blaring horn and bright headlights. "The truck!" He sat up and winced at the tenderness in his ribs.

"Careful." She touched his shoulder. "You may still be a little sore."

Sore from what? He looked her over. "Ye dinna get hit?"

"No, you saved me. And I know I should be grateful, but really, Connor, it makes me angry. You left yourself right in the path of the truck. You have to be more careful. It would have killed me if you'd been run down."

His mouth twitched. "Because ye love me?"

"I'm serious. Don't you dare put yourself in danger like that again."

"How did I get here?" He touched the thick white robe that had fallen into his lap. "And where did this come from?"

"Bunny gave it to you."

His eyes widened in feigned horror as he examined the length of the robe. "That's one hell of a big rabbit."

She laughed. "It's from Buniel. My friend, the Healer."

"I figured that." His jaw shifted as he imagined her perfect angelic boyfriend. "Why was he here? And why was he taking off his clothes?"

"He healed you." She gave him a wry look. "You can thank him later. You had a fractured skull, a concussion, cracked ribs, multiple contusions—"

"I was injured?" He rubbed his rib cage. No wonder it seemed a bit tender. "I was hit by the truck?"

"No. I managed to move you out of the way with a blast of air."

"Och, that's good. Thank you." He smiled. "All yer hard work and practice paid off."

"I suppose." She ducked her head, still looking embarrassed.

He felt his head. There was dried blood in his hair. A fractured skull? No wonder he couldn't remember much. "How did I get injured then?"

"You . . . uh . . ." She pointed up a rocky incline. "The road is up there. You . . . fell down here."

"I fell off a bloody cliff?" How could he have been so clumsy? Why hadn't he simply teleported to safety?

"I . . . it was my fault." She hung her head. "I may have used a little too much force with the blast of air—"

"Ye blew me off a cliff?" he shouted.

She winced. "It's not really a cliff. It's more of a . . . slope."

He huffed. "Is that how ye treat the man ye love?"

"Well, yes." She lifted her chin. "I was desperate to save you. And when Darafer froze you—"

"What?" Connor jumped to his feet. "Darafer was here?"

"Up there." She stood and pointed to the road. "He froze time. He froze you right in front of the truck."

Connor shook his head. This was too strange. "He froze time?"

"Yes. Darafer froze everything except himself and . . . me."

Connor's heart plummeted. She'd been in terrible danger, and he—he had been completely helpless. "I—" He stumbled back, knocking against the tree.

"Careful." She grabbed his arm. "You may be a little dizzy from the concussion."

"Nay." He moved aside, breaking her grip.

Bugger. Anger swelled inside him. She was trying to take care of him, trying to protect him.

That was *his* job! He was supposed to protect her! And he'd failed her.

Just like he had failed to protect his wife and bairn. "How can ye love me? I was bloody useless!"

She stiffened with surprise. "Don't say that."

He paced away. "All this time, I've stayed by yer side in case that bastard showed up. And when he did, I did nothing."

"It's not your fault. He has powers that are beyond both of us."

Connor rushed toward her and grabbed her by the shoulders. "Did he hurt you? If that bastard harmed you, I'll find a way into hell and—"

"Don't say that!" She pressed her hand over his mouth. "Don't ever try to fight him. Please."

Connor took her hand in his. "What good am I to you if I canna protect you?"

"You do protect me. You saved me from the truck. You saved me that first night."

He kissed her palm. "It breaks my heart that I couldna protect you from the demon."

"I'm fine. Darafer can't take me to hell unless I agree, and I will never agree." She rested her hands on his cheeks. "You have never failed me. You have been a blessing to me since the moment you found me."

"Och, lass." He wrapped his arms around her and held her tight. It made his ribs hurt, but he couldn't complain. He would have her for only a short while.

"Shall we go home?" he asked.

"Yes." She picked the white robe off the ground and shook it out. "We were lucky Bunny showed up." She plucked Connor's phone off the ground, and it instantly lit up. "I was going to call your friends for help, but I didn't know how."

"I'll show you later." He dropped the phone into his sporran and pulled her back into his arms. "Let's go."

Connor dropped his torn and tattered kilt on the bathroom floor. It was beyond repair. The T-shirt he'd worn was shredded, too. He examined his leather sporran. Scuffed up a bit, but it would still do.

He took a quick look over his body. Apart from a little soreness, he appeared intact. Marielle's angelic boyfriend had patched him up well. He didn't know whether to be grateful or pissed. Just the thought that he'd been frozen and then later unconscious while demons and angels had dropped by to visit, it was too much.

He stepped into the shower and lathered up his bloodied hair. He decided on being pissed. Aye, that suited him well. He was a vampire, dammit. A supernatural being with his own set of awesome powers. He'd been able to control mortal minds for centuries. He'd been able to defeat any mortal or Malcontent in battle. He was top dog. Top of the food chain.

Not anymore. He could be frozen and rendered helpless? Bloody hell! How could he defeat an enemy who could control him?

How could Marielle trust him? He stood under the showerhead, letting the hot water pound on his head. That was the real problem. He was afraid of failing her. He'd failed before, and he'd lost his wife and baby daughter. And then, he'd lost his soul. He'd become a coldhearted bastard who fed on others to stay alive.

But she still loves you.

He closed his eyes and let the water run down his face. His angel loved him. She called him a blessing.

With a sigh, he turned off the water. She would be with him only a short time.

He dressed in a clean pair of plaid flannel pants and a T-shirt that either Phil or Howard had left behind. It was Howard's cabin, actually. He and Phil used to come here on a full moon so they could shift and hunt. But now Phil was shifting with the other werewolf lads at the school, and Howard was joining them there. Connor smiled, imagining a big bear hunting with a pack of wolves.

He peeked into the bedroom to make sure Marielle wasn't there half dressed. Or undressed. The room was empty. Too bad.

When they'd arrived back at the cabin, all covered with dirt and grime, he'd insisted she shower first. He'd needed a bottle of blood to regain his strength.

He usually showered at his room in the basement at Romatech, but he couldn't leave Marielle alone, so he'd showered here.

He padded into the main room, still drying his wet hair with a towel. He spotted Marielle, lying on the couch with her head resting on the pillowed arm. As he approached, he noticed she was bundled up in Buniel's white robe. The angel sun catcher was in her hands, and she was studying it, running her fingers over the crystal wings.

He sat on the other end of the couch, next to her bare feet. "You miss heaven."

"Yes." She sat up and drew her legs in to make more room for him. "It's been my home since I was created." She tugged the robe closed around her neck, then rubbed her chin against the soft white material.

No doubt, she missed her angelic boyfriend, too. He eyed her damp blond hair that curled on the ends and her freshly scrubbed lovely face. "Do ye look like that in heaven?"

She smiled. "My form is similar, but not this solid or detailed. I'm more of a spirit there."

"Ah." *Good.* Then Buniel couldn't touch her or kiss her.

"I miss my wings." She lifted the sun catcher up to the ceiling light. "I miss the thrill of soaring through the heavens and feeling the air rush by me. I miss the freedom of going anywhere I please." With a sigh, she lowered her hand. "I really missed my wings when you were injured, and I couldn't take you anywhere for help."

"Ye doona like feeling powerless." Connor tossed his towel onto the coffee table. "I feel the same way."

"You have plenty of wonderful powers." Marielle poked at him with a bare foot. "Stop being down on yourself."

He smiled. "I canna fly, but I can levitate. Would ye care to go up a wee bit?" He pointed up in the air.

She gave him a dubious look. "How far can you go?"

He shrugged. "Mars. Venus." When she laughed, he grinned. "Would ye believe the top of the chimney?"

She laughed again, and the sound was music for his soul.

He stood and extended his hand. "Come."

She took his hand and followed him outside.

The grass was chilly on his bare feet. He stopped in the middle of the clearing.

"Good thing ye're wearing this." He folded the voluminous white robe around her. He had spotted a pair of knit pajamas underneath. "I hear it is a bit chilly on Mars."

"Or the top of the chimney." She smiled up at him. "So how does this work?"

"Ye have to hold on to me." He put her arms around his neck, then grabbed hold of her waist.

He started up slowly. Three feet. Five feet.

She peered down. "Is that as fast as you can go?"

He zipped up another ten feet, and she laughed.

She tightened her grip around his neck. "I like it. Thank you."

He slowly rose another ten feet.

She glanced down with a speculative look. "I wonder what would happen if I directed a blast of air down at the ground?"

He frowned. "That doesna sound verra wise."

"Oh, come on." She stretched a hand out and *boom!*

They took off like a rocket, shooting straight up into the sky.

"Bloody hell!" He pulled her close.

She squealed with laughter. "Yes! This is what it's like. Don't you love it?" She flung her arms out and arched her back with her face toward the stars.

"No!" He grappled to keep ahold of her.

They slowed to a stop, hovering in the air. Connor's heart stopped pounding and he glanced down. Holy Christ Almighty, they had to be a mile above the Earth.

"Wasn't that fun?" She wrapped her arms around his neck.

"I was afraid I would drop you."

She traced the line of his jaw with a finger. "Do you really worry so much about me?"

"Aye."

"You sweet man." She kissed his cheek. "I was never worried. I trust you."

His groin tightened. *Great.* He was getting hard a mile up in the air. And as fiercely as he was holding her, she would be sure to notice.

"I want to try something." She stretched a hand out to the side and let loose a little blast.

They flew in the opposite direction. She repeated it a few times more, laughing each time they took off. Soon, Connor was laughing with her. She was right, he did enjoy the wind against his face and the canopy of twinkling stars around them.

She hugged him tight. "Thank you, Connor. I was afraid I'd never fly again."

He rubbed his chin against her temple. "It took powers from both of us to pull it off."

She leaned back and smiled at him. "We make a good team."

Now that they were no longer flying and laughing, he became aware once again of how tightly he was holding her. Her body was molded against his, and they hovered in mid-air, surrounded by stars.

Below them, the world spread out, dotted with trees and lush green pastures. A bird flew by, did a double take at them, then squawked and hurried away.

They both laughed.

"Thank you for this." He kissed her brow. "I'll always remember it."

"So will I."

He studied her lovely face. "I want to touch you, but I doona dare let go."

She leaned forward and rubbed her nose against his. "How is that?"

It was enough to make his groin grow even harder. And his vision turn red. He kissed her cheek. "Do ye really love me?"

"Yes. How do you—" She blinked with a startled look. "Your eyes are glowing."

"Aye. Ye look pink like a rose." His gaze focused on her lips, so red now, so alluring. "I want to kiss you."

Her eyes widened, but she didn't refuse. When he leaned close, her lips parted. When his mouth touched hers, she melted against him. He was lost.

And they plummeted about half a mile.

She squealed, latching on to his shoulders.

He regained control, and they came to a stop, hovering once again.

She took a deep breath. "Good heavens! What was that?"

His pounding heart thudded in his ears. "Sorry. I—I lost my concentration and forgot I was levitating." He glanced at the ground below. "Maybe we should go down. Slowly. Make a gentle landing."

"Instead of a crash? Sounds good to me." She chuckled. "Your eyes aren't red and glowing now."

"Aye. Sheer terror will do that to a man."

She grinned. "It was a wild ride. Thank you."

"Ye liked it?" He brought them down slowly. He could think of other wild rides she might enjoy.

"Where are we exactly?"

"It doesna matter. I can always teleport us back to the cabin."

They landed in the middle of a green pasture, surrounding by forested mountains. The grass was soft and cool beneath his feet.

She let go of him and sauntered across the meadow. "What a beautiful place."

"Shall we stay for a little while?"

She turned. Her hair was wild and windblown, her cheeks pink from the rushing wind.

He walked toward her. "If I lose my concentration now, we willna plummet to our deaths."

She smiled slowly. "What did you want to concentrate on?"

He pulled her into his arms. "I'd like to give you pleasure."

Chapter Nineteen

*Y*ou do please me." Marielle rested her hands on his chest. "I haven't laughed so much in ages."

"Sweetheart, I love hearing ye laugh." He brushed her hair back from her brow. "But I was hoping to make ye sigh and moan."

"Oh." Were his eyes turning red again? Brynley had to be right about her Three-Step Rule. "I don't suppose you're referring to chocolate?"

"Nay." He skimmed his fingers down her cheek to her neck. "I want to pleasure you as a woman."

She swallowed hard and tried to ignore the fluttering of her heart. "I'm not sure I can give you what you want."

He kissed her brow. "What I want is to feel ye shudder in my arms." He kissed her cheek. "I want to hear ye moan and scream."

"Scream?" She tilted her head while he nuzzled

her neck. Moaning she could understand. And shuddering. She was close to doing that right now. But scream? "Why would I scream? Does it hurt?"

"Nay, I willna harm you." He dragged his tongue up her neck, and she shuddered.

"Connor, I cannot become one with you."

"I know." He tickled her ear. "I willna take from you. I will only give." He nipped at her ear.

"Oh!" Her heart lurched. He had sharp teeth. But when he drew her earlobe into his mouth and suckled, she moaned. Her legs trembled, and she had a strange overwhelming desire to lie down.

"Will ye let me touch you? And kiss you?"

"Yes." She clutched at his shoulders. "But I'm not sure I can take very much. I'm feeling so . . . weak."

"Weak?" He gave her a worried look, and his eyes turned back to blue. "Are ye ill?"

"I'm not sure. I just felt limp all of a sudden. And my knees are very shaky."

"Ah." His eyes twinkled. "Perhaps ye should lie down."

She gave him a suspicious look. "I know what you're up to. You want to take me back to the cabin and climb into bed with me. Then the women will arrive and find us there, and it will be very embarrassing. And when you fall into your death-sleep, they'll all fuss at me for not chasing you away."

"Nay. I doona want to climb into yer bed."

Her heart stuttered. "You don't?" Good heavens, that was even more aggravating.

He chuckled. "Doona look so upset with me. I want to lie down with you here."

"Here?" She looked around.

"Aye, under the stars." He slipped off her robe and stretched it out on the grass. He sat on the edge and patted the center. "Dinna ye say yer legs were feeling weak?"

"It only seems to happen when you're kissing me." Without the robe, she felt a little chilly, so she crossed her arms.

"Ye're cold."

"I'm all right."

"Nay, I can tell ye're cold." His gaze focused on her breasts.

She glanced down and winced at the way her nipples were poking out. When she looked back at Connor, his eyes were red and glowing. "Again?"

His mouth twitched. "'Tis a recurring problem."

She huffed. "Brynley was definitely right."

"Nay. She thought she could chase me away, but I'm still here. Still waiting."

"Waiting?"

He arched a brow at her, then reached over, grabbed her pajama bottoms, and yanked.

She gasped when her pajamas fell to her ankles, leaving her dressed only in a T-shirt and skimpy black panties. "Connor!"

He grabbed her around the waist and pulled her down onto the robe.

She squealed and kicked at him. "What are you doing?"

He grasped her thigh to stop her kicking, then leaned over her. "I asked if I could touch you and kiss you, and ye agreed. Have ye changed yer mind?"

"No." Her heart thundered in her ears. "But ye're moving so fast."

"Sweetheart, I doona count time in millennia like you. I'd like to get started. In this century."

"I wasn't taking that long." Her breath caught when he feathered light kisses all over her face. "I'm just a little nervous, that's all." She moaned when he nuzzled her neck. "And you startled me when you pulled my pants down."

He lifted his head. "Right." He kissed her quickly on the lips. "Thank you for reminding me."

"Huh?" She blinked when he suddenly moved down to her feet.

He smiled. "Yer toenails are pink." He kissed her big toe.

"You could have had pink toes, too," she reminded him. He shot her a warning look, but she just smiled. "I thought you looked very handsome with your pink toes."

He nipped at her toe. She squealed and tried to pull her foot away, but he gripped her by the ankle and wouldn't let go. He lifted her leg higher and trailed kisses up her calf to her knee. Her heart raced, and her stomach fluttered.

"So yer knees are giving you trouble, are they?" He lifted her leg higher and kissed the soft skin on the back side of her knee.

She shivered. "That tickles." It more than tickled. It was sending frissons of needy sensations up her leg. She had an overwhelming urge to squeeze her thighs together, but she couldn't when he had one of her legs lifted so high in the air.

He tickled the backside of her knee with his tongue while his hand skimmed up her thigh, closer and closer to her core.

She moaned. She'd never felt so vulnerable. Or so desperate.

He set her leg down, then pulled her into a sitting position. "Lift yer arms."

She started to, then gasped when he whisked her T-shirt off and shoved her back down. She gasped again when he ripped off her panties and tossed them aside. "Good heavens! Aren't you being a little . . . abrupt?"

"Ye think I'm moving too fast?" He settled beside her with a hand resting on her tummy. His gaze wandered over her body. "I've seen you naked before."

"That was different. I was unconscious most of the time." And not so intensely aware of him. Just the way he looked at her made her tremble.

"You're exceedingly beautiful," he murmured.

"Thank you." Good heavens, he was really looking her over. Her cheeks grew warm. "I just need a moment to adjust."

"Ah." His gaze rose to her chest. "I've seen yer breasts before. I've touched them."

She struggled to breathe. "I know."

He leaned closer, studying them. "Yer nipples are hard, ripe for sucking." He moved back. "But I'll give you more time to adjust."

Her mouth dropped open. He wanted to suck on her nipples? A new wave of sensation swept down her body and sizzled in her core. Moisture pooled there. This time she did squeeze her thighs together.

His nostrils flared, and his fingers pressed against her belly. "Lass, if ye adjust any more, ye'll be climaxing without me."

She reached up to wrap her hands around his neck. "Then do it. Please."

He smiled. "My pleasure."

He kissed her slowly and thoroughly, nibbling on her lips and swirling his tongue inside her mouth. She responded, quickly sinking into a world of sensation where his every touch ignited shivers and sparks.

He kissed her neck and each time his tongue licked her skin, she felt a throbbing in her core. It made her desperate, made her want to squirm and press herself against him.

She tugged at his T-shirt. "Let me touch you."

He pulled his shirt off, then leaned over to kiss her breasts. She ran her hands through his hair and along his bare shoulders. When he drew a nipple into his mouth, she groaned and dug her fingers into his back.

Oh yes, he'd been serious about the sucking. More moisture pooled between her legs, and she squirmed.

He moved away from her breasts and grew still.

"Is something wrong?"

"I want to see yer face when I touch you."

"You are touching—" She stopped when she realized what he meant. His hand skimmed down her belly into the thatch of curls. Her breath caught.

He slowly massaged her. "Will ye open yer legs for me?"

She did, and he smiled. "Och, now there's a glorious sight."

She jolted when she first felt his fingers touch her core. She pressed a hand to her chest. "I think my heart will burst."

He lifted his hand. "Ye need a moment to adjust?"

"Don't you dare!"

With a chuckle, he put his hand back on her.

She winced. "Sorry. I don't know what's come over me." She moaned when his fingers traced the folds. "I'm becoming very . . . greedy."

"Ye want more?"

"Yes!"

He flicked a finger over a very sensitive spot, and she squeaked.

He grinned. "Ye might like this, too." He inserted a finger inside her.

"Oh! Oh yes." She squirmed, pressing against him. A buzzing feeling skittered all through her. Her eyes flickered shut.

"Ye're verra tight. And wet." He inserted another finger. When he waggled them, something broke lose inside her. It soared higher and higher. "Connor, I—I—"

He wiggled his fingers again, while his thumb rubbed the sensitive spot.

She screamed. For a second, she thought the world had come to an end, and the stars in the heavens had burst. But then she opened her eyes, and the stars were still there. And she was still alive, her body throbbing with incredible spasms.

"*Qu'est-ce que tu as fait?*" she gasped.

Connor leaned closer, smiling. "Ye're speaking French."

"Oh. *Lo siento.*" She rubbed her head. Spanish? "I think I blew a fuse."

He laughed and gathered her in his arms. "I love you. I love you so much."

"Do you?" She held him tight. "Oh, Connor. I love you, too."

He rolled onto his back, taking her with him. "Lass." He ruffled her hair and kissed the top of her head.

She sprawled across his chest, resting her head over his heart to hear it pounding. She closed her eyes. A vision flashed across her mind. A dark-haired woman, holding a newborn baby. They were beautiful. She pushed the thought away and nestled her cheek against the soft hair on Connor's chest.

If only this moment could last forever.

Her eyes flew open. Was that what she really wanted?

"*Je t'aime,*" Connor whispered.

She lifted her head. "You speak French?"

He nodded. "And Gaelic. What about you?"

"I can speak to any human on Earth."

His eyes widened, then he looked away. "I suppose I'm being greedy to want you all to myself."

She smiled and ran a finger along his jaw. "You make me feel very greedy, too."

He kissed her finger. "Did ye want to scream again?"

Her cheeks grew warm. She really had screamed. "It was much more intense than I had expected."

"We barely got started. I dinna get to taste you or make you come with my mouth."

She blinked. Did he mean oral sex? "You want to give me a blow job?"

He laughed, then winced. "Och."

"What's wrong?"

"Nothing."

She sat up with a gasp. "I shouldn't have leaned on you like that. Your ribs could still be sore."

"My ribs are fine."

"Are you sure?" She smoothed her hands over his bare chest. "You're so muscular and strong." She followed the narrow trail of hair to his navel. "I think you're beautiful."

"Lass—" He gritted his teeth.

She jumped. "Connor, there's something moving in your pants."

"Pay it no mind. Lass, no!"

She leaned over him to pull the waistband of his flannel pants down. His erection popped out, startling her.

"Oh!" She fell across his thighs. "Oh my. Good heavens."

He groaned and dragged his hands down his face. "Ye needna stare at it in horror. It willna harm you."

"It's . . . really big."

He snorted. "It comes in peace."

She giggled, then poked at it with her finger.

It twitched, and he hissed in a breath.

She sat up, amazed by how strong a reaction she had caused. She studied his erection curiously. Could she cause him to scream like he had her?

"Doona touch me again," he muttered. "I'm about to explode."

Explode? That sounded interesting. "You know the problem with me, Connor. I don't follow orders very well." She curled her hand around the staff and kissed the tip.

"Holy—" He gritted his teeth with a strangled noise.

She wasn't exactly sure what to do, but she recalled how much she enjoyed him tickling her breasts with his tongue and suckling her. So she ran her tongue up the length of his staff, then took him into her mouth.

She figured she was doing something right because he was groaning and clutching her hair.

"Enough!" He tossed her down onto the robe and wedged between her legs.

He kissed her hard, rubbing himself against her. The friction ignited her sensitive skin. She wrapped her legs around him and dug her hands into his back.

Moisture pooled, and his movement became slick. An ache throbbed deep inside her, an empty ache that begged to be filled.

"Connor." She wanted him inside her.

And the two shall become one.

He let out a hoarse shout, then shuddered as he found his release. He collapsed beside her, hugging her tight.

She held him, her arms and legs still wrapped around him. Oh God, she hadn't known this sort of love could be so powerful. She'd come so close to begging him to take her.

She rested her head against his chest, listening to the wild thumping of his heart. The vision returned. The dark-haired woman, holding a baby. Connor's baby, she realized with a jolt. She was seeing inside his black pit of remorse. His walls had tumbled down.

Fionnula. That was the woman's name. There was so much love and sadness surrounding her. Why would a woman he loved be in the center of his remorse?

She sat up. "Connor?"

He groaned, his eyes shut. "Give me a minute."

"You didn't tell me you have a wife."

Chapter Twenty

Connor flinched, his eyes popping open. "What?"

"You have a wi—"

"Nay!" He sat up. Holy Christ Almighty, she might as well have punched him in the gut. "I'm no' married."

"And you have a daughter."

His heart raced. He couldn't deny having a daughter. She had lived only a few hours, but for all eternity, she would be his beautiful daughter. He gulped. Would Marielle see his deceased wife the same way?

"I . . . have no wife." He grabbed his flannel pants and cursed silently as he struggled to stuff his feet into the right holes. His damned hands were shaking.

"You did have one."

He glanced at Marielle. She didn't look upset. How could she be so damned calm when he was stunned? More than stunned. Floored with a sucker punch. And now that he thought about it, damned angry. "While I was making love to you, ye were spying on me?"

"No." Frowning, she hugged her knees. "If you must know, the lovemaking is so intense, I can hardly think at all. Just a few fleeting thoughts about how lovely it feels and how wonderful you are. And how much I love you."

His heart filled with longing. It was going to kill him when she left. "I feel the same way."

Her eyes softened with a tender look. "I know you were greatly affected. It made the fortress around your heart tumble down. So when I was hugging you just now, I saw them. Your wife and child."

He finished pulling his pants on. "I doona want to talk about it."

"I thought they were beautiful. And I could feel how much you loved them."

"They died centuries ago. There's no point in—"

"I think there is. Because for some reason, they're at the center of all your pain and remorse. What happened—"

"Nay, I willna discuss it." Damn, he regretted the hurt look on her face. "I'm sorry, Marielle. But I confess nothing."

Her eyes narrowed. "Do you think the Heavenly Father doesn't know?"

"Of course He knows. That's why I'm on the list for hell."

She made a face. "Stubborn man. That list is not written in stone. It can be changed."

"I'm a lost cause. But doona fash. I will still help you get back to heaven."

She snorted. "You think I'm only concerned about myself? What kind of angel would that make me?"

And what kind of man committed the terrible crimes he had? He couldn't tell her. He couldn't bear to lose her love. It was the only light in the darkness where he dwelled.

"We should be going back." He grabbed his T-shirt, then noticed the mess he'd made on Marielle.

"Och, lass." He used his T-shirt to wipe off her belly and thighs. "Doona let this worry you. All my sperm is dead."

She stiffened. "I could have a child?"

"Nay. No' with my—"

"But I have the right body parts for it." She placed a hand on her belly, and her eyes widened with awe. "I could bring forth a living human being."

He gulped. "I thought ye were going back to heaven."

She blinked. "Oh. Yes, I am." She reached for her T-shirt. "I was just . . . surprised for a moment. I hadn't realized . . ." She pulled her T-shirt on.

"We'll have to shower again when we return." He located her underwear and pajama bottoms and handed them to her. "The ladies have keen senses of smell. I know the Vamp women do. I assume the shifter does, too."

She slipped on the clothes. "So they'll know what we did?"

"Aye. After they arrive, I need to go to Romatech

and see Angus. I think we're ready to face the Malcontents."

"I want to go with you." When he started to object, she touched his shoulder. "I'll be there at the battle. I have a right to know what the plans are."

"All right." He stood and pulled her to her feet.

She placed her hands on his cheeks. "Thank you, Connor. I will always treasure this memory. How you made love to me under the stars."

He wrapped his arms around her in a tight embrace. "I'll remember it, too."

"I wish you would trust me with all the pain you've been hiding."

He sighed. He should have known she wasn't going to give up on that. She was a healer at heart. Unfortunately, there was nothing she could do to wash away his sins.

Nothing he could do, either.

An hour later, Marielle sat in a corner of the MacKay security office at Romatech, listening to a roomful of Vamps discuss strategy. She tried to pay attention, but every time she looked at Connor, who was standing nearby, she was reminded of their lovemaking. How truly blessed humans were that they could share an act of love that was so intensely powerful and pleasurable. She'd known for several days that she had a complete set of female private parts, but she'd focused more on denying them and retaining her angelic innocence than on considering the benefits of using them.

She was capable of giving birth. Capable of

having children, like Shanna. It was an intriguing thought, and when she glanced at Connor, her chest tightened.

No, she couldn't do it. She couldn't stay here. She'd known Connor for only five nights. How could five nights make her contemplate giving up an eternity in heaven? She would have to be insane to do that. Or very much in love.

Vanda's words came back to her. How much was she willing to sacrifice for her love? Then Bunny's words flitted through her mind. She had a good heart. If she followed it, she would not regret it.

But he'd also said the human world was too dangerous for her. She had to agree as she watched the Vamps passing out swords and knives, guns and ammunition. Where was the peace and joy she craved? How could she give up singing with the Heavenly Host? How could she give up her wings and soaring through space?

Her gaze returned to Connor. Together, they had managed to simulate flight. And together, he had made her soar to a peak of pleasure she had never imagined. He made love so real, so raw and physical. It was so different from the soft, soothing comfort she felt in heaven. It was like comparing manna to chocolate. One was bland but perfectly sustaining; the other, a burst of delicious pleasure. But one was also constant and eternal, and the other, frightening and unpredictable.

"Damn, what's he doing here?" Phineas muttered, motioning to one of the monitors on the far wall.

From the way the Vamps scowled and cursed,

Marielle could tell the man approaching the front door at Romatech was not well liked.

"Who is he?" she asked Connor.

"Shanna's father, Sean Whelan," he whispered, then raised his voice. "Why is he here?"

Angus sighed. "I asked him to come." When the Vamps started to object, he raised his hands to stop him. "He's been very helpful locating where the Malcontents have been feeding and killing. And he's been using his connections with the government to cover it up. In exchange for his cooperation, he wants to take part in the battle."

"That's whack," Phineas mumbled.

"I've told him how dangerous it is." Angus hesitated. "Tonight, he might change his mind about cooperating with us. Shanna's going to tell him her news."

The room went silent. Everyone watched the monitor as Roman and Shanna greeted her father at the front door, then led him to a room not far from the security office.

Marielle sent up a silent prayer that Shanna's father would be compassionate and understanding, that he would be grateful his daughter was still alive, even as a vampire.

"Everyone understands the plan?" Angus asked. When they all nodded, he continued. "Then we have one last thing to show you. It's a clip from tonight's showing of *Live with the Undead*. Emma?"

She walked up to the wall of monitors and slid a silver disk into a slot. "We checked this out with the manager at DVN, and he says Corky has been feeding these images every night from unknown locations."

"She's traveling with Casimir and recording his journey," Angus added.

Emma punched some buttons. "I think she's having an affair with him."

An image came up on the monitor. A blond, buxom woman was holding a microphone and standing in front of a dark warehouse on a deserted street.

"This is Corky Courrant, reporting live on the road with Casimir. It's been an exciting journey! Thanks to my darling Casimir, I have rediscovered my heritage. No more bottled blood for me! Tonight, I sank my fangs into a handsome young human and drank my fill. You cannot imagine the rush as a mortal's life slips away in your arms. This is our true nature, dear friends, and we should embrace it. Stop drinking that sludge from Romatech! We should take our rightful place as superior beings. We are meant to be conquerors!"

Corky motioned for the cameraman to follow her as she opened a door to the warehouse. "Tonight, I have something very exciting to show you. While it is true that Casimir and his followers, including me, are killing a few people every night, I can assure you that Casimir has plans that go far beyond the slaughter of a few unimportant mortals."

She led the cameraman down a dark hallway, then into a large room. Stacks of wood and pipes could be seen in the dim light. The camera then focused on the floor where dozens of bodies rested.

"These are criminals who have pledged allegiance

to Casimir," Corky explained. "Tonight, they're all in vampire comas, but tomorrow, when these new vampires awaken, they will be ravenous! In the room next door, we have thirty mortals under our control. Tomorrow night, just after sunset, there will be a wild feeding frenzy! I'll be here, of course, to record it all."

Corky grinned. "You will see death and carnage tomorrow, my dear friends! The mortal world will soon bow to Casimir. He will rule the world. And I will be his queen!"

Emma punched a button, and the recording ended. "We've studied this recording, trying to figure out the location, but there were no street signs, no signs of any kind. The land appears to be flat, but other than that, it could be a warehouse in any town."

Angus turned to Marielle. "We'll be counting on you to sense the deaths as quickly as possible so we can teleport in and stop their killing spree."

Marielle nodded. "Just knowing that it's a warehouse will help me find the right place."

"Connor will teleport you there," Angus continued, "and as soon as he confirms ye're in the right place, the rest of us will follow using his tracking device."

"I can understand why I didn't sense their location tonight," Marielle said. "I was searching for death and horror, and it didn't happen there. Those people volunteered and were put into comas—" She was interrupted by loud shouting in the hallway.

On a monitor, Sean Whelan could be seen in the hallway, slamming his fists into walls.

"No' taking the news verra well," Angus muttered.

Emma opened the door, and the Vamps filed out into the hallway. Connor took Marielle by the hand and led her out.

"Damn you! Damn you all!" Sean bellowed at them, his face red with rage.

Marielle winced. Her prayer had gone unheeded.

"It's not their fault," Shanna said quietly.

"Of course it's their damned fault!" Sean pointed a finger at Roman. "I'll kill you for this."

Roman's eyes narrowed, and his fists clenched.

"No!" Shanna cried. "Roman saved me! I would have died if he hadn't transformed me."

"You wouldn't have been at risk if you'd never married him!" Sean spun around, and his gaze landed on Connor. His eyes blazed with hatred. "You're the one. You bloody bastard. You're the one who brought the angel of death here. I'll kill you, too."

Marielle stepped forward to take responsibility, but Connor held her back. "Go ahead, old man. Try to kill me. I'll be doing Shanna a favor, getting rid of you."

"Connor, no," Shanna whispered.

Sean pointed a finger at Connor. "I would be doing the whole world a favor by getting rid of you."

Connor's jaw shifted.

"It was my fault." Marielle lifted her chin. "I'm the angel of death."

Sean's face grew pale.

Connor moved Marielle out in front. "Why do ye no' greet her properly, old man? Shake hands with her."

Sean stepped back.

Marielle pulled away from Connor's grasp and

frowned at him. "That's not funny." She turned to Sean. "I am deeply sorry for what happened to your daughter. I would never knowingly harm any living being."

"That's true," Shanna said. "Marielle was unconscious at the time. I was the one who touched her."

Sean glared at them all, then turned to Angus. "I hear there will be a battle tomorrow night. You will take me."

Angus sighed. "It's too dangerous—"

"I don't give a damn!" Sean shouted. His hands fisted. "I have to kill some vampires. I have to avenge my daughter. If you don't take me with you, I'll start killing you all instead."

Connor scoffed. "Just try it."

Angus lifted a hand. "Enough. We will take you tomorrow night, Whelan. But be warned, the fighting will be fierce and to the death."

Sean nodded. "I'm counting on it."

"Come with me," Connor whispered to Marielle, then dragged her down the hallway to a side exit.

"What's wrong?"

"Everything," he grumbled. He pushed open the door and led her toward a garden area. He released her and paced toward a gazebo.

He turned abruptly. "I doona want you at the battle tomorrow night."

She stiffened. "I have to go. I'm the one who can sense death."

"Aye, but as soon as the others arrive and the battle begins, I want you to leave. I'll ask Emma to teleport you back here to safety."

"But I've been practicing self-defense."

"It may no' be enough!" He walked toward her, his eyes full of pain. "I canna put you in danger like that. I love you too much."

She swallowed hard. "Defeating the Malcontents and Casimir will prove I deserve to be reinstated in heaven. If I run away before the battle even begins, how can I be deemed worthy? If I risk nothing, how can I gain anything?"

His jaw shifted. "I'll get ye back to heaven, one way or another."

"No! I was the one who disobeyed. I have to be the one to earn my way back."

He ran a hand through his hair. "I canna bear the thought of you being hurt."

"I understand. I feel the same way about you. If anything happens to you—"

"I'll be fine, lass. I've fought many a battle."

She groaned. "I know. But you died in one, remember?"

"I dinna die. I was . . . mortally wounded." His jaw shifted. "That was over four hundred years ago. I've improved a lot since then."

Her heart expanded. She loved this man so much. She walked up to him and placed her hands on his face. "I'm going with you tomorrow. And I'm not leaving you alone to face the enemy."

He took her hands and kissed them. "Then I want you to keep this with you." He slid the dagger out of his knee sock and placed it in her hands.

She eyed the dagger with dismay. "Connor, I'd rather not—"

"I know, but I want you to have it. And I want you to use it if ye have to. Otherwise, I canna let ye go with me."

The dagger felt cold and foreign in her hands. She wanted to refuse it, but she needed to be at the battle so she could help protect Connor and prove herself worthy of heaven.

"All right." She accepted the leather sheath Connor handed her, and slid the dagger home.

Chapter Twenty-one

Kick 'em in the balls!" Brynley called from the front porch.

Marielle didn't know how to respond to that, but after seeing Connor close up and naked, she had a good idea what Brynley was referring to. It was her sixth night on Earth, about thirty minutes after sunset, and she was practicing her self-defense maneuvers in the clearing in front of the cabin.

"It is an effective strategy," Connor said quietly beside her. "If one of the Malcontents gets his hands on you, knee him in the groin. Then plunge the dagger through his heart."

She winced. She didn't want to tell Connor she had no intention of killing anyone. Could she make it through the night by simply defending herself with blasts of air? Somehow, she had to. How could she be welcomed back to heaven if she ended a life?

"Can ye sense them yet?" Connor asked.

She closed her eyes and reached out. Deaths in hospitals, deaths in traffic accidents, a few murders. No horrendous mass murder in a warehouse. "No, not yet."

Connor patted her shoulder. "Doona worry. Most likely, they are west of us and still in their death-sleep."

She nodded. Upon awakening, Connor had immediately downed a bottle of blood. Then he'd started strapping on his weapons. A claymore on his back, a dagger in each sock, more knives and wooden stakes in his sporran along with an automatic pistol loaded with silver bullets.

He'd given her a belt to wear that had a leather sheath connected to it. The sheathed dagger was hidden underneath her hooded sweatshirt jacket.

Meanwhile, Vamps and shifters were gathering at Romatech. Angus had called and reported they were ready to move out. Sean Whelan had arrived, armed to the teeth.

While they waited for the sun to set over the Malcontents, Connor insisted Marielle practice. She was happy to stay busy. Otherwise, she would worry too much.

"Take me with you!" Brynley shouted for the third time.

Connor groaned. "I told you, no. Ye're no' trained for battle."

"There's a full moon tonight," Brynley continued. "I have to shift anyway. Phil's going. And three of his boys from school. Carlos is even letting the tiger shifter go. Why can't I go, too?"

Connor glared at her. "They've been trained for battle. Ye havena."

"I can take down an elk in sixty seconds!"

"I can only teleport one, and it has to be Marielle."

"Then tell another Vamp to get his dead ass over here, so he can teleport me," Brynley snapped. "If you let me go, I'll stay close to Marielle and help keep her safe."

That was obviously the right thing to say to Connor, for he pulled his cell phone out of his sporran and made a call.

"Brynley," Marielle said. "This isn't your fight. You don't have to—"

"I want to." Brynley gave her a sad smile. "You deserve all the help you can get."

Connor dropped the phone back into his sporran. "Phineas is coming. He'll take you to Romatech to join up with the others."

Brynley nodded. "Thank you."

"Hello?" a voice shouted from inside the cabin. Phineas peeked out the front door. "There you are." He stepped out onto the porch. Like Connor, he had a sword strapped to his back. Around his hips, he wore a belt with a gun holster and several sheaths containing knives.

He looked Brynley over and smiled. "So is it true that you'll need to take off your clothes before shifting?"

She jabbed him in the chest so hard, he stumbled back a step.

He rubbed his chest. "What the hell was that?"

Brynley glared at him. "That's the stake that a

Malcontent puts through your heart while you're watching me strip, you moron."

Connor chuckled. "She has a good point."

"Yeah, yeah," Phineas muttered. "Like I want to watch a perfectly good woman turn into a dog."

Brynley whipped back a hand to slap him, but Phineas caught her wrist. "I'm faster than you, wolfie-girl."

She narrowed her eyes. "I have a nasty bite."

"So do I." He pulled her into his arms and waved at Connor. "See you later, dude." He vanished, taking Brynley with him.

"That was . . . interesting," Marielle said.

"Aye." Connor gathered her in his arms. "We're alone now."

She embraced him, resting her head on his chest. She felt him rubbing his chin against her hair.

"Marielle, I've asked Emma to keep an eye on you. Ye'll be stationed outside the warehouse to catch anyone who escapes. Some of the newly turned vampires may try to run away. They willna have learned how to teleport yet."

"I want to be with you."

He shook his head. "We'll be fighting hand-to-hand inside the warehouse. Yer blasting power wouldna be helpful there. Ye would be hitting our side as much as the Malcontents."

She swallowed hard. "I hate to be separated from you."

"'Tis for the best. Yer job is to find the Malcontents. After that, let us do our job."

She nodded.

He kissed her on the mouth, a long, fierce kiss that left her knees weak and her thoughts reeling. Was this a farewell kiss in case something happened to him?

Please, God! Please protect him!

He released her and removed his phone from his sporran. "Try again. Can ye sense them now?"

She closed her eyes and reached out. Deaths rolled past her. Death caused by illness. Death caused by accidents.

She stiffened. Memphis, Tennessee. Screams of sheer terror. Thirty people dying all at once. In a warehouse. "I have it."

He quickly made the call. "Angus, we're going. Give us ten seconds." He dropped the phone in his sporran and grabbed her.

She felt a cold stab on her brow as he rushed inside her mind and pounced on the destination. Everything went black.

They landed on a dark street, dimly lit by a street lamp on each end. All the street lamps closer by had been broken. On the right, the street was lined with abandoned stores, the glass fronts smashed and partially boarded up. On the left, a giant warehouse loomed, the same one they'd seen on the news report. There was no one in sight, but screams filled the air.

Dozens of Vamps materialized around them, using Connor's tracking device as their beacon. Some came alone; others brought shifters or mortals with them. Marielle recognized Shanna's father as he arrived with Roman. Sean Whelan pushed away and drew his weapons—a huge pistol and a long, sharp dagger. The Vamps unsheathed their swords.

Robby led a group silently around to the back of the warehouse.

Emma dashed up to Marielle. "This way," she whispered. "We have to guard the shifters."

Marielle gave Connor one last look as she was led away. *May God bless you and keep you.*

He nodded as if he had heard her, then turned to follow Angus into the warehouse.

Her blood ran cold at the sound of their tremendous war cry, followed by gunshots and the clashing of swords.

"Hurry!" Emma dragged her across the street where the shifters had gathered in an alley between two abandoned stores.

"There could be Malcontent guards roaming the area," Emma told her. "I'll watch the other end of this alley. You watch this one. Don't let anyone near till the shifters are ready."

Marielle caught a glimpse of the shifters stripping, then turned her back to stand guard. She shuddered as the sound of the battle in the warehouse grew even louder. Amid the din of gunfire and swords clashing, a scream rent the air. She winced. It had sounded so human. She hoped the mortals wouldn't die. Or the Vamps. Or Connor. Her heart constricted with a sharp pang. She couldn't bear to lose him.

"There's one! Get her!" a man shouted at the end of the street.

She spotted two men just before they vanished. Malcontents. Before she could shout a warning, they reappeared right in front of her. They pounced, but she sent them flying backward so hard, they crashed into the warehouse.

Her hands shook, and her heart thundered in her ears. Good heavens, that had been close!

A tremendous roar sounded behind her.

She spun around. "Ack!" Her heart lurched.

A huge Kodiak bear was standing on its hind legs, growling at her. She stumbled to the side and bumped into a broken sidewalk curb.

The bear dropped down on all fours and dashed toward the warehouse, followed closely by four large wolves, and the largest panther and tiger she'd ever seen.

The bear and panther attacked the two Malcontents she'd thrown against the warehouse, ripping their heads off. The two vampires turned to dust.

Marielle's stomach cringed. The shifters charged into the warehouse, and soon after, more screams pierced the air.

"Good work." Emma patted Marielle on the back.

A lone wolf trotted to the other side of the alley and sat there on its haunches.

"Brynley?" Marielle whispered.

The wolf looked at her, then bared its teeth and growled.

Startled, Marielle stepped back.

"Damn." Emma pulled a knife and threw it spinning through the air right past Marielle.

Marielle whirled around just in time to see the knife thud into a Malcontent's heart and turn him to dust. The knife clattered onto the sidewalk.

"That was close," Emma muttered. "Thanks, Brynley."

Marielle pressed a hand against her pounding heart. Her stomach felt twisted and queasy.

"Are you all right, dear?" Emma asked. "I could teleport you to Romatech in a flash."

She shook her head. "I'm not leaving Connor."

"Oh." Emma's eyes took on a speculative look as she leaned over to retrieve her knife. She straightened with a jerk. "Here they come."

A swarm of newly turned, frantic vampires burst out the front door, screaming and hissing.

Marielle hit them with an air blast that sent them crashing into one another and the warehouse.

Emma dashed toward them, a stake in each hand. She turned four of them to dust before the vampires could even scramble to their feet. Brynley leaped on them, ripping and tearing into their bodies till they turned to dust.

More vampires escaped. Marielle couldn't blast them without hitting Emma and Brynley. She recognized Shanna's father exiting the warehouse, shouting and slashing away at the vampires.

A Malcontent broke loose from the crowd and ran down the street. Marielle knocked him down with a blast of air.

"I'll kill you!" Sean Whelan raced after him.

The vampire jumped to his feet. Sean fired, but

his pistol only made a clicking noise. He tossed the gun down and charged at the vampire with his dagger.

The vampire grabbed Sean's arm, and the two locked in a struggle, falling onto the ground and rolling about.

"Oh God, no," Marielle breathed as she moved closer.

The vampire overpowered Sean, knocked him flat onto the street, wrenched the dagger from his hand, and plunged it into his torso.

Marielle gasped. *No!* She couldn't let Shanna's father die.

The vampire's fangs shot out, and he sank them into Sean's neck. Marielle couldn't blast him away without also hitting Sean.

She looked around frantically. Emma and Brynley were busy killing vampires by the warehouse door. And Sean's attacker was lying on top of him, draining him dry.

She had to do it. Tears filled her eyes as she pulled the dagger from her belt. *God forgive me.* She estimated where the vampire's heart would be, then plunged the dagger into his back. He turned to dust.

She stepped back, and a wave of nausea hit her. The dagger tumbled onto the street with a clatter.

"What are you doing here, Marielle?"

She spun around and saw Zackriel walking toward her. "Is Buniel here? Can he heal this man?" She motioned toward Shanna's father.

Zackriel looked at Sean Whelan, then at the small

battle that Emma and Brynley waged, and shook his head. "There will be no Healers here tonight. Only Deliverers."

She swallowed hard at the bile in her throat. "What about the humans inside?"

"All thirty are dead." Zackriel gave her an annoyed look. "Do you really think this is the way back to heaven?"

She stepped back and stumbled over the dagger she'd dropped. Oh God, what had she done? "Zack—" She turned toward him.

He was gone.

"Help me," Sean wheezed. Blood oozed from his stomach wound and the open gash on his neck. He reached out a trembling hand.

"I'm sorry," she whispered, her eyes filling with tears. She couldn't even hold his hand without killing him.

His hand fell limp onto the hard pavement.

Their strategy had worked, Connor noted with satisfaction as he skewered another Malcontent through the heart. Casimir's followers were falling like flies, caught completely by surprise. Corky Courrant and her cameraman were running about, shrieking, and trying to hide behind stacks of lumber.

He glanced over at Roman to make sure the former monk was doing all right. Roman was holding his own. Jean-Luc Echarpe was watching Roman's back just as he had done during the Great Vampire War.

Angus and Robby were both attacking the ring of Malcontents that surrounded Casimir. Connor wanted to join them, but twice he had to engage Malcontents who came close to killing Sean Whelan. Shanna's father was fighting like a madman, taking such foolish risks that Connor wondered if the man had come to commit suicide.

He knew the battle was over after the shifters charged in, and most of the surviving fledglings ran screaming for the front door, trying to escape. The poor fools had thought they were gaining immortality by becoming Casimir's vampire minions. No doubt they were shocked to find themselves dying the very next night.

With the number of Malcontents dwindling fast, Sean Whelan was having an easier time of it. He was fighting a fledgling with dismal fencing skills. Connor turned to help Angus and Robby as they fought to destroy some of Casimir's most experienced swordsmen.

Robby broke through the ring and made a swipe at Casimir, slicing his shoulder.

Casimir teleported away, then yelled at them from the top of a stack of wood. "I am sick of evading you! You're like a pack of rats, always scurrying about and keeping me from fulfilling my destiny! I want this ended, once and for all. Tomorrow after sunset. Mount Rushmore."

He vanished, and his followers who knew how to teleport followed him. All that was left was a few fledglings trying to escape.

Connor glanced over to where he'd last seen Sean Whelan, but he was gone. The fool must have gone outside to fight more fledglings.

"A final battle?" Robby turned to his great-grandfather. "Tomorrow night?"

Angus sighed. "Most likely a trap."

Connor had to agree, but with the current battle moving out onto the street, his thoughts returned to Marielle. He charged outside, slashing at any Malcontents in his way.

He reached the street and spotted Marielle kneeling beside a body. She was alive! "Marielle!"

When she looked up, he saw the tears on her face. He ran toward her. "Marielle, are ye all right?"

She shook her head. "I've been praying, but none of the Healers will come."

Connor jerked to a stop when he saw Sean Whelan bleeding to death on the street. "Oh no."

"Even Bunny won't come," Marielle cried. "They've given up on me."

Connor looked back toward the warehouse entrance and spotted more Vamps coming out. "Roman! Angus! Over here!"

A group of Vamps dashed over.

Connor knelt beside Marielle. "He barely has a heartbeat."

"God's blood." Roman turned pale as he looked Whelan over. "This will kill Shanna."

Angus turned to Robby. "Bring her here."

Robby nodded and vanished.

"Shit," Phineas muttered. "I knew it was crazy for that dude to come here." He looked at Roman.

"Why don't you take him to Romatech? Give him some blood."

Roman shook his head. "He would be dead by the time we got the transfusion started. And that wound to his stomach—it's not something we can just patch up."

Connor stood. "It would heal if he were a Vamp."

Roman stiffened. "Are you suggesting—"

"Aye," Connor replied. "But if we're going to do it, we'd better be quick."

Robby reappeared with Shanna.

She gasped and fell to her knees beside her father. "Dad!" She touched his face. "Oh God, no! Dad, please don't go like this." She turned a tearful face to Roman. "Can't you do something?"

Roman shook his head slightly. "He only has a few minutes left."

Tears streamed down Shanna's face as she looked at all the Vamps. "I thought you guys would protect him! How could you let this happen?"

Connor shifted his weight. *Bugger.* He'd saved Whelan's life twice tonight. He'd thought the man was safe when only a few fledglings were left.

"I'm so sorry," Marielle whispered. She picked up a dagger beside her. "I used this on the vampire who was attacking him. But I was too late."

Connor's breath hitched. Marielle had killed to protect Whelan? No wonder she looked so pale and devastated.

"He might survive if we transform him," Angus said.

Shanna gasped.

"Dude," Phineas mumbled. "He hates vampires."

"He might see us in a different light if he was one of us," Connor argued.

"That's an excellent point," Angus said. "We wouldna have to worry anymore about him turning on us."

"Unless he gets so pissed by waking up Undead that he kills us all," Phineas grumbled.

"I can't believe you're discussing this like a business decision," Shanna yelled. "Weighing the pros and cons while he's dying? He's my father!"

"Then what do ye think?" Robby asked. "Would yer father choose to be one of us? Or would he rather die?"

Shanna blinked. "I—" She looked down at her father, then back up at the Vamps. "Yes. Yes, do it."

The Vamps glanced at one another.

"What are you waiting for?" Shanna asked. "He's dying! Do it!"

Connor looked at Angus. "Ye do it. It was yer idea."

"Nay, ye were the first one to suggest it. Ye do it."

Connor glanced down at Whelan. Just the thought of sinking his teeth into the bastard made him shudder. "I'm no' touching him." He nudged Phineas. "Ye do it."

"I don't even know how!" Phineas poked at Robby. "You do it."

"Why me?" Robby turned to Angus. "Ye're the expert. Ye do it."

Angus grimaced. "I'm no' doing it. I hate the bugger."

"Stop it!" Shanna screamed. "You— Forget it! I'll do it myself."

"Shanna, you don't know how," Roman said. He closed his eyes and groaned. "God's blood. I guess I have to do it."

"You *guess*?" Shanna cried. "He's your father-in-law. Are you going to just let him die?"

"He threatens to kill me every time he sees me." Roman knelt on the other side of Sean. He leaned over him and shuddered.

"What's wrong?" Shanna asked.

"I'm having trouble getting my fangs to come out," he muttered.

Shanna touched his hair. "Do it for me."

Roman hesitated. "I'm trying."

"He hates you," Shanna said softly. "He told me he wants to plunge a hot poker through your heart and dance on your ashes."

"Bastard!" Roman's fangs sprang out, and he sank them into Sean.

Marielle flinched. The other Vamps nodded with approval, but she looked away.

Connor pulled her to her feet. "Ye doona need to watch. Let me get ye out of here."

"Will he be all right?" she asked.

"We willna know for sure until tomorrow night." Connor led her down the street. "Ye look like ye've been through a wringer. I'll take you back to the cabin. Ye can shower and eat."

"I can't eat."

"Then ye can rest." He touched her cheek. "Ye did verra well, sweetheart."

She shook her head. "I'm afraid I've ruined everything. The Archangels will never let me back into heaven now. I killed a living being."

"Nay, ye killed a vampire, an unholy creature who was already half dead and attacking a mortal. Yer act of bravery may have saved Shanna's father."

"I know he was a vampire, but he had a human soul, Connor, just like you. And I killed him! They'll never let me back into heaven."

"Of course they will! So ye killed one nasty, murdering Malcontent. 'Tis no' like ye slaughtered a dozen men in a fit of rage!"

She gasped.

He winced. *Bugger.* He'd gone too far. "Come on. Let's go back to the cabin." He gathered her in his arms so they could teleport.

"Wait." Her eyes narrowed. "Is that what you did, Connor? Is that the secret you've been hiding?"

Chapter Twenty-two

Bugger. She'd never let up now. For a sweet angel, she could be very stubborn. Connor ignored her question and teleported them to the cabin.

"Off ye go." He immediately herded her toward the bedroom. "Ye'll feel better after ye've had a shower."

"But I—"

"Hurry up! I need a shower, too. I'm covered with blood and guts and dead vampire dust." When she grimaced, he continued quickly, "I'm no' fit to be around. So go!" He shoved her into the bedroom and closed the door.

He breathed a sigh of relief when he heard the water running in the bathroom. How long could he keep this up?

He warmed up a bottle, then sipped the blood from a glass while he disarmed himself. The battle had gone well. As far as he could tell, they'd killed over half of Casimir's small army. And with the exception of Sean Whelan, they'd suffered no serious injuries.

It was a bloody shame they hadn't been able to save the mortals.

"Rest in peace," he murmured and drank a toast in their honor.

He wandered into the kitchen and placed his empty glass in the sink next to the bottle. In the pantry, he found a can of soup, so he warmed it up in a pot on the stove. He set an empty bowl and a spoon on the counter, then heard the water turn off.

He dashed into the closet to find a clean T-shirt and pair of flannel pants, then peered into the bedroom. Empty.

He knocked on the bathroom door. "Are ye done?"

She peeked out with a towel wrapped around her.

"My turn." He pushed the door open and sauntered inside. "Do ye have clean clothes?"

"Yes." She motioned toward the bedroom.

"Good." He maneuvered her out the door. "There's soup on the stove for you."

"You know how to cook?"

"I know how to open a bloody can. See you later." He closed the door.

"But Connor—"

He turned on the shower to drown out her voice. He stripped and stepped into the shower stall. How long could he stay in here? Three hours? He snorted.

Him and his big mouth.

He closed his eyes and let the hot water sluice down his body. He would just have to be firm.

"I confess nothing," he whispered.

Images of that night flitted through his mind, but he shoved them away. What was the point? He'd probably wasted a century of his existence, wandering aimlessly about while he wallowed in shame and regret. Eventually, he'd tried to start over. He bought a small estate in the Highlands, far away from any mortals who would see him as a shameful creature. He teleported every night to a town like Inverness or Aberdeen to steal a few pints of blood. Then he returned to his home and roamed about the grounds. Slowly, the misery and loneliness drove him to despair.

He sought out Roman, who had sired him over a hundred years earlier. And that led him to Angus, and then Jean-Luc in Paris. Their struggle against Casimir became his own. It seemed that finally, his existence had a noble purpose.

But he could never escape what he had done.

With a sigh, he grabbed the soap. Poor Marielle. She felt guilty for killing one lousy Malcontent while he'd lost count centuries ago of how many he had killed. And he never suffered any remorse for their deaths. Not when he considered how many mortals they had drained dry over the years. Besides, while he was killing Malcontents, they were generally trying their best to kill him, so it was a simple matter of self-defense.

He rinsed off. How easily he dismissed all those killings. So why was he so haunted by that one night in 1543? *It was wrong. Ye knew it was wrong, and ye did it, anyway.*

He toweled off and pulled on the clean T-shirt and flannel pants. Then he hauled the laundry hamper into the kitchen.

Marielle was setting her empty soup bowl in the sink. Her long hair was loose and damp. She was wearing plaid flannel pajamas.

"Did ye enjoy the soup?" He tossed the kitchen towels into the hamper.

"Yes, thank you. Can we talk now?"

"We need to do the laundry." He dragged the hamper into the nearby utility room and tossed some towels and clothes into the washing machine. His chest tightened at the sight of her clothes mixed with his T-shirts and socks.

She followed him into the room.

He poured some soap into the machine. "Did the ladies show you how to do this?"

"No."

He snorted. They had time to tell her about blow jobs and paint his fingernails pink. "Ye turn the knob here, then—" He froze when she leaned forward to watch, resting a hand against the machine.

Nothing happened.

"Then?" She gave him a questioning look.

Her touch no longer made something work? "Ye push the button here." He started the machine. What had happened to take away her magical touch? Was the demon right when he said the longer she stayed on Earth, the more human she would become?

Bugger. What if she ran out of time before he could get her back to heaven? A part of him didn't want her to go, but a bigger part cringed at the thought of failing her. He'd failed everyone else in the past.

"Can we talk now?" she asked.

"Nay, we need to . . . load the dishwasher." He padded into the kitchen and took his time rinsing everything in the sink before stacking it into the machine. He even scrubbed the pot he'd warmed the soup in.

When he closed the dishwasher, she was waiting there, holding a mop.

She offered it to him. "Do you want to clean the floors now? And sweep the porch? I think the antlers on the moose head need polishing."

"Are ye mocking me now?"

She leaned the mop against the kitchen cabinets. "I want to talk. I'm sure you know what I want to talk about."

"And I'm sure ye know I doona want to talk about it."

She tilted her head, studying him a moment. "Fine." She turned and went into the bedroom.

He exhaled with relief. Was it really going to be that easy?

Less than a minute later, she exited the bedroom, carrying a blanket. She'd added a jacket over her pajamas and fuzzy slippers on her feet.

No, it wasn't going to be easy. He folded his arms across his chest. "Are ye going somewhere?"

"I'd like to go back to the meadow where we made love last night. You can teleport us there, right?"

"I . . . suppose I could."

"Good. You owe me a blow job."

"What?"

She gave him an impatient look. "You said you didn't get to taste me or make me come with your mouth. I assume that offer still stands?"

His groin tightened. "I—" He ran a hand through his damp hair. The clever minx was learning very quickly how to be human. "This is yer strategy, then, to trick me into talking? I'm no' going if that's what ye're up to."

She shrugged. "Fine. I guess you don't want a blow job, either."

Seconds ticked by.

"I'll get my shoes."

A minute later, they arrived at the green meadow nestled in the midst of forested mountains.

Marielle spread the blanket on the ground, kicked off her shoes, then stretched out, gazing up at the stars.

"Do ye have any idea how beautiful ye are?" he asked softly.

She propped herself up on her elbows. "Aren't you going to lie down?"

He sighed and kicked at the ground. "I'm no' worthy of you. Ye know that. Ye've already figured out the terrible things I've done."

"I've done terrible things, too. I healed a child who grew up to become a serial killer. And tonight, I ended a life."

"In order to save another man's life. And ye healed that child out of compassion. Yer heart has always been good. Whereas mine . . ." He turned away.

"Are you ashamed? Is that why you refuse to talk about it?"

He snorted. "Shame and remorse weigh heavy on my soul, but they doona prevent me from living my life. They dinna stop me from falling for you."

"Then why are you reluctant to talk to me?"

He swallowed hard. "I'm . . . afraid."

"Of being punished? Of going to hell?"

"Nay." He turned to her. "I'm afraid of losing yer love. Yer respect. I could bear anything but that."

She remained silent for a while. "I believe I've been insulted."

"How?"

"You must think my love for you is very small. Shallow and . . . undependable."

He stiffened. "I dinna say that."

"Then try me. Give me a chance to prove myself."

"And a chance for me to lose you?"

"You won't lose me." She patted the blanket beside her. "Trust me. Please."

With a heavy heart, he sat beside her. He'd held the pain inside for so long, he hardly knew how to let it out. "If ye hate me, I willna blame you."

She rubbed his back. "You've hated yourself more than enough. I won't add to it."

He bent his legs and folded his arms across his knees. Could she still love him? With a pang, he realized he'd reached a point where he needed to know. He needed to put an end to the pain. And he needed the certainty of her love.

He took a deep breath. "I was thirty years old, proud to have my own land and a lovely young wife. But the land was along the border, and an English lord was claiming it for his own. So in 1542, I went to fight at Solway Moss."

"And that's when Roman found you dying?" Marielle asked.

"Aye. After he transformed me, he and Angus warned me no' to go home. They said my wife wouldna be able to accept me. That's what happened to Angus, ye ken. But I dinna listen. I went home, and my wife . . . she welcomed me."

"That's good." Marielle patted his back. "I'm glad."

He sighed. "At the time, I thought I was the luckiest man on Earth. There I was, a terrifying, blood-sucking creature, and she still wanted me. Now, I wonder if she really had any choice. She was six months' pregnant when I was transformed. Her parents were deceased. She had no other place to go."

"I'm sure she loved you," Marielle whispered.

" 'Twould have been better for her if she had rejected me. The news spread through the local village, and the people feared for their lives and the lives of their children. I would work the field at night, but they would come and throw stones at me and yell at me to leave. I had to find secret places for my death-sleep so they wouldna try to kill me while I slept."

"I'm so sorry."

He shrugged. "I drank blood from our livestock and worked hard on the farm. I thought after the babe was born, and the villagers realized I meant no harm to anyone, they would leave us alone. The night my wife gave birth, I was there to help her."

He hugged his knees. "I will always remember the joy I felt, holding our wee babe in my arms. I thought my heart would burst. I fell into my death-sleep thinking no man could possibly be more blessed than I."

He stood abruptly and walked away from the blanket.

"What happened?" Marielle asked.

"I awoke the next evening and rushed to the house to see how Fionnula and my daughter were faring." He shut his eyes briefly as the memory flashed through his mind. "The men from the village had killed them both."

Marielle gasped and rose to her feet. "How could they? Why would they do that?"

"They figured I was only staying there because of my wife and child. So they killed them to be rid of me."

"Connor, I'm so sorry." She touched his arm.

He scoffed. "Do ye think the story ends there? That I cried for my wife and daughter, then quietly made my leave?"

Marielle's eye widened.

"Oh, I cried, all right. I shouted and screamed. I tore the house apart. I flew into a rage that ye canna imagine. A cold rage that turned the world blue and froze the blood in my veins. I took my claymore and went to the village. And I slaughtered every man there."

Her face grew pale.

"I knew it was wrong, but I dinna care. I did it anyway."

"You were distraught," she whispered.

"That is no excuse!" He gritted his teeth. "I killed them all, and I found great satisfaction in it."

"You—you don't mean that."

"Aye, I do! There were women and children screaming in terror, begging me to stop, but I kept going till every man in the village was dead."

Tears glimmered in Marielle's eyes. "You were in terrible pain."

"Love can do terrible things." He rubbed his brow. "My wife died because she loved me. Then I took her love and the innocent love of a wee babe and twisted it into an ugly rampage for revenge. I doomed my soul."

A tear ran down Marielle's cheek. "I'm so sorry for all the pain you've endured—"

"What about the pain my wife and child endured? What about the widows and orphans I left behind? After a few nights, I realized the true impact of my crime. Women and children slowly starving to death because of me. I would go hunting every night and bring them a deer or a handful of rabbits. And they screamed in terror whenever I came. Eventually, they all left, running away from the nightmare I had foisted upon them."

He sighed. "The village disappeared. There's nothing there now but empty fields. And the grave where I laid my wife and daughter."

"I am truly sorry," she whispered. "For everyone."

He tilted his head back and gazed at the stars. His heart felt lighter just for sharing the secret of his crime, but his punishment was about to begin. Any minute now, she would rebuke him for being a cruel and vicious monster.

She was silent.

He glanced at her and saw that her eyes were shut. Tears glistened on her cheeks, and her mouth moved silently as if in prayer.

He took a deep breath, preparing himself for rejection. He'd known all along he wasn't worthy of her. It didn't stop him from loving her, though. And it wouldn't stop him from keeping his pledge.

Her eyes opened, and she regarded him sadly.

His heart squeezed. For the first time, he could see her age in her eyes. Millennia of pain, joy, and wisdom.

"I want to be clear on this," she said softly. "I never want to hear you say again that your soul is doomed. Do you think you are God that you can make such a judgment?"

He blinked. "But I am doomed. Even the demon said I was on his list."

"A demon will say everyone is on his list. But he is not God, either. The decision is not his."

Connor swallowed hard. "Ye're no' . . . appalled by what I did?"

"I am constantly appalled by what humans do. And constantly amazed." She sighed. "Why should I point out the seriousness of your transgression when you already know it? You have great remorse for what you did. You should ask our Heavenly Father to forgive you. And then begin your life anew."

"I doona deserve it."

She smiled. "You can feel that way, but He still loves you. I love you, Connor Buchanan. I will always love you."

His heart stuttered. "Ye—ye canna mean that."

She made a face. "Oh, you're right. I changed my mind. I hate your guts now."

"What?"

She swatted his shoulder. "When I say I love you, you should accept it. If you don't, then you're calling me a liar."

"Nay, I—" Tears stung his eyes. "Ye still love me?"

She gave him an impatient look. "Only a man with a good and noble heart would punish himself for centuries. Your wife and daughter would not be pleased to see you wallowing in misery."

"I'm no' wallowing," he grumbled. "I fought a battle earlier tonight."

"You've kept a black pit of suffering in you for so long, you have trouble accepting love when it falls in your lap. It's time to stop the suffering. You have a woman here who loves you." She crossed her arms with a huff. "And I'm getting really tired of waiting for my blow job."

He laughed.

She gave him one of her radiant smiles. "That's more like it. You have centuries ahead of you, Connor Buchanan. They should be filled with love and laughter."

He pulled her into his arms and buried his face in her hair, his tears mingling with her damp hair. "Ye are the light in my darkness. I love you more than I can say."

"Will you become one with me?" she whispered.

He leaned back. "We . . . canna . . ."

"I want to." She caressed his cheek, wiping his tears away. "If I ever make it back to heaven, I want to know that I gave you everything I have."

"But what if it . . . soils yer—"

She touched his mouth. "I've come to realize that joining with you could never be a soiling of our love, but a celebration of it."

His heart swelled and he squeezed her hand. "I like the way ye think."

She smiled. "I thought you would."

Marielle jolted when she felt his tongue against her private parts. Good heavens! She clutched the blanket in her fists.

Connor was amazing her with his speed and determination. In a frenzy of movement, he had undressed her and himself in just a few seconds. Then in a whirlwind of sensation, he'd tumbled her down on the blanket and kissed her all over. Her nipples were red and hard from his suckling. Her heart pounded from the wild things he'd done with his fingers. Still reeling from that climax, she'd watched him kiss his way up her bare legs to her thighs.

And then . . . his tongue. Good heavens, the things this man did with his tongue. She gasped. She moaned. She cried out for mercy, and he kept going, kept taking her higher and higher. She was spiraling toward the heavens, flying without wings. She screamed, but instead of plummeting to Earth, she landed in his arms.

"Oh, Connor." She gasped for air. Her heart thundered, and her body rocked with spasms.

He leaned over her, smiling. "No speaking in tongues?"

She smiled back. "*Magnifique.*"

"Wrap yer legs around me."

"Mmm?" She did as he asked, then jolted when she felt him pressing against her. *And the two shall become one.* "You didn't want your blow job?"

"I want inside you. Now."

"Oh."

He looked at her closely. "Did ye change yer mind?"

"No." She gasped when he nudged at her. Her grip tightened on his shoulders.

"Am I hurting you?"

She shook her head. "No. It's just strange. As an angel I never even noticed this sort of thing. It seemed so . . . unimportant. But now, it . . . it seems like a really big thing."

"Aye. It is."

She searched his eyes and saw so much love and tenderness there. "I love you."

"I love you, too." He rested his brow against hers.

He plunged into her. She gasped. He gasped, too, their breaths intermingling.

"You're inside me," she whispered, then hugged him tight with her arms and legs. Even her inner core squeezed tightly around him.

He groaned.

The small amount of pain she had felt faded away. The discomfort of feeling overly stretched melted away. She smiled. *And the two shall become one.*

She patted his back. "I'm comfortable with you now. Thank you."

"Comfortable?" He propped himself up on his elbows and frowned at her. "Ye're no' excited?"

"Excited?"

"Aye. I'm so excited, I'm about to explode."

"Oh. Of course." That was how a man spilled his seed inside a woman. "You can finish up whenever you like. I'll be fine."

"Fine?"

She smiled. "Yes."

He cursed under his breath.

She wondered what was wrong. They were one now. How could she be confused about what he was thinking if they were one?

"Ye want to feel *fine*?" He pulled out a bit, then plunged back in.

She gasped.

"Was that fine?" He ground himself against her.

"Oh!" She clenched his shoulders.

He dragged himself out slowly, then slammed back in.

She squeaked.

He set a steady pace. "Are ye feeling fine yet?"

"Yes!" Good heavens, he was doing it to her again, making her fly, but now it was even better. He was soaring with her.

He pounded into her, and when she screamed her

release, he shouted and let himself go. The feel of him climaxing inside her made her own release go on and on.

He collapsed beside her, breathing heavily.

She smiled, gazing at the stars overhead. She'd done it. She'd become one with Connor. For all eternity, she would know they were one.

Her smile faded. If the Father could forgive Connor, He might forgive her, too, and tell the Archangels to let her back into heaven.

But how could she leave Connor?

Chapter Twenty-three

*W*hen Marielle fell asleep in his arms, Connor didn't see any reason to move her. He folded the blanket over her and let her sleep, sprawled across his chest, while he gazed up at the stars.

It was a miracle she still loved him, and a part of him wanted to hold on to her forever. But it was her heart's desire to return home to heaven, and he had sworn to help her. He wouldn't break his pledge. He was haunted, though, by the thought that time was running out. If she became too human, would the Archangels accept her back?

After a few hours, she stirred. They gathered up their clothes, and he teleported them back to the cabin.

There were three missed calls on his cell phone and an angry text from Angus. *Where the hell are you?*

Connor warmed up another bottle of blood and made the call.

"Where the hell have ye been?" Angus demanded. "Ye missed our strategy meeting for tomorrow night."

"I had to guard Marielle."

"Ye could have brought her with you. And ye should have answered yer damned phone. We were worried something had happened to you."

"How is Shanna's father?" Connor asked, attempting to change the subject.

"He's in a vampire coma, but his wounds appear to be healing. We'll know for sure tomorrow night if he's going to make the transition."

"Did everyone make it through the battle all right?"

"Aye, just a few cuts and scrapes that will heal in death-sleep," Angus answered. "I ripped my kilt, and when I tried to order a new one online, they said it would be three months before I could get it."

"Three months?" Connor had never heard of it taking so long.

"Aye, apparently there's been a sudden rush on kilts. Forty-three orders from some town in New York."

Connor grinned. The lad from the ice cream shop must have told a few friends, and the news had spread.

"Anyway, I want you and Marielle here tomorrow after sunset," Angus ordered. "Everyone's gathering here at Romatech. We'll have some time to prepare before the sun sets at Mount Rushmore."

"Ye think it's a trap?" Connor asked.

"Aye. So we'll be arriving in two different groups. If the first group is trapped, the second group should be able to set things straight."

"Makes sense to me. See you tomorrow." Connor rang off.

He settled on the couch next to Marielle. "We know where to find Casimir tomorrow. Ye could stay here—"

"I want to be with you."

He brushed her hair back over her shoulders. "I hate to put you at risk."

"I have to be there when Casimir and the Malcontents are defeated." She rested her head on his shoulder. "I don't think it's a coincidence that Casimir asked you all to come to Mount Rushmore. I lost my wings near there. I believe I will get them back at the same place."

He groaned inwardly. Then she was hoping to leave him tomorrow night. He was sorely tempted to beg her to stay with him. But how could he? How could he expect her to give up an eternity in heaven for the short life of a mortal? If he truly loved her, he would let her go.

"Not again," Marielle grumbled when Connor handed her a dagger.

"Aye, ye're no' going without a weapon." He strapped a belt around her waist.

It was Marielle's seventh day on Earth, the day humans called Friday. Just before dawn, the ladies had brought Brynley to the cabin as usual, and she had guarded the cabin during the day.

Just after sunset, Connor had emerged from the closet and guzzled down a bottle of blood. Now he was arming himself and Marielle before teleporting to Romatech.

"I want to go, too!" Brynley announced. "I kicked ass last night."

Connor gave her a worried look. "Can ye shift again tonight?"

"Yes! I can shift for three nights at the time of a full moon. Tell Phineas to get his tight ass over here and pick me up."

Connor arched a brow. "I'll pass yer message on to him." He grabbed on to Marielle. "Let's go."

"Don't forget about me!" Brynley shouted. "I'll kick Phineas's ass if he doesn't . . ."

Everything went black, and Brynley's shouts faded away. Marielle stumbled when they arrived on the grounds at Romatech.

"Come." Connor led her through the side entrance.

So many Vamps were arriving, the MacKay security office and hallway were jammed.

"Once ye're fully armed, go the cafeteria!" Angus shouted.

Marielle accompanied Connor to the cafeteria. He introduced her to other Vamps along the way: Jack, Zoltan, Mikhail, Kyo, and a man Connor referred to as Russell, the new guy. They had come from Eastern Europe, Russia, and Japan, and Connor explained how they'd spent hours teleporting west and following the moon in order to be at Romatech at the correct time.

Then he introduced her to Jean-Luc, Dougal, J.L., Rafferty, and Colbert. They lived in Texas, California, and Louisiana, so they had spent the night at Romatech.

Connor was introducing her to the cat shifters, Carlos and Rajiv, when she spotted Phineas and waved him over.

"Yo, what's up?" Phineas did a knuckle pound with Connor.

Marielle lifted her fist, and with a grin, Phineas tapped her knuckles softly. "Looking good, angel."

"Brynley wants to fight again," Connor said. "Do ye have time to teleport her here?"

Marielle tried to remember Brynley's exact words. "She said you should get your tight ass over there and pick her up."

Phineas's eyes widened. "Is that what she said?"

Connor snorted and gave Marielle a wry look.

"I was trying to be accurate," Marielle replied. "I believe those were her exact words."

"Tight, huh?" Phineas smirked. His cell phone rang and he pulled it out of his pocket. "That's probably her now." He put the phone up to his ear and deepened the tone of his voice. "Hello, baby. The Love Doctor is at your service."

He jumped. "Oh, hi, Angus. Sir. Yes, sir. I'm right on it." He turned off the phone. "Shit!"

"What's wrong?" Connor asked.

"Stan's emergency button went off in the office," Phineas grumbled, his face showing a hint of red. "I have to see what's going on." He vanished.

"Who is Stan?" Marielle asked. She didn't like the worried look on Connor's face.

"Stanislav is our mole at the Russian coven in Brooklyn," Connor explained. "Maybe he knows something about Casimir's plan for tonight."

"You still believe it's a trap?"

Connor shrugged. "It could be. But Casimir is still in a bad position. He lost over half of his men last night. We have plenty of excellent fighters, so we shouldna let this chance go by. The bastard needs to be killed once and for all."

Marielle nodded. There was no denying the fact that the world would be a much safer place once Casimir was gone. "Oh, there's Roman."

As Roman walked into the cafeteria, he was greeted with multiple questions about his wife and father-in-law.

Roman raised his hands to quiet down the crowd. "I just left Shanna and her father. He's doing as well as can be expected. His stomach wound is completely healed."

"What about his rotten personality?" Jean-Luc asked.

Roman snorted. "I'm afraid there's no cure for that."

"Is he pissed?" Jack asked.

Roman smiled. "He's adjusting. He had one bottle of blood, then asked for some Blissky. He's . . . upset, but not just because he's Undead now. He's angry about missing the battle tonight."

Roman worked his way through the crowd, greeting the Vamps and shifters. He pulled out his cell phone and frowned at it, then approached Marielle and Connor. He smiled at her, then nodded his head at Connor.

Connor nodded back.

Marielle sighed. Things were obviously still tense between the two men.

"Shanna asked me to thank you for your help in saving her father's life," Roman told her.

"I am so pleased he is doing well," she replied.

"Shanna was too upset last night to realize what you had done." Roman gave her a sympathetic look. "I'm sure it was not an easy thing for you to do."

Marielle nodded. She didn't want to admit her fear that taking a vampire's life had ruined her chances of returning to heaven.

"After we returned here last night, Father Andrew came by to console Shanna and pray with her," Roman continued. "He has an unusual view on the situation. He believes you were meant to save Sean, just like you did me, and that your destiny will continue to be linked with ours."

Marielle glanced at Connor. "Perhaps." She still wasn't quite sure she could actually leave him.

Connor's eyebrows lifted with a questioning look.

Roman glanced at his phone again and sighed. "I don't know why he's not answering. There must be some sort of emergency at his church."

"Ye're trying to call Father Andrew?" Connor asked.

"Yes." Roman frowned. "He should be here by now. He wanted to give us a blessing before we go."

"Is everyone ready?" Angus shouted as he entered the cafeteria.

Everyone let out a loud whoop.

"Take a seat," Angus ordered. When everyone was seated, he continued, "Ye've either been assigned to my team or the second much larger team, led by Robby. The second team, comprised of Vamps and shifters, will arrive ten minutes after the first. So if we get in trouble, first team, remember we have to last ten minutes."

Connor took Marielle's hand and squeezed it.

"Phil has contacted his werewolf friends in the area, and they have set up a beacon in a wooded area close to the monument," Angus explained. "That is our focal point for teleporting."

Phineas rushed into the cafeteria, and everyone sat up.

"News?" Angus asked.

"Yes," Phineas replied. "Stan reports that Nadia received a call from Casimir. She and her coven have been ordered to go into battle."

Angus nodded. "Casimir is desperate to increase his number."

"Stan said if he has to kill anybody, it'll be a Malcontent," Phineas continued. "So he's asking everybody here to remember which side he's on and not to kill him."

Angus snorted. "So the main reason he called you is he's worried about his own skin."

Phineas shrugged. "Partly. He's also worried about Nadia. Casimir has given her a special assignment to carry out. Stan doesn't know what it is, but he says she's dizzy with excitement over it."

Angus muttered a curse under his breath.

Phineas stiffened. "Oh, I gotta go."

Angus frowned. "We're about to leave."

"I'll hurry. Big bad wolfie-girl needs a ride." Phineas vanished.

"Is he talking about my sister?" Phil called out.

Everyone chuckled.

Seconds later, the Vamps and shifters all turned to look out the cafeteria window. Marielle assumed it was due to their superior hearing, since she hadn't heard anything.

Outside by the basketball court, Phineas had returned with Brynley. An angry Brynley who was shouting at Phineas. She shoved him, then he grabbed her arm and dragged her to the cafeteria door.

"Don't ever leave me waiting like that again!" Brynley yelled as Phineas opened the door.

"Don't ever attack me again!" Phineas pushed her inside.

Brynley raised a hand to strike him, but he caught her wrist.

"Snout-face," he hissed.

"Bloodsucker," she growled.

Angus cleared his throat.

Brynley looked around and saw everyone watching them. Her face turned a shade of pink, but she gave them a big smile. "Hi there! I'm ready to fight."

"We can see that," Angus said dryly. "Brynley, ye're on Team Two. Phineas, ye're Team One."

Phineas nodded and released Brynley's wrist. "Be careful," he mumbled.

She cast a worried look his direction. "You, too."

A timer went off, its peeping noise filling the cafeteria.

Angus punched a button on his wristwatch, then motioned for his wife, Emma, to join him. "That's it. The sun has set on Mount Rushmore. Team One, time to move out."

Marielle accompanied Connor to where the first team was gathering.

Shanna dashed into the cafeteria and ran to her husband in the first group. "Are you leaving now?"

"Yes." Roman embraced her and kissed her brow. "Did Father Andrew make it?" When Shanna shook her head, he looked at Marielle. "Would you say a blessing for us?"

"Of course." Marielle nodded, not wanting to admit that she feared her prayers were no longer heeded. Last night, she'd begged in vain for a Healer to help Sean Whelan.

She cleared her throat. "May the Lord bless us and keep us. May His light shine upon us, and may He return us all safely to our loved ones."

Everyone mumbled an *amen*. Some crossed themselves.

Marielle hugged Connor tight. "Please, be careful."

"If it gets ugly, hide in the woods. Stay alive." He kissed her temple.

Roman cleared his throat.

Marielle turned to see him and Shanna watching her and Connor curiously.

"I have to hold her to teleport her," Connor grumbled.

"I have to hold him, too." Marielle slipped her arms around his neck.

"Why do you have to go?" Shanna asked her.

"I have to do my part to make sure Casimir is defeated," Marielle replied. "I believe it will convince the Archangels to let me back into heaven. And I don't think it's a coincidence that this is happening by Mount Rushmore, where I lost my wings. It should be where I can get them back."

"Oh, I see." Shanna gave her a sad look. "Then you might be leaving us tonight?"

"Perhaps." Marielle felt Connor's arm tighten around her. "I can't be sure this will work."

Shanna embraced her, then hugged her husband again.

"Ye think ye're leaving tonight?" Connor whispered.

"I'm not sure. I don't really know if I can ever get back."

"But if they come for you tonight, ye'll go?"

The thought of leaving Connor brought tears to her eyes. "I guess."

"That was why ye wanted to be with me last night. Ye thought it was our last chance?"

She blinked away the tears and nodded. "I will always love you, Connor."

"Time to go," Angus announced.

Connor pulled her tight in a fierce hug, then everything went black.

Chapter Twenty-four

*C*onnor eased forward and peered around a tree. Casimir and a small group of his minions were at the base of Mount Rushmore on a small stage. In front of them, aluminum bleachers ascended a hill to the lookout terraces and buildings that housed gift shops and restaurants for tourists.

He spotted Corky and her cameraman midway up the hill on the first lookout terrace. Below her, people sat on the bleachers. Some were Malcontents holding knives. Others were mortal, and by the blank looks on their faces, he assumed they were all under vampire mind control.

He moved quietly past Casimir's inept guards, then dashed back to Angus and the first team.

"Hostages," he whispered. "About fifty-five mortals. Sitting on bleachers, eleven to each row. Behind each row of mortals, there's a row of Malcontents, armed with knives."

Emma winced. "If we attack, they'll start killing the mortals."

"Casimir is surrounded by five bodyguards," Connor continued. "There are three guards on this side just inside the woods, and probably a few more on the other side. We should take out them out first."

Angus nodded. "Jean-Luc, take three men and teleport to the other side. Kill any guards over there. Quietly."

"Got it." Jean-Luc motioned for Dougal, Ian, and Phineas to follow him. The four men sped up the hill.

"I'll surrender to Casimir," Roman whispered.

Angus flinched. "Nay."

"I'm the one he wants the most," Roman argued. "I'll offer myself if he lets the mortals go. It'll buy us some time till the second team arrives, and if we can get the hostages released, then our guys can attack."

Angus sighed. "We'll do that as a last resort. First, let's get rid of the guards."

"I'll show you where they are," Connor whispered as he pulled a dagger from the sheath beneath his knee sock.

He weaved through the woods back toward the monument. Angus, Emma, Roman, and Marielle moved alongside him. He stopped when he spotted the three guards.

A twig snapped beneath Marielle's foot, and the guards turned toward them. She hit them with a blast of air, but it barely knocked them back a few feet.

Connor noted the shocked look on her face before he threw his dagger. It thudded into the heart of the first guard, turning him to dust.

Before the second guard could yell out a warning, the third one snapped his neck and plunged a knife into his heart.

Angus froze, his arm raised and ready to throw his dagger.

The third guard dropped his knife and held up his hands. "Don't kill me," he whispered in heavily accented English. "I am Stanislav."

"Aye." Angus lowered his arm. "What can ye tell us?"

"Casimir thinks you will surrender to save mortals." Stan looked them over, frowning. "Is all the men you have?"

"Nay," Angus said.

Stan nodded. "Casimir make big mistake. He set Malcontents behind mortals to slit throats, but last row is all Malcontents. We teleport behind them—"

"And take out the whole row at once. Good plan." Angus removed his cell phone from his sporran. "I'll text the plan to Jean-Luc, and see if they've finished off the guards."

While Angus waited for a reply, Connor turned to Marielle. "What happened to yer blast?" he whispered.

She winced. "I'm afraid I'm losing my power."

She was becoming human. And far too vulnerable to be here. "Stay here in the woods," he told her.

"The other side is ready. Let's go." Angus motioned for his team to follow.

Connor glanced back to make sure Marielle was staying put. She lifted a hand in a halfhearted wave.

They moved up the hill to be even with the last row of bleachers. A flash of light came from the woods on the other side. Jean-Luc and his group were ready.

With their swords drawn, the Vamps teleported behind the last row of Malcontents and stabbed them all through the chest.

Casimir and his bodyguards yelled, and the rest of his army faced the Vamps with weapons drawn. The mortals sat eerily still and facing front, their minds still under control.

"Drop your weapons!" Casimir yelled at them. "Drop them or I start killing mortals!"

The Vamps hesitated.

One of Casimir's bodyguards pointed at Stanislav. "Traitor!"

Casimir's eyes narrowed. He held his left arm close to his chest, bent at a strange angle with a glove on his left hand, but with his other arm, he motioned to another bodyguard. The guard casually walked up to the bleachers and slit a mortal's throat.

Connor cursed silently.

"Do I need to kill another?" Casimir asked.

Roman dropped his sword with a clatter. "I surrender. It's me you want. Let the mortals go."

Casimir smirked. "I'll let a mortal go for each one of you who dies."

Connor glanced at his watch. The second team would arrive in a few minutes. They needed to stall. They'd killed off more than a dozen of Casimir's men, but he still had forty more.

"I doona believe ye'll let any of the mortals go," Angus shouted.

"I'll prove it." Casimir pointed at Roman. "After I kill you, I'll let the first one go."

"Agreed." Roman walked slowly down the steps toward the stage.

Casimir grinned and glanced up at Corky. "Be sure to get this recorded. I want to watch Roman's death every night."

"Will do, sweetheart!" Corky yelled back.

Roman reached the stage.

"Check him for weapons," Casimir ordered.

Two of his bodyguards frisked Roman and found two knives, which they tossed onto the stage.

Casimir snorted. "Did you think you were going to kill me, monk? You were always a weakling." He motioned to his guards. "Bring him closer. Make sure he's facing the camera."

The guards dragged Roman over to Casimir.

Connor checked his watch. *Bugger.* Still two minutes to go. He caught Angus's eye and motioned with his head toward the stage.

Angus nodded.

Connor teleported to the stage along with Angus, and they killed two bodyguards.

Casimir clutched Roman with his gloved hand and moved Roman in front of him as a shield. "Kill three mortals!"

Three Malcontents in the bleachers slit the throats of their captives. The remaining mortals still sat there, expressionless.

"Drop your weapons, or I'll kill three more!" Casimir shouted.

Connor and Angus tossed their swords on the stage. A group of Malcontents ran up onto the stage. Some grabbed their swords and took their weapons, while others seized them and pinned their arms behind their backs.

Casimir smiled. "Angus and Connor. Thank you for joining us. Now I can record myself killing you when I'm done with Roman." With his good arm, he put a knife to Roman's throat. "Are you recording, Corky?"

Corky screamed as her cameraman suddenly fell off the balcony and plummeted twenty feet to the next level.

Connor spotted Marielle slipping back behind a tree. She must have blasted enough air to make the cameraman fall.

Corky levitated down to her fallen cameraman. "You stupid fool!" She whipped out a knife and stabbed him, turning him to dust. "How dare you fail our king!"

She picked up the camera and grinned. "It's still working, sweetheart!"

"Thank you, my queen." Casimir glanced at Angus when a beeping sound came from his watch. "What is that?"

"The sound of yer final defeat," Angus replied.

With a loud whooping noise, Vamps and shifters erupted from the woods. The Malcontents forgot all about slaying their mortal victims when they saw a huge Kodiak bear, five wolves, a panther, and a tiger charging toward them.

Screams, roars, and the clashing of swords filled the air. Connor ripped Roman from Casimir's grasp. Casimir jumped back, flailing his knife. Connor looked about for a weapon. He recalled the sword he'd left at the top of the monument, but that was too far away. Empty-handed, he jumped at Casimir, but the coward vanished.

"Dammit!" Connor ducked when a Malcontent took a swing at him with his sword.

On the bleachers, the mortals came to and began screaming. Casimir's mind control over them had broken when he teleported away.

"You will drop your weapons!" Casimir bellowed from the top of Mount Rushmore. "Drop them or I will kill your priest!"

Connor looked up and gasped.

The fighting stopped. The mortals ran screaming up the stairs to the exit.

Casimir stood on top of George Washington's head, his knife in his right hand. Nadia was dragging Father Andrew toward him.

"Oh God, no," Roman breathed.

"Drop your weapons and surrender!" Casimir screamed as he pulled Father Andrew close.

"Don't do it," the priest yelled.

Roman tossed down the weapon he had managed to grab from a fallen Malcontent. "Let him go! Take me instead!"

The Vamps dropped their weapons. The Malcontents pointed their swords at them.

Casimir glared at them. "Now swear your allegiance to me."

"Let him go!" Roman yelled. "Let him go, and I'll swear."

"No!" Father Andrew shouted. "Don't do it, Roman!"

Casimir laughed. "This reminds me of the good old days. You remember, don't you, Roman? Remember the time when I invaded your old monastery and killed all the monks? All those innocent old men who had raised you?"

Roman paled.

Casimir sneered down at him. "I'm going to kill you anyway, so I might as well watch you suffer first." He stabbed Father Andrew in the chest and tossed him off the monument.

"*No!*" Roman levitated up to catch the priest in his arms.

Rage erupted in Connor, snapping his vision blue, freezing the blood in his veins. He teleported to the top of the monument and grabbed the claymore he'd left behind a week ago. With a war cry, he beheaded Nadia.

Casimir whirled around. His eyes widened with fear.

"Stop!" Corky shouted.

Connor glanced back, his vision still tinted blue.

Corky had teleported to the top of the mountain with the camera. "If you kill him, I will spread the video all over the Internet and tell everyone that vampires are real." She lifted the camera. "I'm recording now."

"Drop your sword," Casimir hissed. "You don't want the whole world to know about us. It would be the end of us all."

Connor shook with rage. He turned to Casimir. "It is yer end tonight." He stabbed him through the chest and turned Casimir to dust.

"No!" Corky screamed.

Connor whipped around to kill her, too, but she vanished, taking the camera with her.

Marielle screamed when she saw Father Andrew stabbed and thrown off the cliff.

"Bunny! Can you hear me? Please come. Please save him." She repeated her plea over and over as she scrambled down the hill, dodging the trees.

Meanwhile, the battle had started up again. Vamps and shifters attacked the Malcontents, shouting and roaring their fury. Thank God the mortals were managing to flee.

She reached the bottom and weaved her way through the fighting to where Roman knelt on the stage with Father Andrew in his arms.

"Father!" Marielle fell to her knees beside him. Tears filled her eyes. "I'm praying for a Healer to come. Please stay with us!"

Roman had a bloodstained hand pressed against the Father's wound, but blood was still seeping out. "Let me take you to a hospital."

The priest shook his head. His face was pale and clammy with sweat. "My time has come."

"Don't say that!" Roman shouted. "Oh God help me, I should have never dragged you into my world."

Father Andrew gave him a weak smile. "I don't regret a moment of it."

Connor materialized beside Marielle, his face haggard.

She reached up to touch him. "Are you all right?"

He shook his head slightly as he regarded the priest. "I have avenged you. I hope it will give you peace."

"You killed Casimir?" Roman asked.

Father Andrew coughed, then lifted a trembling hand to Connor. "My son, you know what I really want from you."

Connor's mouth twisted, then he fell to his knees and clasped the priest's hand. "Forgive me, Father, for I have sinned. It has been . . . almost five hundred years since my last confession."

"Tell me," Father Andrew whispered.

A tear rolled down Connor's cheek. "I . . . have murdered in a fit of rage." He glanced up to the top of the monument. "Twice."

Father Andrew nodded. "I will pray for you." He looked at Marielle. "Now I wish to finally be touched by an angel."

"Father, no." Tears streamed down her cheek.

Blood trickled from the side of his mouth. "I'm in pain, child. Please let me go."

Marielle glanced at Roman through her tears, and he nodded. A pink tear ran down his face.

"Dear soul, your Father loves you greatly." Marielle laid a trembling hand on the priest's brow.

He didn't die. His soul didn't open for her. He merely sighed and fell into a painless coma. With a gasp, she lifted her hand. Was she no longer a Deliverer?

"Marielle." Zackriel appeared close by. "I have come for this soul."

"Have I ceased to be an angel?" she whispered.

"Who are you talking to?" Roman asked.

Zackriel knelt beside her. "You are very close to being completely human."

Another tear slipped down her face. "You're not taking me with you tonight, are you?"

"It is not yet your time." Zackriel rested a hand on Father Andrew's brow. "Dear soul, your Father loves you greatly."

Marielle saw the priest's soul open and his spirit lift out. Zackriel stood and moved close to the spiritual form of Father Andrew who was smiling at her, Connor, and Roman.

She stood and bowed to the priest. "God be with you, dear soul."

Zackriel wrapped an arm around the priest. "It is time for us to go."

"Will I ever be able to go back?" Marielle asked.

Zackriel smiled at her sadly. "It is still possible. But only if you really want to." His wings fluttered out, and he vanished, taking Father Andrew's soul with him.

"What just happened?" Connor asked.

Marielle gazed up at the stars while tears rolled down her face. "Father Andrew is going to heaven."

Chapter Twenty-five

*A*n hour later, they were all back in the cafeteria at Romatech. Marielle sat quietly in a corner, watching the friends she had made in the seven nights that she'd been on Earth. They had succeeded in defeating the Malcontents, but there was no celebrating.

The Vamps sipped from bottles of Blissky and Bleer. The shifters indulged in real whisky and beer.

After Connor had teleported her back, he'd hugged her fiercely. "I thought ye were leaving."

"Not tonight."

He slumped into a cafeteria chair. For the last hour, he hadn't moved or spoken a word.

At the end of the battle, the Vamps and shifters had quietly cleared away all signs of the struggle. Piles of dead vampire dust were swept into the woods. Weapons were gathered and returned to Romatech. Bloodstains were washed away. A group of

Vamps swept through the area, looking for mortals and wiping their memories of the night's events.

Roman had teleported Father Andrew's body back to his church. Now he returned to the cafeteria, his eyes red and swollen.

Shanna ran up to embrace him. Her eyes were red and swollen, too. "What did you tell the other priests?"

Roman sighed. "That he was attacked by a criminal."

Shanna nodded. "I suppose that's true."

Phineas slammed his Blissky bottle down. "At least we got rid of Casimir once and for all."

Heads turned to look at Connor.

He remained silent, gazing blindly into space.

"Do ye think Corky will really do it?" Ian asked.

"Do what?" Radinka asked.

Ian shifted in his chair. "Corky had a camera. She threatened to expose our existence on the Internet if Casimir was killed."

"Damn," Gregori muttered. "I'll get a laptop and see if anything has come up." He dashed from the room.

Connor's jaw shifted, and he rubbed his brow.

Marielle was relieved just to see him move. He'd been motionless for nearly an hour.

"Well, I think Connor did the right thing," Phineas mumbled.

The room grew silent.

"I agree," Brynley said. "Connor had a chance, and he took it. Who knows when another chance would have come up?"

Another silence stretched out.

Gregori returned with a laptop and began scouring the Internet.

The shifters wandered into the kitchen to look for some food.

Roman drank some Blissky. "Father Andrew's funeral will most likely happen during the day. We won't even get to see it."

Shanna patted his arm. "We'll have a memorial for him here."

Roman stood and lifted his glass. "To Father Andrew. May we remember him always, and may he rest in peace."

Everyone stood and lifted his glass to Father Andrew. Then silence pervaded the room once more.

"Oh shit," Gregori muttered, drawing everyone's attention. "Corky posted a video on YouTube." He clicked on it, and Corky's strident voice filled the room.

"Here it is! Proof positive that vampires are real! See the blue glowing eyes on the vampire with the sword? And see what happens when he kills the other vampire? Dust!"

Brynley snorted. "No one's going to believe that. No one will even see it."

Gregori winced. "It's been up three minutes, and it already has a thousand views. If it goes viral, we could be screwed."

Connor stood abruptly and exited the glass door into the garden.

Marielle followed him. "Connor!"

He headed toward the woods.

"Connor, please. Talk to me."

He slowed to a stop.

He kept his back to her, but she could see the tension in his stiff spine and clenched fists. "I know you're upset."

"Do ye have any idea what I have done?" He spun around to face her. His eyes were filled with pain. "I have sentenced all my friends to death."

She flinched. "It can't be that bad."

"It is. For as long as vampires have existed, our first priority has been to keep our existence a secret." He snorted. "God, how many times have I preached that to my friends? I would have never believed that I would be the one . . ."

She stepped toward him. "We'll figure something out."

"The world will want to destroy us." Connor's mouth twisted with pain. "I have failed my friends. I have failed everyone I have ever known."

Her vision blurred with tears. "Connor, please. Don't do this to yourself."

He squared his shoulders. "But I willna fail you. I will get you back to heaven." He vanished.

"No!" She ran forward, but he was gone. "Connor! Connor!" She collapsed on the ground, crying.

What if she had lost everything? Connor. Her wings. Her heavenly home.

Eventually, she heaved herself to her feet and walked back to the cafeteria.

"I am so sick of crying." She wiped her face. She felt old. And tired. And human.

She let herself back into the cafeteria.

Everyone was talking about the new problem. Someone had turned on the television, and a news station was reporting on the video. A ticker ran across the bottom of the screen. *Vampires are proven real!*

Sean Whelan strode into the cafeteria. "Quiet! This is no time to panic."

The room grew silent.

Sean glared at the television. "What a stupid mess. I'll get ahold of my contacts in the government and get them to declare this whole thing a hoax."

"Will they do that?" Roman asked.

Sean snorted. "They'll do anything for a price. I may have to let a few key people know that vampires are real, but I'll make it to their advantage to keep the secret."

Angus's eyes narrowed. "Why would ye help us, Whelan?"

He glowered at Angus, then at Roman. "Because I'm one of you now." He turned and marched toward the exit. "I'll start negotiations immediately."

"We're coming with you." Angus and Emma dashed after him.

Everyone started talking again, but this time there was a hint of hope in the air.

Marielle sighed. If only Connor had stayed.

The next night, Marielle wandered through the garden at Romatech. Her eyes felt dry as sand from too much crying. Her heart thudded with a constant throb of pain.

For the first time in her existence, she understood the pain of mourning. Before, she took souls to heaven, and it was a time of joy and reunion.

Now she felt the separation. Sharp and severe. Father Andrew was truly gone from this world.

And where was Connor? Was he alone and suffering? Had he retreated into his black pit of despair and remorse?

She walked through the rose garden, plucking a rose here and there. The other Vamps and shifters had gone on to their homes. She had spent the night at Romatech. Shanna had given her a room in the basement, for she had nowhere else to go.

She found a cement bench beneath a tree and sat. Her heart ached for all her new friends who were grieving. Her heart ached for Connor. Why didn't he contact her? Didn't he know she loved him, and he didn't need to suffer alone?

"How are you?" Shanna asked as she approached.

Marielle sighed. "Tired of crying."

"I know how you feel." Shanna collapsed beside her on the bench. "It's Saturday night, and there's no Mass. What will we do without Father Andrew?"

"I picked these flowers for him." Marielle lifted the bouquet.

"They're lovely. We'll put them in a vase in the chapel."

She lowered the bouquet, and her shoulders slumped. "They're still alive. They didn't turn brown and die."

Shanna regarded her curiously. "Were you expecting them to?"

Marielle nodded. "That's what used to happen when I was a Deliverer."

"You're no longer an angel of death?"

Tears stung her eyes. *Not again.* "I don't think I'm an angel at all."

Shanna drew in a sharp breath, then rested a hand on Marielle's back. "I'm so sorry."

Marielle wiped a tear away.

"Is it so terrible to be human?" Shanna asked.

"It's . . . hard."

"I know, sweetie." Shanna rubbed her back. "You don't think you can go back to heaven?"

Marielle sighed. "Zackriel said it was possible."

"Well, there, you see!" Shanna smiled. "You mustn't give up hope."

"I had thought that helping to defeat Casimir would get me back to heaven, but I was wrong. Zackriel said I could go back if I really wanted to, but I don't know how."

Shanna's eyes narrowed. "If you really want to. Maybe that's the problem." She gave Marielle a pointed look. "Do you really want to?"

A chill skittered down her spine, and her skin pebbled with gooseflesh. Good heavens. Was it doubt that was keeping her earthbound? No, not doubt.

Love. Love for Connor.

Sunday night, shortly after sunset, Marielle woke to a banging on her bedroom door at Romatech. She peered outside and found Angus and Emma.

"Connor just called," Angus told her. "He wants me to take you to him."

"Oh." Her heart lurched.

"Dress quickly," Emma said. "You need to leave right away."

"Yes! Yes, of course." She shut the door and ran to the bathroom. Connor wanted to see her! She washed her face, brushed her teeth and hair, and tossed on some clean clothes that Shanna had given her. She stuffed her feet into shoes, grabbed her jacket, and ran into the hallway.

"Good." Angus grabbed her around the waist. "I have to teleport you there."

"Good luck," Emma said with a worried look.

"Is something wrong?" Marielle asked.

Angus sighed. "He dinna sound good on the phone. Hold on to me, lass."

She grabbed his shoulders. "Where are we going?"

"Connor's home in Scotland," Angus replied, then everything went black.

Chapter Twenty-six

*M*arielle ran across a pasture in the moonlight. Angus had dropped her off by a large house of gray stone. Then he had pointed north.

"Connor said he would be at the henge. That way, over the hill." Angus gave her a worried look. "I'll come back tomorrow night to make sure ye're all right." He vanished.

Marielle was gasping for air by the time she reached the hill. It was chilly here in Scotland, but the run had warmed her up. She climbed the hill, wading through heather that reached her knees. The blossoms opened and filled her nostrils with a sweet scent. She reached the top of the hill and stopped.

It was beautiful. A green meadow stretched out below her, surrounded by mountains. Stars sparkled overhead. In the middle of the meadow, a circle of gray stones stood. She spotted a lone figure in the middle.

"Connor!"

He turned toward her. He smiled, although his face looked pale and tense.

She ran down the hill to the henge. The stones were ancient and beautiful, and she rested a hand against one while she caught her breath.

A surge of warmth swept up her arm. It was the stone, recognizing her as another ancient entity. She leaned against it, and it loaned her some strength. Beneath her hand, a small patch of brown withered lichen turned green.

She blinked. Were her healing powers back?

"Are ye all right, lass?" Connor asked.

"Ah—yes." She pushed away from the stone. "I've been worried about you."

"I had some matters to take care of." He squared his shoulders and lifted his chin as if he were going into battle. "Marielle. It has been a week since I found you, but the love I have for you will last forever."

She walked slowly toward him. "I love you, too." A frisson of alarm crept up her spine. Something was wrong.

"I made a promise to you, and I found a way to keep it." He smiled, but the pain in his eyes made her stop.

"What have you done, Connor?"

He motioned behind him.

Darafer stepped around a stone and into the circle, his green eyes gleaming with victory.

She gasped. "No."

"I discovered if I called them by name, they would come." Connor motioned to his right.

Zackriel and Buniel moved into the stone circle.

"Connor," she whispered. "What are you doing?"

"I'm making things right. Darafer said he had the power to erase all the news about vampires. 'Twill make the world safe again for my friends."

She trembled. "Don't believe him."

"And it dinna really cost me anything." His back stiffened with determination. "I was on the list for hell, anyway."

She shook her head. Tears crowded her eyes. "Don't do it. I'm begging you. Don't go with him."

Connor's eyes filled with tears. "I'm sorry. 'Tis the only way."

Darafer stepped forward and his black wings unfurled. He stretched a hand out to Connor. "Come with me now."

"No!" Marielle screamed.

Connor turned to the demon. "There is one condition. Ye will never attempt to take Marielle to hell again." He looked at the angels. "And if I go to hell, ye have to take her back to heaven with you."

Darafer cursed and slammed a fist against one of the stones. His wings folded in with a snap.

Zackriel smiled.

Buniel chuckled. "You'll never get to hell that way, Connor."

Zackriel nodded. "There's only one condition where a demon is not allowed to take a willing soul to hell— when that soul is sacrificing himself to save another."

"But—" Connor stepped toward the angels. "Ye have to take her back."

A blinding white light filled the henge, and Marielle squeezed her eyes shut.

When the light softened, she opened her eyes and saw an Archangel floating down to the ground.

"Gabriel," she whispered.

Connor moved close to her, a stunned look on his face. "Is—is he here to take you back to heaven?"

"I don't know." She bowed her head to honor the Archangel.

Connor noticed her doing it and bowed, too.

Gabriel inclined his head toward Marielle. "Dear angel, our Father loves you greatly." He smiled. "You were never abandoned. He has been with you always."

"Are you saying she's no longer banished?" Buniel asked.

"She never was truly banished," Gabriel said. "She has always done exactly as her Father hoped she would do."

Darafer snorted. "I told her she was being used."

Gabriel gave the demon a hard stare.

Darafer shifted his weight and grimaced with a pained look.

Gabriel turned back to Marielle. "If you are concerned that you have somehow been manipulated, I can assure you that you have not. It is true that the Father hoped you would do as you have over the centuries, and it is also true that the Father created you with an inclination to rebel and do as you have done. But you also have free will, and your decisions were always your own. Because they were your own, that makes them even more precious to the Father. He is most pleased with you."

Tears slipped down her cheeks. "Thank you."

"Blessed is he who finds his destiny and fulfills it." Gabriel gave Darafer a pointed look.

Darafer turned pale. "I'm out of here." His wings unfurled and he vanished.

"If Marielle was never banished, then she can go back to heaven?" Connor asked, glancing nervously at the Archangel.

"She can if she wishes to." Gabriel smiled. "Connor Buchanan. It was never about Marielle's redemption. It was about yours."

He flinched.

Gabriel laid a hand on Connor's head. "Dear soul, the Father loves you greatly."

"I can be forgiven?" Connor whispered.

"You have proven yourself worthy. Ask the Father and you will receive." Gabriel stepped back and looked at Marielle. "Have you made your decision?"

She nodded and wiped away her tears. "I'm staying here with Connor."

"What?" Connor turned to her. "No! Ye canna do that."

"It is my decision."

"Nay. I willna let ye do it. Ye canna give up heaven for me. It is yer home."

She smiled. "My home is here with you."

"No! Ye canna give up yer immortality. I canna forgive myself if ye die because of me. I lost one wife that way. I canna bear to do it again!"

"Hush!" Gabriel gave them an annoyed look. "This is a simple matter. Marielle Quadriduum, do you wish to take Connor Buchanan as your husband?"

"I do."

"And Connor, will you have Marielle as your wife?"

"Aye, but—"

"Enough!" Gabriel placed his hands on their heads. "You will be husband and wife, each living as long as the other and remaining as you are now." He stepped back. "Are we done now?"

"She—she's still immortal?" Connor asked.

"As much as you are." Gabriel gave him a wry look. "You can still die, but I'm not in any hurry to see you again."

"Thank you." Marielle bowed.

Gabriel grinned. "Thank you. Our Father is greatly pleased." He spread his wings and with a flash of light, disappeared.

"Congratulations!" Buniel ran forward to hug Marielle.

Zackriel approached her slowly. "I hope you can forgive me. I was told to take your wings. I didn't want to hurt you, but I was hoping you would help bring about Casimir's defeat." He smiled at her. "Well done, Marielle."

"Thank you, Zack."

He inclined his head. "May your days be blessed." His wings unfurled and he vanished.

"You're married!" Buniel grinned at her.

She laughed. "I guess I am." She glanced at Connor,

who appeared stunned. "You're all right with that, aren't you?"

"Aye." He ran a hand through his hair. "Holy Chri— Sorry." He gave them an apologetic look. "I thought I was going to end up in hell tonight."

"You are," Buniel joked. "It's called marriage."

Marielle swatted Buniel on the shoulder. "How dare you. Marriage is a holy sacrament."

Connor stared at her in amazement. "I thought I would go to hell, but I'm in heaven."

Marielle hugged him. "We're married, Connor!"

He grinned. "Aye, we are."

Buniel laughed. "I'll leave you with a final blessing." He rested his hands on their heads, then stepped back. "There. You are completely healed. Go forth and multiply." He gave Connor a pointed look. "Tonight."

Then his wings unfurled and he disappeared.

"Bye, Bunny," Marielle whispered.

"What did he mean by tonight?" Connor asked. "And he said I was completely healed?" He felt his fangs. "Nay, I'm still a Vamp."

Marielle smiled. "I believe it was your sperm that was healed. At least until you fall into another death-sleep."

Connor's eyes widened. "Ye mean tonight? We could— Holy Christ!" He swung Marielle up in his arms and strode away from the henge.

She laughed. "That's why he said, 'Go forth and multiply.'"

"Aye." Connor ran up the hill with her in his arms. "For once I think we should follow orders."

She laughed again.

He reached the top of the hill. "That's yer home down there. I hope ye like it."

She glanced at the large stone house. "I love it."

Connor started down the hill toward the house. "Bugger. I should have just teleported you straight to the bedroom."

"I like being carried by my husband."

"Aye, but we could be there already. I could have yer clothes off by now. And I could have you naked in bed."

She nodded. "I see the Three-Step Rule is still in effect."

"What is that?"

She laughed. "I'll tell you later." She kissed his cheek. "I love you, Connor Buchanan."

He grinned. "I love you, Marielle . . . Buchanan."

At Avon Books, we know your passion for romance—once you finish one of our novels, you find yourself wanting more.

May we tempt you with . . .

- **Excerpts** from our upcoming releases.

- Entertaining **extras**, including authors' personal photo albums and book lists.

- Behind-the-scenes **scoop** on your favorite characters and series.

- **Sweepstakes** for the chance to win free books, romantic getaways, and other fun prizes.

- Writing **tips** from our authors and editors.

- **Blog** with our authors and find out why they love to write romance.

- **Exclusive content** that's not contained within the pages of our novels.

Join us at
www.avonbooks.com